SWAN WITH THE WIND

ELLEN RIGGS

BOUGHT-THE-FARM
MYSTERIES

Free Fun Story!

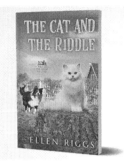

Can this sleuthing sheepdog solve a riddle in time to save a missing cat?

Ivy, Edna and Gertie team up with Keats and Percy to outwit a wily catnapper in this EXCLUSIVE Bought-the-Farm story. Join Ellen Riggs' author newsletter today to receive *The Cat and the Riddle* FREE at **ellenriggs.com/fun**

Swan With the Wind

Copyright © 2021 Ellen Riggs

ISBN 978-1-989303-74-0 eBook
ISBN 978-1-989303-73-3 Book
ASIN B08W75VCDK Kindle
ASIN 1989303730 Paperback
Publisher: Ellen Riggs

www.ellenriggs.com
Cover designer: Lou Harper
Editor: Serena Clarke
2109021059

CHAPTER ONE

Runaway Farm had never looked more scenic and serene than it did on the morning I had to leave it behind. There were pale pink apple blossoms in the orchard, purple wildflowers in the meadow, chartreuse buds on the trees and green lawns studded with aggressively golden dandelions. Only an important mission could make me give up this fragrant slice of heaven after a brutal winter.

I strolled around the pastures with Keats, my sheepdog, and Percy my fluffy marmalade cat. Soon the place would swarm with people and I wanted to soak in the silence for as long as I could. Not that a farm was ever really silent. Right now, the bleating of the new baby goats competed with the braying of the donkey thugs. In the barn, Clippers, the miniature horse, gave a shrill whinny to get my attention. There was never enough of me to go around and sometimes that weighed on me. Especially when I was going to become an absentee farmer for the next week or two.

As excited as I was about my road trip with Jilly, I was already homesick. Farm-sick, I supposed. The thought made me smile. A year ago, I spent my days in a corporate tower firing people in my human resources job. Coming home to Clover Grove had never been in my plans, let alone taking over a hobby farm and inn. Life had delivered some hard punches and sweet kisses since then. Overall, I called it a win.

"Boys, there's something missing here," I said, staring around at the gorgeous property. "We need a pond. A sweet sapphire pond for ducks and frogs. And goldfish! Imagine seeing flashes of orange coming out of the depths."

Keats, my normally chatty dog, said nothing. I looked down to find him glaring at me with his eerie blue eye. His warm brown eye had grown chilly, too. The only thing my fearless border collie hated more than his winter coat was water, whether that came in the form of rain showers, a bath or the swamps that pocked the local terrain. We'd stumbled into a few fetid bogs and it never ended well. The dog shook himself from head to toe as if to dispel the memory and Percy gave a plaintive meow. The two often differed but on this they agreed fully.

"Just a thought," I said. "You know it's only a matter of time before the Rescue Mafia dumps waterfowl on us. I'm surprised it hasn't happened already."

The band of pet rescuers from nearby Dorset Hills had already placed many critters in need here. It wouldn't shock me to come home and find a rhinoceros in a pasture they'd built on the fly. Ducks would be the least of my troubles.

Keats gave one of his odd mumbles and it carried a note of alarm. He ran this farm with an iron paw and the only person who got around him was Cori Hogan, a tiny tyrant of a dog trainer who led the Rescue Mafia. Keats' blind adoration of Cori allowed her to make regular and unauthorized deposits in our farm bank. If she showed up with waterfowl, he'd change his opinion on ponds pronto.

The dog's mumble morphed into a grumble. Apparently, his love for Cori did have limits. He'd take the rhino over the pond any day.

"A farm needs ducks, that's all I'm saying. Quacking adds to the ambiance. But since you feel strongly, we'll leave it in the hands of fate." I smiled and then sighed. Fate had given my butt a kicking since I rescued Keats from a criminal and left the city for farm country. Clover Grove might look like a watercolor painting but there were shadows I'd never seen as a child. Bodies had practically been strewn in my path since my return. It was like fate had been waiting for me.

For us. Keats was my partner in crime-solving and his instincts improved every day. We had plenty of backup from Percy, along with my best friend, Jilly Blackwood, and octogenarian preppers Edna Evans and Gertie Rhodes. Not to mention my boyfriend, Kellan Harper, chief of police, and my brother Asher, also a cop. There was a terrific team here and I was a little nervous about the trip ahead. Jilly's grandmother had resurfaced recently to say she felt uneasy in her upscale gated retirement community. All Jilly could discern was that a new arrival—a vicious swan—was menacing the residents. Keats' wary blue eye told me there was more to the story. Either way, going down south to help was the right thing to do.

It was a long drive to the Briar Estates, and perhaps Jilly would be more forthcoming about her family on the way. She'd never said much about her past and I didn't press her. I'd been reticent to discuss family, too, until we were overrun with my unruly clan. Jilly managed the many shades of Galloway better than I ever could and was adored by my brother. It was likely just a matter of time before she officially became one of us.

Strolling from pasture to pasture, I said goodbye to my favorites. Of course, they were *all* my favorites. Some were more challenging than others, and that only made them more special. It meant I needed to put in extra time studying their unique personalities. My goal was to make every animal under my care feel safe, valued and happy.

Keats gave his classic sneeze of laughter that basically said, "Knock yourself out." He had bigger priorities than coddling barnyard divas.

The roar of an ATV ended my rumination. Edna Evans was rolling through the fields at top speed burning off some morning steam. Eight months ago, she spent most of her time in a recliner or spying on me from her living room window. Now she'd revealed herself as a prepper and rode around in fatigues in case the apocalypse arrived without warning. She still did what she called routine surveillance on the farm, but also helped me with both livestock and criminals. In short, there was no one better to hold the reins at Runaway Farm in my absence.

She hopped down from the ATV with impressive ease, pulled off her helmet, and patted her gray perm. "I'm still annoyed at being left out of this road trip, Ivy. In case you're wondering."

"Good morning to you, too," I said, leaning my back against the camelid pasture fence and crossing my arms. "If you came with us, I'd spend the whole time worried about the farm. I'll be able to focus on Jilly's gran's problem knowing this place is in your capable hands."

"You've got an army to run the farm," she said, pouting. "Meanwhile, you and Jillian may be at risk. Without me, you're babes in the woods."

"We're neither naïve nor alone," I said. "Keats is our secret weapon."

"How do you know his so-called magic will work outside Clover Grove?"

"Because it worked in Boston. Edna, we'll be fine. Jilly's gran lives in a gated retirement community. How dangerous could it be?"

Edna gestured from her ATV to her fatigues. "If you're suggesting retirees are harmless, think again. Plenty of us have incredible second innings."

"These are more typical seniors," I said. "You and Gertie didn't retire to gated communities."

She waggled silvery eyebrows at me. "That's where they'll come first, you know."

"Who? The zombies?"

"Creatures who thrive in lawless times. The first rule of survival is to keep moving. No gates. No routine. Leave the enemy guessing."

"Well, I'm actually looking forward to spending time behind this particular gate. There's a store, a café, a pub and even a spa." I looked at my shabby nails, knowing they were beyond redemption. "It'll be great to kick back for a few days. Jilly really needs this."

Edna puckered her permanently puckered lips a bit more. "True. She's losing her looks."

"That's a terrible thing to say! Jilly is gorgeous."

"She's been wilting like an old rose, Ivy. Her color is gone and so is her spark."

I stared at her, wondering if I'd missed the signs. "If that's true, seeing her family will surely help."

"Family is more of a liability than a comfort, remember. Or has your tune changed?"

"Not really. If the zombies get me, it will be because I stopped to deal with my mother."

Mom was in a state over the recent return of my father, Calvin, after a decades-long absence. They had silently agreed to give each other space and rarely ended up here at the same time. Since Calvin was an experienced farmhand and I needed help, Mom was staying at her apartment in town to do therapeutic sewing. I still wasn't sure what to make of Calvin, but it was nice not having to share a roof with my mother full-time.

"Exactly," Edna said. "The Calvin drama kept you from noticing Jilly fading before your very eyes. I wouldn't be surprised if things fall apart between her and your brother."

"That will never happen. He adores her."

"No doubt about that, but she's questioning if he's up to the job of protecting her."

"He's a cop, Edna. Of course, he can protect her."

"Your hotstuff cops can't keep you safe from your own families. They're the insidious enemy we can't escape." She tapped her temple. "Because they're in here. Attacking from behind whatever gates we've built."

The truth of her words struck me. Memories were the enemy. Nothing disabled me faster than thinking about the past, and while I'd made great strides there was no wiping the slate totally clean.

"All the more reason for this trip," I said. "Jilly needs a chance to make peace with her past. You've done it, I'm doing it now, and it's her turn."

Edna nodded. "Before there's peace there's war, and that's why I should be riding with you. I thought you said we were—"

"Real family. Chosen family. Yes. But in this instance I

need to put my furred and feathered family first, Edna." I gestured to the driveway, where vehicles were pouring in. There was Bridget Linsmore's lime green van, containing members of the Rescue Mafia, Gertie's white van, Charlie's pickup, a few sedans, and at the end, a police SUV. "Someone has to keep these people in line."

Her chin lifted as if someone had placed an invisible crown on her wiry curls. "I'm the CFO," she said. "The Chief Farm Officer."

"Exactly. And your special mission, if you choose to accept it, is to figure out why Drama Llama and the thugs are so agitated. They've been calmer lately but they're milling around today. You might want to cycle Byron through here."

"Which one is he? Honestly, Ivy, I have too much going on upstairs to remember the names you assign. It's worse than the roster in my school vaccination program."

"Byron is the livestock guardian dog who hangs with the pig. If there's a predator riling the donkeys, maybe he should move out here."

"I see what you're doing," she said. "Trying to placate me with a problem to solve."

Car doors slammed and people came toward us. "Maybe I'm coming up with a problem that will keep *me* here, where I belong."

"How about you do that while I drive down to show those seniors what old age can look like? Then we'd all be happy."

"Except Jilly," I said. "She needs her best friend by her side, and I won't let her down."

Edna glanced over my shoulder and said, "Better keep your wits about you."

"Yeah. The savage swan situation sounds strange."

"I mean now." Edna's camouflage glove shot out to grab my shoulder but big teeth beat her to it.

The trio of donkey thugs had skulked up behind me. Two of them yanked me along the fence while Drama Llama got into position.

"Noooo..." It came out of my mouth in a howl of despair and Keats threw himself at the fence with no hope of reaching my camelid assailant. A stream of putrid spit shot at me and I only managed to turn away in time to take it in the side of the head.

"On the bright side, it didn't hit your eyes," Edna said. "You wouldn't be able to see the road today."

I shook my fist at Drama and mopped my head with my other sleeve. "That felt like a bad omen."

"Ivy, let me share a little retiree wisdom," she said, towing me toward the crowd in the parking area. "Sometimes spit is just spit."

CHAPTER TWO

As usual, Cori Hogan was dressed all in black except for the orange middle fingers on her knit gloves. She raised both hands now and said, "Stop right there, farmer."

"Permission to approach, captain?" I asked.

The orange fingers fluttered. "Denied. Report to the decontamination chamber immediately."

"I don't have time to shower. We promised to get there by tomorrow night."

"You can't shut Jilly in a small space stinking like that," Cori said. "Not if you want her alive on arrival."

"Agreed," Edna said. "Although I was hoping to see what happened when Chief Hotty McSniffalot went in for the goodbye hug."

Jilly was coming down the front stairs dragging a huge suitcase. Did she really need that much stuff for a weeklong visit, or was she secretly planning to stay longer? Maybe the Briar Estates was like an ocean cruise with formal nights. I should have asked earlier.

I'd packed heavy, too, but with different goals. On Edna's advice, I'd assembled a go-kit with shovels, rope, an ax and life jackets for the beach. A farmer-sleuth came prepared.

Edna collected Jilly's suitcase just as my uniformed brother came forward to do the same. There was a brief tussle before Jilly spoke up. "Asher, let Edna do it. She's got a flair for packing."

Now I couldn't help but see the truth of Edna's words. My best friend had lost her spark, despite many hours in her kitchen happy place cooking for our army.

"Jillian is right, young man," Edna said, yanking so hard on the suitcase that Asher nearly lost his balance. "Better stick to being handsome."

Kellan walked over, also in uniform. "Miss Evans, let's be respectful of the people who serve and protect this town."

Edna muttered something disrespectful that included the words dagnabit and Chief Haughty McSnobalot and then continued on to the truck. Kellan ignored it, letting his slow, gorgeous smile spread over his face as he came toward me. Our fingers had nearly touched when a smaller animal grabbed my shoulder. A wolverine in red clothing.

"Stop right there, Ivy Rose Galloway," Mom said. "I can hardly stand to touch you and I delivered you into this world. Get inside and shower. Kellan and Jilly deserve better."

I might have argued but Keats was herding me to the stairs. Apparently, I stunk too much even for him. "Fine. We'll be late leaving."

"Kellan," Mom said behind me. "Have you considered one of my other daughters? I have three very much available. All clean and relatively tame."

Poppy, Iris and Violet offered a joint protest. "Mom!"

"What? It's a compliment," she said. "You're practically

identical, thanks to my genes, but Calvin's came out in Ivy. They're both content to sleep in a barn, whereas Chief Harper is a man of refined tastes."

Kellan laughed. "You overestimate me, Mrs. Galloway."

"I don't want to be called that anymore." She frowned as she saw Calvin's truck pulling in. "Especially not with *Mister* Galloway in the vicinity."

"Keats," I said, "get Mom before she makes me really glad to leave home."

Even Jilly smiled when Dahlia jumped away from the dog's herding nip.

"You owe me for another set of nylons, Ivy," Mom said as she followed me up the stairs.

"Take it off your unpaid rent."

"I've spent my pennies on products for you." She gave me a little shove. "I recommend the tea tree and pine body wash today. You'll smell like a man, but I doubt you'll be dating one any time soon."

She kept me in the shower longer than I wanted, but eventually I was back outside downloading instructions for farm management to the team. Cori finally got her sheepdog, Clem, to join forces with Keats and herd Jilly and me to the truck.

"We were running this place before you got here, remember?" she said. "Go, already. Fix this savage swan issue and try to have a little fun while you're at it."

"Fun? In a retirement community?" Edna said. "Impossible."

Remi Malone wove through the crowd carrying Leo, her beagle, like a spotted handbag. She neatly cut off everyone but Kellan and Asher, pushing the others back with nothing more than a sweet smile. It was a natural grace she shared with Jilly.

"You'll want a moment to say your goodbyes," she said, before smothering Leo's silky ears with kisses. It was a blatant attempt to decoy Cori, who espoused a "four on the floor" rule for canines. The trainer's instant tirade gave Kellan and me the cover we needed for a hug.

Then, easing me to arm's length, he gave me that smile again—the one that had melted the iceberg in my chest since my homecoming. Our high school romance had been simple and sweet. Back then, we'd imagined a life together in the city, with corporate careers and plenty of kids. Now I had plenty of kids but all of them had hooves and rectangular pupils. My days revolved around manure, although my HR skills were hardly wasted managing diverse personalities among livestock and occasional psychopaths.

Meanwhile, Kellan carried a gun and the lines on his face told tales of horrific experiences he hadn't shared. There was a lot of water under the bridge since our youthful romance broke down, but I wouldn't change a thing. Sometimes I wondered if he felt differently, but he answered every challenge I issued with more conviction. It was time I started believing that he accepted me just as I was. Moreover, it was time to start accepting myself as I was and stop seeing myself through my mother's eyes—as the smelly daughter who was like her longtime deadbeat dad.

"I'd ask you to be careful but I suppose that's useless," Kellan said.

"I promise to be more careful than usual," I said. "It's one thing to take risks on my turf surrounded by my army, and quite another to play cowboy in a strange place."

His smile said he wanted to believe me. "That sounds encouraging."

I squeezed his hand. "I take more chances here because I know you're on duty."

"I don't know whether to be flattered or frustrated," he said, but his gaze warmed.

"I can only do what I do because of my prince on his white charger." There was an indignant rumble below, so I added, "And my canine charger, of course."

"For once I came first," Kellan said, pulling me close again. "Take that, Keats."

The next mumble was insolent, and Kellan jumped away suddenly. The dog had no doubt deposited another bruise on my boyfriend's calf. I frowned at Keats. "At least let me fill up my hug bank to last a week. You hate hugs and Percy only likes them from Jilly."

In fact, I could see the cat cradled in her arms now as I stared right through the truck's cab to where she stood on the other side. Asher was trying to fill *his* hug bank, but Jilly appeared to be using marmalade fluff as a barricade.

Since Calvin resurfaced, a cold front had rolled in between Asher, who'd welcomed him, and the rest of us, who hadn't. In time, hackles would settle and Mom's golden boy would prevail in winning everyone back. Jilly and Kellan had been caught in the middle and it hit her the hardest. A week away would give me time to right that wrong. I didn't want my family issues coming between a couple who had always felt destined to me. To Keats as well, it seemed, because he ran around the truck and tried to herd the two together with sheepdog moves. When that didn't work, he took a leap at Percy. The cat gave an angry yowl and jumped from Jilly's arms into the truck. After that, Asher made his move but her arms hung limply over his shoulders.

There was confusion in my happy-go-lucky brother's

blue eyes when Jilly pulled away. Keats must have felt the chill, too, because he drove her into the truck, and then parked himself on her lap.

Kellan gave me a worried glance as I climbed inside. "It'll be fine," I said. "There's an ugly duckling that needs our attention. Once we've turned it into a beautiful swan, things will look brighter."

"Just don't bring it home," he said.

Closing the door, I rolled down the window. "If you really loved me you'd dig me a pond while I'm gone. I was just telling Keats that we need some quackers."

He shook his head, laughing. "At least they can swim when your ark sinks."

Laughter helped ease the dull ache in my heart as we started rolling away from my happy place.

Keats wasn't moping at all, however. He placed white paws on the dashboard, ready to take on swans and whatever else lay ahead. Without turning, he mumbled something that made me smile.

"What did he say?" Jilly asked.

The question revealed her state of mind because she typically spoke "Keats" almost as well as I did.

"He said this is the most fun he's had in ages." I took my hand off the stick shift to pat her arm. "And he thanked you for making it happen. You're a sheepdog's dream come true, Jilly Blackwood."

Finally, my friend's easy laughter filled the truck. "At least I can make someone happy."

Keats offered another mumble that I translated automatically for her. "That was the doggy equivalent to buck up little camper, adventure awaits."

And with that, I geared up and cruised toward the highway.

CHAPTER THREE

For the first hour of our drive, Keats kept up his eager panting. He was the only one without mixed feelings about the trip. Percy was disgruntled over being relegated to his carrier. Both animals should have been restrained, but Keats had probably never seen the inside of a crate and would be greatly affronted to start now. All I could do was hope for the best and trust my improved truck handling skills. It was encouraging that Jilly no longer clutched the door handle for dear life when I drove. That left her hands free to stroke Keats' sides rapidly as he perched on her knee. She probably wasn't aware of how that revealed her nerves.

When her fingers slowed and Keats' lolling tongue retired to his mouth in a state of relaxed alertness, I glanced at my friend. No matter how stressed, she'd pulled a nice outfit together, topped with a lightweight blue wool jacket and matching silk scarf.

"Nice earrings," I said. "They have an antique look."

She nodded and the dangling pearls swung. "They've been in my family for generations."

"I'm sure your gran is going to be happy you're wearing them."

The pearls bobbed again, catching a little light and creating a warm glow. "Probably. I tried giving them back to her when our family broke up but she wouldn't hear of it."

"Broke up? Was the rift as big as that?"

"Massive. My mom and my aunt had an epic fallout when I was a teen and Gran was caught in the middle. Aunt Shelley wanted Gran to move out of the old family manor so that she could take over herself. Mom tried to stop that from happening and failed. Shelley's the younger but she's a force of nature."

"Is that when your gran moved down south to the retirement community? She couldn't have been very old at the time."

"She was the youngest person there and it took a long time to adjust. According to Mom. They still keep in touch."

"Then your aunt took over the old house?"

The pearls bobbed a yes. "Plus all the responsibilities that came with it. It's old and needs a lot of care."

"What about your mom?"

"She moved to California when I left for college. We chat now and then. That's about it."

"Sounds like she was sad about losing the home."

Jilly's hands picked up speed on Keats' sleek sides. His mouth opened in a pant that didn't have the same happy quality anymore. "Mom complained about the old house but later I think she felt..."

"Exiled?" I suggested.

"Exiled and yet relieved. Also hurt Gran didn't or couldn't side with her. Aunt Shelley and Janelle won that battle. We all lost the family."

"Janelle? That's another name I haven't heard."

"My cousin. Shelley's daughter. We were like twins growing up, but when she hit high school something changed. That's what started the whole ruckus."

I looked around to get my bearings. We were coasting past town after town in the hill country range. There were at least 30 of them, and while each had a unique identity in my youth, lately they were more homogenized like Clover Grove. Dorset Hills had started that ball rolling by becoming "Dog Town." They attracted tourists in droves and the rest of us cast a net to hold them longer.

"What change could cause that much trouble?" I asked.

"Janelle transformed practically overnight," Jilly said. "She started getting into trouble and Aunt Shelley said I was a bad influence."

"You! A straight A student who sang in show choir and managed the yearbook? You're a perfect role model."

Jilly laughed. "Not my aunt's idea of perfection. She's eccentric. Bohemian." Her index finger traced a pattern in the paw prints on the side window. "A rebel, unlike me."

"And Janelle?"

"Dropped out of college and from what Gran says, still drifting from job to job."

"Sounds like she suffered most from all this."

"I don't know about that," Jilly said. "But she hasn't tried to make things right."

"Family," I said. "You know I empathize."

She nodded. "It means so much that you'd come along, Ivy. Reliving all this will be tough. I'd made peace with the situation and was glad to be done with the drama."

"Maybe you'll get a surprise. You know how unnerving Calvin's arrival was, but now I see it as a good thing.

Mostly. Releasing old demons is giving me room to breathe and I hope it will do the same for you."

Staring out the passenger window, she shrugged. "Maybe it will do some good."

"That's more like our Jilly." Keats turned and gave Jilly a rare lick on her cheek. "Keats agrees. And he wants to know what's going on between you and Asher."

The dog mumbled huffily over my using him to cover my own nosiness.

"Everything's fine," she said. "I'm just focused on my family right now."

"Fine? I saw my brother's face today. It was like someone stole his NFL football signed by a quarterback I can never remember. He feels you drifting away from him and doesn't know what to do about it."

"Not drifting away—just taking a road trip that'll apparently give me more capacity to enjoy life. Let's see what next week brings."

She rolled down the window and pulled in a breath of spring air that held the effervescent tang of the hills, although we were nearing the end of the range.

I geared down and grabbed the hand that compulsively stroked Keats' sleek side. "You're going to rub the fur off my dog and I don't want your gran to meet him bald. I may not care about my own appearance, but I like my pets to be pretty."

That got a laugh out of her and she squeezed my hand back. "Would you be mad if things didn't work out with your brother?"

I shook my head. "You're the best thing that ever happened to him, but if he doesn't make you happy, then I support you in whatever you choose."

Her lips folded into a thin line and she blinked a few

times before speaking. "I'm afraid we don't have what it takes for the long haul. My family resurfacing changes everything."

"Did Asher's reaction to my father's resurfacing change your mind?"

Asher had welcomed Calvin with open arms, acting like a free agent instead of pulling with the rest of us. I thought I knew my open, genial brother, but Calvin's arrival had shown a different side. If I was recalibrating, Jilly must be doing the same.

"I haven't been upfront with him about my family, either," she said. "That's what gives me pause. If we can't be honest about things like that, what does it say about our future?"

"It says you should take your time, just like I'm doing with Kellan. Sometimes I want to fast-forward to a happily ever after, but it's not realistic with all the baggage I carry."

"Kellan has his own, too," Jilly said. "He walks as if the weight of the world's on his shoulders. Then his eyes light on you and he straightens up and smiles."

My heart had squeezed like a fist in my chest and the pressure released with her words. "Thank you for saying that, Jilly. How about we both just see how things go?" I felt a shift in the atmosphere through our open windows. "I have faith my brother would always support you, but it's *his* job to prove that to you. Whatever happens, you and I will be besties forever. You're my real family, remember."

"You have no idea how much comfort that gives me." She gestured to a road sign for the turnoff to Wyldwood Springs. "I spent a lot of summers in this area, you know. Before Gran moved away."

"In Wyldwood Springs? You're a hill country girl and never told me?"

She laughed. "Wyldwood hardly qualifies. There's barely a bump in the entire county. But I loved staying at the old family manor."

"Before your aunt stole it out from under your gran?"

"Yeah. Mom and Shelley never got along, but Mom wanted me to spend time with Gran and especially Janelle, since we were both only children." Her window went down even more. Two noses competed for fresh air, only one of which snorted. "It was magic. I mean, everyday magic. Just running through wildflowers till the fireflies came out."

"Idyllic," I said. "We rarely get fireflies in Clover Grove. That's the upside of the downside of hill country, like Wyldwood Springs."

"It really is pretty." She stuck her fingers out the window and let them trail in the breeze. "There are brooks and waterfalls and old bridges everywhere. Janny and I tried to take a picture on every bridge but we never made it before..."

Her voice drifted off and I prodded her gently. "Before detonation?"

She nodded. "Mom came to drop me off that summer and there was a summit. I'm still not exactly sure what happened. Janny had stayed in Wyldwood that year and got in trouble. Gran took the blame and Shelley basically lost it. The next day, Mom pulled the car around and gunned us out of there." She rolled up the window so fast Keats protested. "That was the last visit."

"Do you want to do a little drive-by?" I asked. "I'd love to see your old family home."

"No." The answer was quick and decisive. "Maybe on the way back if things go okay with Gran."

"Sounds good." I adjusted my seat for the next leg of the journey. Now that we were out of hill country, I was more relaxed. Jilly seemed to feel the same and we lapsed into the comfortable silence of old friends.

Keats settled too, curling into a ball in Jilly's lap. His eyes never fully closed, however, and his nose twitched constantly, picking up signals on the light breeze from my window. Even when it was freezing, I gave him fresh air to monitor our surroundings. He was my early alert system.

A few hours later, that's exactly how I came to notice we were being followed. The car behind us was far enough back that there was nothing to see but a glint of late afternoon sun off chrome and glass. But Keats had gotten twitchy. His muzzle lifted and swiveled. Then he stood and looked over Jilly's shoulder. And finally he grumbled something under his breath to Percy, who turned around in his carrier to face the back of the seat. There was nothing for the cat to see, but plenty to feel.

"What's going on?" Jilly asked.

I flicked my eyes from mirror to mirror a few more times before answering. "If I didn't know better, I'd say we're being tailed."

CHAPTER FOUR

"Tailed? Are you kidding?" Jilly's voice spiked. One of her strengths in the corporate world had been her even, melodious tone that rarely gave away her emotions. Farm life had stolen that from her.

"There's a car way back that nearly drops out of sight every time I look. At first I didn't think much of it because it seems like it's different cars. I haven't been able to get a fix on a vehicle, so I may be wrong."

Now she reached for the handgrip. "Percy and Keats say you're right."

The dog's ruff had risen, and his ears flattened. Something was amiss.

"I can't imagine why anyone would tail us now," I said. "Unless it's Jim Moss, that private investigator whose sinister client came after Calvin."

"You said Kellan dealt with that."

"He did, at least as much as he could. The roots of crime run so deep in hill country that it's like playing whack-a-mole. Kellan can't even disperse funds from the recovered treasure until he's sure it won't cause more harm than good."

Jilly loosened her scarf with her free hand. "Do you really think someone would come this far to keep track of us? We've been driving most of the day."

"It's so weird. They could have gained on us any time, yet they stay just far enough back. It's almost like they sense when I'm checking the mirror."

Her hand moved from her scarf to touch one pearl earring. "Maybe it's not about Clover Grove at all. Maybe it's about the Briars."

"The Briars? What do you mean? No one knows us there. Barely even your gran."

Her lips twitched into a ghost of her usual smile. "Our reputation could have preceded us. Social media isn't our friend, Ivy."

Percy let out an eerie moan. I had no doubt his orange fluff had puffed to fill the carrier.

"Jilly, what's really going on at the Briar Estates? You sounded more worried about your gran than a pesky swan seems to warrant."

There was a long pause as my friend collected her thoughts. "Gran gave me nothing to go on, but I am worried. Our family used to have enemies."

"Like the Swensons and Milloys in Clover Grove?"

She nodded. "Maybe worse."

"Do you think an old enemy could have surfaced at the Briars?"

"It's a secure community. But it's also the first time Gran's felt uneasy."

I glanced at Keats and said, "Should we initiate evasive maneuvers?"

His paws pounded a brisk yes on the dash, so I wasted

no time in taking the next exit without signaling. Edna had taught me that quick, unexpected turns were the best way to shake a tail, but it was harder in flat farm country like this. Before long, we found a lane nearly blocked by vines and drove into it. I pulled a U turn, and we settled to wait.

Just as we were about to breathe a sigh of relief, two cars shot past. The vine curtain prevented us from getting a model, let alone plates, but both looked like dark sedans. There was silence in the truck, but a buzzing energy suggested four brains at work.

We waited until Keats' flags settled before venturing out of our hiding place. After that, Jilly used her phone to navigate a deliberately convoluted route through the country side roads. The fields were gorgeous in the magic hour before sunset but now they held the faint hint of menace.

"What should we do?" she asked at last. "If we go back to the main highway, they can find us again."

"How about we stick to the back roads and then find a pet-friendly motel?"

Our plan had been to spoil ourselves with a nice dinner and an overnight stay in a boutique hotel but getting tailed was bad for the digestion.

"Maybe we should just keep driving," Jilly said.

"I'd agree if we were on the highway but it's so confusing out here and would be worse in the dark. Plus it would add hours to our commute. I say we start fresh in the morning. Besides, Percy and Keats will need a break."

"Fair enough," she said, and searched online till she came up with a motel that turned out to be just what we needed—low profile, but not low enough to qualify as fleabag. Within half an hour, we found the place and checked in.

"It's not horrible," I called to Jilly after sticking my head into the room.

She was behind me, lugging her suitcase up the stairs to the second-floor balcony. "At times like this, you know who I miss?" she said.

"Asher?" My voice was hopeful.

"Edna. Her weapons are more diverse and her regard for the law so flexible."

I laughed as I went back to help her. "So true. Yet her sense of good versus evil is refreshingly inflexible. Gertie is the same. But for the next week we'll need to make do with the weapons we have." I shoved the door open and let those weapons walk into the room ahead of us. "They're exceptional long-range danger detectors and an asset in any altercation. But I do wish I'd thrown a pig poker into the truck."

My favorite farm tool was a long wooden pole with a hook on the end. Despite my clumsiness, I'd become adept at wielding it. Edna said recently that there was a swordswoman inside me waiting to get out. High praise indeed.

"I'm sure we'll be fine with Keats and Percy," Jilly said, as we heaved her suitcase onto the stand beside the bed. "They'll let us know if something's wrong and we'll rely on conventional methods."

"You mean calling in a regular emergency rather than a Zombie 911?"

"Exactly." That was what we jokingly called a crisis better suited for our octogenarian apocalyptic army than the regular police. "Any port in a storm."

Before unpacking, I said, "How about we run down to that little country store we passed and grab some snacks? Otherwise, we're competing with the pets for kibble."

"I'll stay here with Percy," she said, as the cat examined

every inch of the room. "Like you said, they deserve some downtime."

"Okay. Keep the door locked and your phone handy."

"Yes, ma'am." After a second she added, "Isn't life strange? We could never have imagined our lives now when we worked in corporate towers."

I stopped with my hand on the doorknob. "Back then I could predict exactly what would happen every single day with mind-numbing accuracy. Now I can't see five minutes ahead, whether we're on the farm or off it." Stepping outside, I called back, "Can't blame you for having some regrets, my friend."

"No regrets. You?"

"I was dead inside and didn't know it. I'd rather be running for my life with my besties any day." I tossed her a grin. "But a short vacation from trouble would have been nice."

"Yeah, we earned it." Percy meowed in apparent agreement. "Get me some barbecue chips, okay? And corn chips, too."

"Chocolate to finish?" I asked.

"For sure. I'd suggest a bottle of wine but I guess we need to stay sharp."

"We'll raise a glass with your gran tomorrow," I said.

"Do *not* let her drink," she said, as the door closed. "The eccentricity magnifies tenfold."

I was still smiling when Keats stopped at the top of the stairs and went into a point. Much of the light had left the sky now but his white paw and muzzle were easy to see.

"What's wrong, buddy?" I peered out over the railing across the parking lot. There were four other vehicles—two trucks and a couple of old sedans. I was surprised a motel so out of the way got even that much business.

Near the entrance to the lot a big dumpster sat half-shrouded in scrub bush. Beside it something stretched out on the asphalt. It looked like a man on his side, but it was hard to tell. Had someone fallen? Passed out?

"What do you make of that?" I said aloud. Keats' tail had bristled and brushed my leg as he started skulking down the stairs. "Wait, buddy."

Lifting my phone, I snapped a photo. Then I stretched the image so I could get a better look before walking into trouble. The picture was dark and grainy, but from what I could tell, it was human, not animal.

Texting Jilly, I started down the stairs after Keats. She came out onto the balcony and I called, "Get ready to phone for help. Someone's fallen over there by the dumpster."

She followed me, with Percy at her heels. "Be careful," she called. "Slow down. You're going to—"

I tripped. Of course, I tripped. If there was something to trip over, I always did. If there was nothing to trip over, I tripped then, too. It was one thing I could count on. This time, there was nothing but a handful of big pebbles like marbles.

"I'm okay," I said, scrambling to my feet.

Jilly's heels clattered on the metal stairs behind me. "Wait for me. It could be a setup. What if you lean over the body and someone grabs your leg?"

"Keats won't let that happen," I said, circling my truck at a run.

"Ivy, please. I've got a bad feeling about this."

I did too, but I couldn't leave anyone suffering if I could help. "Wait! *What?*"

By the time I reached the dumpster, the body had vanished.

If it had ever been there.

Had it been a dusk-induced optical illusion?

I might have convinced myself it was never real, were it not for Keats. He lifted his paw in another point, hesitated, and then set it back down. For once, my perceptive dog seemed confused as well. There *had* been something worth seeing, that much was clear from his stiffened tail. Only his muzzle moved as he applied eyes, ears and nose to the mystery.

Flicking on my phone light, I walked around the side of the dumpster. There was no sign anyone had been here. No broken branches, no footprints in the damp earth under the bushes. Keats' ruff and tail settled somewhat, although his eerie blue eye scanned continuously.

The click of Jilly's heels brought us back around to the pavement.

"Nothing?" she asked.

"I saw someone lying right here. At least I thought so, and Keats did, too. Now they're gone."

"Just lying here? Drunk, maybe?"

"I doubt someone that inebriated could have moved away so fast."

"A prank, maybe. Something local kids pull on guests to spook them. They'd know an escape route."

"Possibly, although Keats would know where they went." I gestured toward him. "Have you ever seen this dog so baffled?"

His ears went up and down, and he spun several times, sniffing and snorting.

She shook her head. "Obviously you both saw something. What about a deer? Maybe it got hit by a car and was stunned for a second."

I led her into a circle of light from the motel and held

up my phone. "Come and look. I took a photo to see what I was getting into."

Our heads collided and we rubbed our temples as we stared at the hazy, pixelated image. There most certainly *had* been something beside the dumpster.

"It looks like a middle-aged man," Jilly said. "Balding a little, right?"

"Looks like it. Can't see much else, except..."

"What?" she asked.

I angled the phone. "Is he wearing some kind of uniform? There's a hint of yellow on the chest. Can you see it?"

Jilly stretched the image and then took the phone and held it up to her nose. The phone trembled as she lowered it. "It might be."

"It's not a police uniform," I said. "Some kind of security company, maybe. Or a local legion."

She stared at me and pressed her lips together for a moment. Then she said, "Let's get out of here."

"Leave now? We paid for the room."

"Something's wrong." She gestured toward the dumpster. "Really wrong. Look at Percy."

The cat was scraping invisible litter over the approximate spot where the man's bald head had rested.

"Oh no! But if that man were dead, there's no way he could have moved or *been* moved in the time it took me to cross the parking lot."

Jilly started back toward the stairs at a brisk clip. "Only if there was a team. And we don't want to stick around to find out what they were doing here."

"Like a rural biker gang?" I snapped my fingers at the animals and followed. "It didn't look like *that* kind of uniform. Country thugs would wear leather. Or at least denim."

"Let's grab our stuff and talk in the truck."

I had seen Jilly move fast any number of times but tonight there were rockets under her stilettos.

I jogged up the stairs behind her. Even in work boots, I could barely keep up. "We should call the police, right?"

"I don't want to stay here while they investigate," she said. "We could be stuck for days. You know how these things work." Opening the door to our room, she went inside. "Let's call from the road. Find a pay phone." Throwing things into her suitcase, she added, "Ivy, for once, let's not get involved."

I paused in the doorway with Keats and we both cocked our heads. Was that the sound of a motor receding, or my pounding heart?

"Jilly, we're already involved," I said, walking into the room. "Percy thinks a man died here. I should send the cops the photo, at least. It may be someone they know."

Latching her suitcase, she swung it off the stand as if it were now as light as a feather. "I guess. But then they can trace us."

Closing the door, I leaned against it and checked my phone again.

"That won't be a problem," I said. "Because the photo is gone."

"You must have deleted it accidentally. Check the trash."

"Gone," I repeated, after scrolling and clicking. "Just like the body."

She hauled her suitcase to the door. "Just like *us*. Let's roll."

CHAPTER FIVE

The twisting roads would have been tough to navigate in daylight let alone after dusk. We missed a couple of turns before realizing that Keats could do the heavy lifting as copilot. I thought his talent for sniffing out directions was confined to hill country but he seemed confident he could get us back to the main drag, albeit the slow way.

On the upside, watching for cars was easier at night. There were no headlights coming up behind us. Every so often I slowed to be sure. Both Keats and Percy were at ease, and gradually Jilly and I let down our guards, too.

"Well," I said at last. "That was strange. And coming from us, that's saying something."

Jilly raised her hand and pointed. "There's a phone booth. Looming out of the mist in the middle of nowhere."

"Creepy," I said. "For a creepy report. You ready?"

"Yeah. Let's get it over with."

We got out of the truck with Keats and crowded into the old-fashioned booth.

"I'll try to keep it short so we can keep moving," I said, staring out at the road. "Why is it so foggy all of a sudden?"

"Because we've stepped into a horror movie," she said. "Obviously."

We both started to laugh, stopped, and then started again.

Keats yapped a sharp reproof. "Sorry buddy, you're right. We're a little giddy."

I shook off the feeling too literally and accidentally shoved Jilly out the door. That only got us laughing again.

"How about I go sit with Percy?" she said. "So you can focus."

Things went better after that. I got through to reception at the local police department and spilled the story of the mysterious prone figure, adding all kinds of qualifiers. Maybe it was a kid playing a prank. Maybe someone had fallen and then staggered off. Or maybe a deer took a nap and got startled. I offered even more options, stopping just shy of suggesting an alien invasion.

At no point did I mention Keats' reaction or Percy's litterbox move.

The skepticism on the other end was to be expected, but it still made me miss Kellan. He tried hard to take me seriously no matter how implausible the story. In the end, they agreed to send someone out to the motel to look around.

Just as they asked for my contact information, I pretended the line cut out and hung up.

"That could have gone worse," I said, getting back into the truck. "Let's try to put some miles under the wheels."

"Roll on," Jilly said, letting Keats resume his navigator position.

"This is a first," I said. "In all our years of friendship we've never done an overnight drive."

"We were far too practical for that, I'm afraid."

Back then, we believed vacations were for sissies. We'd taken exactly two, when Flordale Corp refused to cash out my credits. Then we spent our time working beside a pool, eating resort meals that couldn't rival Jilly's cooking on her worst day. What was the point?

I rubbed my forehead to still my spiraling thoughts. "I need to text Kellan at our next stop. Maybe he's got an idea of who was tailing us earlier. My money's still on the private investigator and his shady client."

"Possibly." Jilly waited a few minutes before continuing. "After the weirdness at the motel, I'm inclined to think it's about me. Well, not me, per se. More likely my gran or Aunt Shelley, but they could try to get to my family through me."

I glanced at Keats, who was giving Jilly the full force of his warm brown eye. She probably didn't see it, but she'd have felt the comfort. Then his eerie blue eye flashed at me to suggest we were circling something important.

"Tell me more," I said. "I'm beginning to think the roots of organized crime might stretch from Clover Grove down to Wyldwood Springs and even beyond."

"Scratch the surface anywhere and there's rot underneath," she said.

I eased the seat back to get more comfortable for a long night. "What would they want from your gran, though? Does she have money?"

"Yeah. It's not cheap to live in a place like the Briar Estates," Jilly said. "But what they really want is something she *doesn't* have, as much as she might wish otherwise."

"Color me curious." This felt foreign territory in more ways than one. After more than a decade of loyal friendship, Jilly and I were finally exposing dark truths about our pasts, and how they'd shaped who we'd become.

"It's complicated," Jilly said. "I mean really complicated, not cliché complicated."

"More complicated than my family with its generations of mysteries and enemies?"

She patted my arm and her fingers were cold even through my sleeve. "We have generations of enemies too, but with a special twist."

I flashed her a reassuring smile and found her staring at me intently. Maybe she was evaluating whether I was ready to hear her story. "Just tell me, Jilly. You know I have an open mind."

Now she sighed. "My mind is closed about this. Blinds down and locked up tight."

I gestured with my right hand to the dog in her lap. His eyes were trained on Jilly but his posture was relaxed. "Keats isn't worried, so I'm not worried."

"Okay. Well." She took a deep breath and then a couple more, just as she'd taught me to do in times of trouble. "There's a chance that an old family enemy has located Gran, in what's supposed to be a secure community, to get what she has."

"Cash? Old jewels like your pearl earrings? A treasure map?"

"Secrets. She has insider information on generations of true eccentrics. People who think they're... well, magical."

"Magical? Like witches?"

"No one uses that word. At least not around me."

I had prepared myself for all sorts of things, but not magic, understandably. Jilly sounded skeptical herself, but I was determined to live up to my promise and roll with whatever she told me. Keats still wasn't worried, even with a word like "witches" floating around the cab of the truck.

"And *is* your gran, er, magical?" No way was I calling Jilly's gran a witch, even in jest.

"Gran claims to have second sight."

"As in, ESP?"

"Clairvoyance, telepathy, a sixth sense... There are so many words for mind-reading."

"And does she? Read minds, I mean."

Jilly's curls swished back and forth. "Not to my knowledge, and I'm sure she'd be poking around in my head if she could. Never have I seen one of her prophecies come true, other than that her daughters would fight many battles." She laughed a little. "Even the mailman could predict that."

"If she doesn't have a track record for prophecy, why would anyone bother coming after her?"

"She may not be psychic, but she does have an encyclopedic mind about the past. It could be that, or it could be that her predictions used to be so off base she infuriated people. Powerful people who didn't take kindly to having incorrect thoughts or actions attributed to them."

"I would guess not." I digested the new information before adding, "Is this why your aunt sent her away?"

Jilly nodded. "The Briar Estates is a gated community geared to eccentrics like Gran."

"Like witness protection."

"Sort of. That's a nicer way of putting it than a modern, secure facility."

"Couldn't they just sell the house and move?"

"The old manor was built for us nearly two hundred years ago and we made a commitment not to sell it. Ever."

"A commitment to whom?"

"Each other, I guess. I never got the full story because Mom didn't want me to know. I was okay with that."

Okay in the way I was okay with my father leaving my

mom to struggle with six kids, no doubt. I couldn't get away from my family fast enough and that was the case for Jilly, too.

"And why exactly were *you* given the boot, if you don't mind my asking?"

Her fingers ran over Keats' sleek side to draw on his strength and comfort. "Because I don't have what our family calls 'the gift.' Gran, my mom and I don't have it, whereas my aunt and Janelle do. Allegedly. It's never been proven to my satisfaction but I didn't stick around to find out."

"So your aunt's a witch," I said, grinning.

Jilly laughed more easily, as if her throat had loosened. "Shelley's a witch, all right. Janelle never was, even if she is. But if there's any truth to the story, the responsibility for the house and its legacy rests on Shelley's shoulders, so I can see it's a lot of pressure. Especially with Janelle on the run."

"Literally on the run?"

"Remember I said she got into some trouble? Shelley dealt with the issue, but it seemed wise for Janelle to put some distance on the past, too."

"It seems like your Gran is stuck between a rock and a hard place. Not magical, but still attractive to the wrong people."

"That's how I see it. The myth is as dangerous as the real thing. It attracts a dubious element we're not equipped to fend off. So the banishment is apparently for our own protection."

"It's like the buried treasure," I said. "They think you have answers and they're prepared to fight hard for them."

"Exactly. And in gran's case and mine, there's no gold at all." She shook her head. "At least *I* know it, unlike Gran."

"So this is why you kept a low profile in Boston?"

"I didn't buy into the whole thing, but crazy's crazy, whether it's magic or not." She touched my arm again. "There's never been a sign of trouble since. I wouldn't knowingly put you or your family and animals in harm's way."

I gave her a grin. "Whereas I've knowingly put you at risk plenty of times."

"That's different. Those situations have been about regular sociopaths."

Now I laughed out loud. "Regular murderers versus witchy murderers?"

"Exactly." She laughed, too. "Although remember, we don't use that word."

"Right. People used that word to punish people for all kinds of things for centuries." I waited a few beats and asked the big question. "Jilly, do you think your gran is, well, crazy? For lack of a better word."

"Quirky and eccentric, most definitely. Deranged, no. She just has some strange ideas."

"Don't we all?" I reached out to touch Keats' ears and felt the usual tingle of energy flow into my fingertips. Who's to say it wasn't magic of sorts? I explained it away with my concussion, and his superior sheepdog senses and powers of observation. Some days I believed it was a profound bond with a phenomenal dog. Other days I believed it truly was magical. "Not everything can be easily explained."

"I know. But when my aunt cut my mom and me off, I decided to keep my feet on the ground. To stay practical and pragmatic."

"Hence the degrees in psychology and human resources," I said. "I shared the same goal. To understand people better and keep my eyes wide open."

"But we can't outrun our pasts forever. They've caught up with us both this year."

I shrugged. "That's okay. Whatever your relatives have to throw at us, we'll handle it, just like we've handled every murder investigation."

"It's the magic I worry about, or more specifically the lack thereof. Gran's really just a regular old lady who doesn't even have Edna's combat skills. A sitting duck."

"Let's just go in with an open mind. Use the powers of observation we've honed over the past decade and just see what's what."

"I don't want to keep an open mind about this."

"Just like I didn't want to keep an open mind about Calvin. But throwing logs on my fires of resentment held me back."

"And how do you feel now?" she asked. "Did the fire go out?"

"Not completely, but it's so much better. Basically it feels like I've faced the thing I dreaded most and survived. Calvin's back and he's just a man with issues."

"Lucky for you, Calvin doesn't think he's a warlock."

Now I truly laughed and Keats joined in for the first time with a happy pant. "No one says that word, do they? Can you imagine what my mom would think of all this? She would so love to be an official witch."

"I love Dahlia," she said. "Eccentric in just the right ways."

"I bet your gran is, too. You might look at her differently now. We've seen plenty of things that can't easily be explained away."

"I won't." Her jaw set stubbornly, but I knew my friend was more flexible than she seemed in this moment.

"Jilly, think about it. The way we chat to Keats and Percy makes people speculate about us."

"Just our sanity," Jilly said. "Not about our witchiness."

"That's what I'm trying to say... that witchiness is a matter of perspective. This may stretch our horizons a little, that's all."

She flung herself back in her seat in a sulk. "There was a good reason I ditched my family."

"The problem with family is they won't stay ditched." Once again I patted her arm encouragingly. Keats laid one white paw over my hand to add his vote of confidence. "Just remember... they're not your real family. We are."

Percy added a plaintive meow from the back seat and Jilly nodded. "If we're going to be knee-deep in crazy, there's no one else I'd rather have behind me."

I glanced into the mirrors in what was becoming a compulsive ritual. "Let's hope we're the only ones behind you until the gates of the Briars lock behind all of us."

CHAPTER SIX

I had no idea what to expect from a deluxe gated community. Such things didn't exist in Clover Grove, where most seniors either stayed home with their families or entered Sunny Acres Retirement Villa, which was neither high end nor high security. I was in and out of the villa regularly to visit seniors I'd befriended over the past few months.

The Briar Estates was indeed gated and at least partially surrounded by high brick walls with elaborate ironwork on top featuring barbed briars.

"It looks like a prison with a classier design," I said, reaching out of the truck to press the security button. "Is it to keep people in or keep people out?"

"Both," Jilly said. "From what Gran tells me, there are day trips that are accompanied by a security detail."

My eyes widened as I turned to her. "A security detail?"

"Bystanders probably see them as attendants or care-givers, but they're apparently armed."

"Armed! Oh, my. Seems like a savage swan might be

the least of their worries. I hope I can help with that, at least."

"I'm sure you will. With all the safety measures in place, only a rogue swan could get inside and scare people."

"Well, you leave the swan to Keats and me, while Percy helps you with your grandmother." I turned to look at the cat, who'd demanded to be out of his carrier on the last leg of the journey. "Do your fur baby thing. It keeps Jilly calm."

Percy climbed over the headrest and down to perch right on top of Keats, which the dog hated. A skirmish started in Jilly's lap and stopped just as suddenly as a voice came over the intercom demanding our names. When I answered there was another long pause before the double doors creaked open to allow us into the fortress.

Inside, two men stood waiting in knockoff police uniforms. There were epaulets on the shoulders and pockets embroidered with green barbs.

"Welcome to the Briars," the taller man said. He had a warm smile and eyes that seemed to twinkle. "I'm Special Constable Larry Helms and this is my colleague, Special Constable Doug Farrows. Mrs. Brighton wasn't expecting you until this evening. My call woke her up."

"We decided to drive straight through," Jilly said, introducing herself, then me, and finally Keats and Percy. "It was easier on the pets."

"Didn't Mrs. Brighton tell you about our no-pets policy?" Doug Farrows said. "If the board of directors made an exception, we didn't hear about it."

"They're very well behaved," I said, summoning my best HR smile. "Mrs. Brighton asked us to help with your swan problem and we need our best team on the job."

"Ivy's an animal whisperer," Jilly said. Catching herself, she added, "I just mean she's a hobby farmer with

expert practical skills. The sheepdog is her magic weapon."
Now her fingers fluttered. "Not magic of course. Or a
weapon. Although a sheepdog at work always looks like
magic. Doesn't it, Ivy?"

Jilly was babbling, which was also completely
unlike her.

"It sure does," I said. "Well, it's nice to meet you,
constables. We look forward to our vacation here. It's a
lovely place."

I couldn't actually see much of it yet. Tall trees with
broad canopies mostly blocked the sun's early rays. The
atmosphere didn't feel welcoming, either. Hair prickled on
my arms and the back of my neck. Looking down, I saw
both pets had fluffed, too.

"You'd be better leaving the swan problem to us, Ms.
Galloway," Doug said, chilling me with blue eyes that
seemed as eerie as Keats' in the weak light. "Unless you
have specialized swan skills. This bird has a ten-foot wingspan and one heck of a temper." He glanced at Keats and
the collision of blue eyes sent the officer backward a step.
"Swans have been known to drown dogs, you know.
They're ruthless."

I expected Keats to shudder at the prospect of an
aquatic demise, but he kept staring at Doug until the man
took another step backward.

"We'll figure something out," I said. "In the meantime,
we'd best get moving. Mrs. Brighton is waiting."

"Ladies, come back this afternoon for a full briefing on
our operating rules," said Constable Helms. "The security
of our residents is paramount."

"Of course, Special Constable Helms," Jilly said.

"Call me Special Constable Larry," he said. "Everyone
does."

I wanted to laugh but pressed my lips together instead as we got back into the truck. If I hoped to flit around under the radar here, I'd need to respect the laws of the land.

The men stood with arms crossed as we drove off and followed their directions to Mrs. Brighton's house. The streets were wide, short, and lined with flowering trees that gave off a heavy, almost cloying fragrance. Nearly identical white bungalows with blue shingles sat side by side. Only a few subtle touches set them apart—a bird fountain here and a gnome or two there.

"Do people own their homes?" I asked Jilly. "It looks like a regulated compound."

"They own the house but not the land," she said. "Like a condo. There's a board with elected officials to speak on behalf of owners. Overall things seem to run smoothly."

"They must pay an arm and a leg in fees. Everything is impeccable."

"That's the upside. Residents barely need to lift a finger. But if you do want to plant anything other than regulation flowers, you need to petition the board." She gave a nervous laugh. "It must be tough on someone like Gran, who has her own opinions. Unless she's changed."

Ahead on the left, a woman with long silver hair stood at the end of a short driveway waiting for us. The sun had shoved itself higher on the horizon and made the woman's curls gleam. She was wearing a flowing blue dress that almost touched her ankles and a navy shawl with white tassels. I didn't see a hint of Jilly in her face or figure, but they both had gorgeous curls and when she smiled, the resemblance became clear. Jumping out of the truck, I saw that her eyes were also as green and sharp as my friend's.

Jilly came around the truck, arms crossed. She wasn't planning on hugging her grandmother, but Keats had other ideas. He circled both women and tightened his sheepdog knot until Jilly relented. He didn't release them for about eight seconds. It would be harder to hold a grudge against anyone after a hug that long.

Squirming away at last, Jilly gestured to the rest of us. "Gran, I want you to meet my best friends. Ivy Galloway, Keats, the brilliant border collie, and Percy, the best cat in the world and my surrogate son."

"I'm Bridie Brighton," she said, offering me a hug that felt normal and grandmotherly. She had a lovely, melodious voice. "I've never been a fan of pets, Ivy. I hope you won't hold that against me."

"Not at all," I said. "I love them enough for both of us, Mrs. Brighton."

"Call me Bridie. It's really Birgitta, but no one's ever called me that."

"I hope my pets won't be a big imposition, Bridie. If so, I could look for a pet-friendly hotel nearby."

She gave a dismissive wave. There were plenty of rings on her fingers studded with stones I didn't recognize, bangles on her wrist, and a blob of amber dangling from a long pendant around her neck. Her bohemian style certainly clashed with Jilly's conservative polish. No wonder Bridie had handed over the classic pearl earrings.

"Don't be silly, dear," she said. "You're here to help our community. Jilly told me all about your mystical touch with animals."

Jilly scowled. "I never said 'mystical.'"

Bridie ignored that and continued. "I'd never relegate guests of any species to a hotel. Besides, the Strathmore Hotel and Resort is the only one in the vicinity and it's quite swanky. I doubt animals are welcome there."

"Well, we're definitely not swanky," I said.

"Your overalls gave me the first clue," Bridie said, with a chuckle. "I suppose they were comfortable for a long drive." She gave Jilly an appraising glance. "You both look a little worse for wear, though, girls."

"We drove straight through, remember," Jilly said.

"You didn't need to do that. The swan is a problem but not life or death. At least, not yet. With a few residents over the century mark, it could come to that, though."

"We'll get right on it," I said. "In fact, let's go meet this grumpy swan now."

"You need breakfast, a shower and a nap in that order," Bridie said. "The swan can wait a little longer."

She tried to shepherd us to the house while our black-and-white shepherd did the opposite. I don't think Bridie noticed the tide had turned to carry her down the driveway instead of up.

"Why on earth would you drive all night, Jilly?" she said. "It wasn't safe to push yourselves that hard."

"It wasn't safe *not* to," Jilly said. "We decided to keep moving after getting tailed."

"Tailed!" Bridie's eyebrows shot up. "Tailed by whom?"

"That's the question," Jilly said. "We thought we'd shaken them so we stopped at a motel. Then Ivy saw something odd there, and we got back on the road."

Bridie turned to me so fast that her chandelier earrings jangled. "What exactly did you see, Ivy?"

I described the incident at the motel. Now that it was well behind us, it seemed less ominous. If it hadn't been for the reaction of the animals at the time, I might have dismissed it completely. But Percy's litterbox move had never been wrong yet.

"It was the strangest thing," I said, at the end of the

story. "I wish I still had the photo, but I must have deleted it by accident."

Bridie's green eyes pinned me and her brow creased. "You said this mysterious figure was wearing a uniform?"

"It seemed so, yes. There was a crest on the chest pocket in yellow. At least I thought so. The image quality was poor, though."

She wrapped the fringed shawl around her shoulders and shivered. "Is there a chance trouble followed you from the farm, Ivy? I know you've had some dangerous run-ins."

"It's possible," I said. "Crime in Clover Grove runs a little deeper than I knew growing up."

"In all of hill country," Bridie said. "The roots are twisted and impossible to uproot, I'm afraid. I'm sure Jilly's told you about our—"

"House in Wyldwood Springs?" Jilly interrupted. "My best summers were spent there with you, Gran, but I haven't shared the tall tales, yet."

"Why on earth not, Jillian? You two have been friends since college. And with all that's happened since rescuing that dog, it's clear Ivy can handle herself."

"I roll with what comes," I said. "How about you fill me in on what's happening here while we go meet the swan, Bridie?"

"All right, then," she said as we reached the road. Her smile was back but the fact that she set off in bedroom slippers told me she was more flustered than she let on.

"Gran." Jilly gestured toward the slippers.

"Oh my goodness," she said. "The Mighties would have a field day with that."

"The Mighties?" Jilly asked, as Bridie went back up the drive and slipped her feet into a pair of sandals sitting on a rack by the door. They had floppy white leather daisies on top, which sealed the deal on the hippy look.

"The High-and-Mighties. Mighties for short," Bridie said, joining us again. "The clique that can demolish your reputation in three seconds flat."

"Sounds like Clover Grove," I said. "Or any small town, I suppose."

"The Briars is a small town, for good and for ill," she said, leading us down the road. "It's barely six a.m., yet I guarantee people are already talking about your overalls, Ivy."

I laughed. "I'm used to gossip."

A frown battled with her smile and won. "You've never experienced gossip till you've gotten on the wrong side of the Mighties. The impact can be... catastrophic."

"Are you on their wrong side, Gran?" Jilly asked.

"Today, yes. I ride the line with wobbles either way. If you manage to vanquish the swan, it might push me back over." Now she grinned for the first time and it made her look years younger. "No pressure."

"We're good under pressure," I said. "All of us."

Up ahead a woman took her time collecting the newspaper from the end of her driveway.

"Mighty?" Jilly asked.

"One of the Mightiest," Bridie said, lifting her hand in a merry wave. "That's Cherise Heatherington, and greeting you first will be a badge of honor for her."

Cherise was wearing a fuchsia jumpsuit with a long zipper. It was an ambitious choice for someone who was well over 80 and nowhere near as robust as our apocalyptic octogenarians back home. Her flyaway hair and sloppy makeup suggested speedy preparation. Opalescent pink lipstick was colored way outside the lines.

Bridie made the introductions while Cherise blatantly appraised us through oversized glasses with green sparkly frames.

"Hello, girls," she said. "Jillian, you're the spitting image of your grandmother, I must say. Roland always says Bridie could stop a clock."

It was light enough now to see color rising in Bridie's cheeks. "Roland is Cherise's husband," she said. "He's kind to all the ladies."

"Some more than others," Cherise said. "All more than me, I'm afraid."

"Oh, Cherise," Bridie said. "Rollie is devoted to you. But the ratio of women to men here would turn anyone's head."

"It's at least ten to one," Cherise said. "Our dance nights are interesting, girls."

"Dance nights?" Jilly asked. "Sounds like fun."

"We have a full calendar, thanks to our volunteer social convenor, Charlotte Greenwich," Bridie said. "She never stops."

"Never stops talking, you mean," Cherise said. "Honestly, I don't know how Lottie gets anything done with all her poking around."

"Yet she accomplishes so much for us. There's never a day without an activity." Bridie turned and gave Jilly and me an exaggerated smile. "Busy seniors are happy seniors."

"Apparently," Cherise said. Her eyes dropped to stare at Keats, who stared right back. His tail and ears had drooped. "What a strange dog. You do know we have a no-pets policy here, girls?"

"A rule with exceptions," Bridie said. "It would be cruel to part people from the pets they owned before coming. The rule really applies to new pets, Cherise."

"Informally. On the books, it's still the law of the Briars. And this one"—she gestured at Keats—"makes me uncomfortable."

"We won't be here long, Mrs. Heatherington," I said. "Keats and Percy, my cat, are a big help in dealing with disruptive animals, so I'm hoping we can sort out this cranky swan problem together."

"Good luck with that." Cherise let her glasses slide down her nose. "That flapping monster chased my Rollie and knocked him over yesterday."

"Throwing rocks wasn't Rollie's best idea," Bridie said. "I guess he didn't realize how fast swans can move."

Cherise gave a grunt. "He learned that lesson with the alligator. Sometimes men like to push their limits."

"Alligator?" Jilly's voice was a little raspy. "There are alligators here?"

"It's sub-tropical and similar to the everglades," Cherise said. "All kinds of creatures lie in wait."

Tugging each of us by the sleeve, Bridie said, "We'll speak again soon, Cherise. Looks like we have a few stops on our way to the pond."

Indeed, half a dozen women were already outside, moving at a snail's pace to gather their newspapers. That probably had less to do with age than meeting us as we passed.

Bridie kept up a brisk clip, calling out greetings while trying to keep our little parade moving. One woman hurried down the driveway leaning on an ornately carved wooden cane.

"Stop right there, Bridie Brighton," she called, waving the cane. "I want to meet this granddaughter of yours and her swan whisperer friend."

"I'm hardly an expert," I said, after Bridie introduced us

to Elsie Cornwall. The woman's hair was so decidedly mauve that it had to be a choice, rather than an accident. She was wearing a floral caftan that was as roomy and garish as my artist friend Teri Mason's collection back home. "I hope I can help."

"Oh, you can, sweetheart," Elsie said. "It's in the cards."

"The cards?" I asked.

"I do tarot readings. I'm sure Bridie's already told you. My accuracy rate is considered the best in the Briars. Give me an hour and I'll prove it to you."

Bridie pinched my arm in the way Jilly often did and spoke for me. "Ivy doesn't believe in such things, Elsie. She's a simple farmer."

"I'm always curious, Mrs. Cornwall," I said. "I'll take you up on that offer another time."

"Wonderful," she said. "A sensible girl, not a simple girl."

"Not simple at all," Jilly said, and it was nice to see one of her brilliant smiles. They'd been in short supply, and I relied on them like sunshine. Vitamin Jilly offered a constant infusion of optimism.

"I'm sure I can provide you girls with sufficient insight," Bridie said. "There have been messages from beyond."

"Gran," Jilly said. "It's not a competition."

"Sweetheart," Elsie said, "it's always a competition around here. Everyone thinks she has some sort of insider knowledge about the future or the past. Tea leaves, trances, crystal balls, you name it."

"There's precious little to predict around here," Bridie said. "One day looks pretty much like the next. Except for the swan, and no one predicted that."

"Don't forget I saw a bird in a dream last month," Elsie

said. "I mistook it for a raptor, I'm afraid. Visions get a little muddled sometimes."

I looked down at Keats, who tipped his head this way and that, taking everything in and standing down on judgment for the moment. His ears were twitching and his tail moderately high. Percy's posture was also relaxed. They'd slept enough on the drive to make a good showing. Still, Keats was swiveling constantly, checking all sides.

"What about the men?" I asked. "Don't they have these abilities?"

Elsie's caftaned shoulders rose and fell. "Some probably do, but not my Carlisle. He'd rather mock us, I'm afraid. Men are allergic to woo-woo."

Bridie towed us out of earshot. "If Rollie Heatherington had any foresight, he wouldn't have been mowed down by the swan. His toupee fell off and Charlotte Greenwich got a picture for her next newsletter. Cherise was beside herself."

She kept us moving after that, despite many attempts to stop us. One equally fit woman trotted after us down the street.

"I'm Alice Cheevers," she said, puffing slightly. "One of Bridie's best friends, although you wouldn't know it today."

Alice was petite and the only woman we'd seen so far with brown hair. There was a salon on site that probably got steady business.

"No offence, Alice," Bridie said. "The girls have been driving all night. I want to give them a quick look at the troublemaker and get them home for a rest. There will be time to socialize later. I bet they'll join us for bingo tonight."

"Absolutely," Jilly said. "I look forward to chatting with you, Mrs. Cheevers."

"Miss," Alice said as she trotted along. "Never met the

right fellow, unfortunately. But you'll make a beautiful bride, Jilly. I predict it before the year's out. And fair-haired babies in your arms after that."

Jilly's face practically exploded in flames. "I'm not engaged, Miss Cheevers."

"That's coming very soon." She pushed back tendrils of dark hair. "I was the first to call this one and my record on romance is stellar. All I had to do was hold a photo of you, although normally I do palms." She turned thick bifocals on me. "As for you, Ivy, you're about to be distracted by a handsome ginger."

I gestured to Percy. "This one?"

She laughed. "The one bearing arms, not claws."

"No armed gingers for me, thank you. I'll show you my palm later and I bet you'll see someone else."

Falling back suddenly, Alice let her hands drop and then wrung them. "One more thing," she called after us. "Ivy, listen to the donkey."

"The donkey?" My brow furrowed. "I have several of them back home."

Bridie gave a sudden jerk, turning left onto a short dead-end street. "Never mind Alice. I love her dearly but she's overconfident in her predictions."

"So Jilly won't be marrying soon and having a blond brood?" I asked, grinning.

"I do hope so," Bridie said. "There's rough water to cross first, and we're almost there."

The interruptions weren't over yet, however. A man of about our age came down a driveway and waved. This time Bridie stopped and smiled. "Well, good morning, Casey. Please meet my granddaughter, Jilly Blackwood, and her friend, Ivy Galloway. Girls, Casey is the owner and property manager for the Briar Estates. Our big boss, as it were."

Casey was handsome, with plenty of dark hair and a pleasant smile. "Ladies, I'm just a pawn," he said. "First to my father, the real owner, and then to the board. I can't decide what to have for breakfast without extensive consultation." He looked down at my pets. "No one asked me about these two, for example. I hope they're well behaved."

"Very," Jilly said, offering him her brightest smile. Casey melted a little under its heat, like most men and any objections he may have had seemed to fade.

"Were you consulting with Saundra Milby about cereal?" Bridie said, proving herself as nosy as everyone else.

"Her sprinkler system went haywire overnight. I pulled the darn thing apart before giving up and calling a plumber." He flexed his hands and rubbed one wrist. "I hate losing, but the cold got to me." He smiled again. "What brings you ladies out so early?"

"The girls wanted to see the pond," Bridie said. "It's our main attraction, especially since the goldfish arrived. They're like flashes of fire."

"Someone freed them instead of flushing," Casey said. "And they spread like... well, wildfire. Expect the unexpected at the Briars, you two, and enjoy your stay."

"Thanks, and see you soon," Jilly called, as Bridie pressed forward again.

"Don't encourage Casey, dear," Bridie said. "He's not in the cards for you. I support Alice's prediction of blond grandchildren."

Tossing Jilly a grin, I let Bridie hurry me along till we reached the end of the road and stepped over a curb onto a well-worn trail. I expected Keats and Percy to frolic ahead as we made our way down the path to the water, but neither one left our sides.

"Uh-oh." I pointed at my puffy dog. "Someone's not thrilled about meeting the swan."

The pond looked quite pretty with dawn's flattering light. Reeds and tall rushes surrounded the oval body of water that was about a quarter of a mile long and half as wide. An old wooden pier that was more picturesque than practical sat off to our right.

"That dock looks like a deathtrap," I said. "I'm surprised they keep it around."

"It's quaint," Bridie said. "At least according to people who like that sort of thing. We put it to a vote at a board meeting, and it stays. There's a hazard sign, now, at least. You'd think people would avoid it on their own, but some are more capable than others."

Keats ran back and forth in front of us and nearly tripped Bridie.

"I'm sorry," I said, grabbing her elbow for a change. "He's trying to keep us safe."

"I don't even see the swan," Bridie said, scanning the water. Then she spun right around. "It's snuck up on dry land before and attacked." She led us closer to the pond. "Dee-Dee Trask took quite a tumble off her walker. Nearly broke a hip. But then, she's been sanctioned for leaving out poisoned bait for raccoons so who knows what she was doing."

"The plot thickens," I said, slipping past Keats and signaling him to hold the others back. "We'll get to the bottom of it."

I squinted at the gleaming water in search of our white, winged adversary. Keats gave a sharp yap of warning just as my right boot started sinking. Water gushed in around the laces and then right overtop as it sank into the silty muck bordering the pond. In seconds I was in over my knees with both feet.

Keats let out a wail, as if I were about to drop to oblivion.

"Buddy, I've stepped into worse," I called out.

Staring around, I saw that might not actually be true.

Less than two yards away, a body was lodged in weeds.

CHAPTER SEVEN

I'm not sure if I screamed or not. My throat felt raw as Bridie and Jilly closed in to pull me out of the sludge. Likely Keats had herded them forward to help. They were too focused on their footwork to notice the floating woman.

"What's wrong?" Jilly said. "I've never seen you get so worked up over mud before."

I managed to hoist my arm and point.

"Oh my gosh!" Jilly said. "Gran, don't look."

Then she hauled both of us back so fast that Bridie lost a sandal, and I tripped and landed on my backside. The ground was mushy in a few spots even yards away from the water. It was like the marshes that dotted our county back home. Sneaky.

Craning to get a better look, Bridie sucked in so much air that she had a coughing fit. "Girls, *do something*," she sputtered. "She needs help."

Percy stood well back from the water's edge making elaborate sweeping gestures with one orange paw. After a few seconds, he switched paws. The classic double litter box maneuver told me this woman was past needing help. Jilly noticed too, and our eyes met.

"It's no use, Bridie," I said, still seated in soggy grass. "She's gone. And we should leave her exactly as she is till the police come."

Jilly fumbled for her phone. "Any idea who it is, Gran?"

"It looks like Lottie," Bridie said. "Charlotte Greenwich." Her voice sounded strangled and she clutched her throat. "I've seen that dress before. It always reminded me of my mother's bedroom curtains. The swan must have hated the hibiscus print, too. So garish."

Jilly glared at her. "Gran, don't say things like that. It's no time for jokes."

"Oh, I know. I'm just..."

"In shock," Jilly said. "Strange things come out of the mouths of shocked people. So let *us* do the talking when the police arrive."

As Jilly spoke to the police on the phone, I looked up at Bridie's pale face. "We've had some experience, unfortunately."

"They'll shoot the swan," Bridie said. "The board will accept nothing less."

That got me up on my feet. I walked over to the decrepit dock and said, "Where is this bird?"

Almost on cue, a flash of white emerged from the screen of heavy vines on the other side of the pond and the swan swam toward us. Its wings were up and curved in what appeared to be a warrior pose. When the bird came closer, I saw it was a mute swan with its orange beak bordered in black. I'd done a little homework in advance and while they weren't actually mute, this species tended to be quieter than other swans. Not to mention more aggressive. Special Constable Doug hadn't been wrong about its impressive size. This bird could swat us like flies.

"Keats, stay with Jilly and keep an eye on Percy," I said. "We need to be careful."

After a second, I gave the bird a little bow. I don't know why. It just seemed like the polite thing to do before such a magnificent beast.

"Did you just curtsy to that bird?" Bridie asked.

"I was aiming for a bow but my knees are wobbly," I said. "The point was to show him—or her—that we mean no harm."

I looked around for goldfish but if they were there, they'd turned off their high beams.

"You'd better come back," Jilly said, dropping the phone in her pocket. "Keats is having a conniption."

"The poor dog," Bridie said, as he skulked over to me when I left the dock. "He's all busted up about Lottie."

Keats shuddered convulsively and I shook my head. "Actually, he's more busted up about being this close to water. He's the bravest dog in the world... except when it comes to the bathtub or anything larger. Good thing I packed a life jacket because we might be spending some time down here."

The dog whined and stared up at me pleadingly.

"It's almost like he understands you," Bridie said.

"He does, at least some of the time," I said. "Sheepdogs are bred to read every flicker of an eyelid or twitch of a finger. Keats and I are attuned to one another."

"Now I see what Jillian meant about your magical connection."

"Just practical farm magic." I listened for sirens and Percy picked up on them first. He climbed up the back of my overalls and sat on my shoulder. "The police aren't far off. My policy in these situations is to say little. Let them do the talking."

"Exactly," Jilly said. "We were just in the wrong place at the wrong time. Saw nothing. Heard nothing. Right, Gran?"

"Of course, Jillian. That's the truth."

"No speculation. No gossip. It's their job to figure out what happened."

"Lottie fell into the water and drowned, that's what happened," Bridie said. "Probably trying to get some photos of the swan or feeding it crackers. Those hibiscus petals couldn't keep her afloat."

"Gran, that's the kind of commentary to avoid. There may be more to this story than we know."

"More to the—" Bridie covered her mouth, and then murmured, "You don't think Lottie was...?"

"Don't even say the word," Jilly said. "It's possible she fell prey to the swan... or someone else."

"Why would you even say such a thing?" Her grandmother lowered her hand and a dozen bangles tinkled. "It wouldn't have occurred to me and now I can't unhear it."

"We're not sure, Bridie," I said. "But we have seen how the pets behave in such situations. So you'll want to be careful about what you say to the police. Be honest, but careful. Do you know if Lottie had enemies?"

"Enemies?" Bridie's green eyes darted all around. "Of course. We're all enemies here."

"You can't *all* be enemies," Jilly said.

"It's more like an armed neutrality, I suppose. You never know who you can trust, and it changes by the day. There are factions like the Mighties and others. I have no doubt people will try to throw each other under the bus if the swan *isn't* the villain."

"Gran, surely it can't be that bad. What a horrible place to live."

"Oh, Jilly, it's home. They're my family now. We bicker, we make up. Nothing like this has happened before. I mean, if it's what you think it is."

I looked down at Keats, whose convulsive shuddering had stopped. His flags had risen again, telling me we weren't out of the woods yet. "So this Lottie had enemies..." I prompted.

Bridie glanced out at the water and then looked away. "More than many. As our social convenor, she knew everyone. Their likes, their dislikes. Even their secrets." She shuddered, as Keats had earlier. "In a place like this, information is currency. Lottie always had the nicest garden. People dropped off cuttings, and casseroles and little gifts. She walked around like there were springs under her shoes."

"Okay, now you know what *not* to say," Jilly said, watching the police drive right up onto the grass. Four officers spilled out of two cruisers and ran toward us. "Remember your script, Gran. Please."

"I will, don't worry." She turned and her eyebrows shot up. "Well, I'll be. Alice was right about your armed ginger, Ivy."

The cop in the lead had auburn hair. He would most certainly be considered handsome by someone who wasn't lucky enough to have a tall, dark and handsome chief of police waiting at home. Thinking of Kellan now made me cross my arms and hug myself. He would be upset when he heard what had happened. While it had nothing at all to do with the farm or Clover Grove, somehow I'd stuck my foot in trouble again. Both feet, actually. There was grit between my

toes and despite more pressing concerns, it was uncomfortable.

"Don't go there, either, Gran," Jilly said. "Ivy's happily
taken by a wonderful man. And this isn't the right time to
be thinking about romance."

"It's long past time for you two to be thinking about
romance." Bridie found a sly smile. "I consider you an
honorary granddaughter, Ivy. The way you're trying to help
is more than most family would do."

That was probably a jab at Jilly for her long absence but
Bridie was smart enough to be indirect.

"My mom calls Jilly her best and favorite daughter," I
said. "And there are five Galloway girls."

"You're all wonderful daughters," Jilly said. "And
Dahlia knows that full well. How many times have you
helped her out of situations just like—" Her voice cut off
suddenly and she finished the thought with a slight flick of
her fingers toward the pond. Now the police were gathered
around the body, one officer in the water up to his waist.
Another was stuck in the muck not far from where I'd been
trapped. It was surprising that senior residents hadn't been
pulled into the depths permanently. Or maybe they had.

"Here we go again, Jilly," I said. "Crime sticks to us like
a bad smell."

"Quiet now," she said, as Officer Auburn walked over.
"New place, new rules."

Indeed. Here we didn't have Kellan or Asher to take the
lead. Nor would these men necessarily understand us—our
humor, our camaraderie and our unique bond with Keats
and Percy.

"Normal," I muttered. "We need to act normal."

Keats offered a little sneeze that sounded like, "Fat
chance."

"We need to try, at least," Jilly said. "And *you* keep quiet."

"Jillian. That's no way to speak to your friend." Bridie's tone was severe.

"I'm speaking to the dog," Jilly said. "But you're right, anyway. Sorry, Keats."

His mouth dropped open in a happy pant and he mumbled something along the lines of, "We're all family, here."

"Exactly," Jilly said.

"*Jillian.* And you were worried about me. Don't speak to that dog in front of—" She stopped and offered a wide smile. "Hello, officer. I'm Bridie Brighton, a resident here." She introduced us and then added, "I'm sorry to say that we're the ones who discovered Charlotte Greenwich in this desperate predicament."

"I'm Chief Gillock," he said, curtly. "Please tell me exactly what happened."

We looked at each other and silently voted Jilly to be official spokesperson. She accepted the responsibility, knowing that her grandmother and I both had a little problem with oversharing. Bridie might be one brick short of a full load, but I was traveling light, too.

"Chief, it's all so shocking," Jilly began. "My friend Ivy and I only arrived at the Briar Estates an hour ago after a long drive. We wanted to stretch our legs and Gran decided to show us the pond and the swan. Unfortunately, Ivy walked too close to the edge and sunk in the silt. Right in front of her was... well, this woman. Gran seems to think it might be Charlotte Greenwich, a long-time resident here."

"Lottie was our social convenor," Gran said. "She organized some wonderful events and life is going to be terribly dull without her."

"Gran, we don't know for sure it's Lottie."

"I've been staring at the back of Lottie's head for over ten years, Jillian," Bridie said. "She was in the front row of every single board meeting and on her feet half the time arguing with the executive. Never could get herself elected, no matter how hard she tried. She deserved that role."

"Gran." Jilly's voice was low and insistent. "We haven't let Chief Gillock get a word in edgewise." She offered him her best headhunter smile—the one that charmed the most aggressive corporate sharks. "I'm so sorry, sir. As you can tell, we're all rattled."

The chief's jawline was as pale and chiseled as a marble bust, but the light dusting of freckles made it less formidable. Those flecks probably worked to his advantage when he wanted to be disarming, but right now they undermined his severe expression. I couldn't help thinking of a kid dressed up for Halloween.

Shaking my head to dispel the image, I covered my mouth. A smirk would get me in big trouble, at least with Jilly. Fatigue made me giddy.

"Have I missed something amusing, Ms. Galloway?" the chief asked.

My hand dropped and took the smirk with it. I had been a corporate soldier for too long to let silliness get the best of me. "Of course not, Chief. As my friend said, we're tired and shocked, but there's nothing amusing about Lottie dying in a pond."

"If indeed it is Charlotte Greenwich," he said.

"As I told the girls, I recognize her dress," Bridie said. "My grandmother had—"

"Never mind," Jilly said. "The chief will confirm the woman's identity."

"If indeed it is a woman," Gran muttered, mimicking the chief.

Keats was the only one who gave a mumble of laughter and her eyes dropped to him with a startled look.

The chief shook his head. "We'll take your contact information and come by later to chat. In the meantime, expect a call to assemble at the recreation center so that we can brief everyone at once." He glanced around. "Since I don't see a vehicle, I'll have one of my officers drive you home."

"That won't be necessary," Jilly said. "Gran's house is just a short walk."

"They're lying in wait, Jillian," Bridie said, gesturing to the crowd assembling at the entrance to the park. "Worse than turkey vultures."

"Gossip and speculation are exactly what we want to avoid," Chief Gillock said, as he beckoned one of his men. "Please get in the car peacefully."

Bridie bristled at his implication. "I'd like to see you take me by force, young man. I have special abilities that might give you the shock of—"

"Gran!" Perpetually cool Jilly lost her composure. "I'm so sorry, Chief. Gran studied martial arts, but I'm quite sure she wouldn't use her moves on you."

For the first time, his lips twitched, ever so slightly. He wasn't completely immune to the Jilly Blackwood magic after all.

"Just go home, ladies."

"Chief, I lost a shoe, in case you haven't noticed," Bridie said. "Maybe you could get it for me."

Only the daisy on Bridie's sandal was visible in the muck and Chief Gillock frowned. Before he could do the gallant thing, however, someone else beat him to it.

Normally Keats hated getting his paws dirty, but he evidently wanted to impress Jilly's grandmother. Seizing the shoe by the petals, he delivered it to her.

"Well, thank you, Keats." Bridie's voice was almost a purr. "Still, I can't put that filthy thing on. I'll need to hop over to the car. Chief... would you?"

Sighing, Chief Gillock allowed Bridie to wrap one arm around his waist and half-carried her to the police car.

When he left, she smiled at us. "That'll make a much better story for the Mighties, girls. They'll think I was faint from the ordeal. We need to be strategic."

"Gran, just slide over," Jilly said. "We all need to fit, including the pets."

I turned to follow the chief and Jilly came, too.

"Let us know if you need help with your investigation," I said. "If you suspect foul play, this is the dog for you. He has a great nose and even better instincts."

The chief tipped his head. "Now why would you ever imagine it was foul play?"

The pinch Jilly gave me reminded me not to tell him the cat now cradled in my arms had said so. "I think everyone will blame the swan, don't you? Fowl play."

"Ah, got it," he said. "Although, it's a poor time for jokes."

"It wasn't the swan," I said, staring out at the bird. The whole time we'd been talking, it had essentially paced back and forth, the loops getting shorter and shorter till it stopped now and faced me. "The poor thing is just distraught that it happened in his backyard, as it were."

"Ivy." Jilly's next pinch would leave a little bruise, like Keats' herding nips. "Everything will come out in the wash," she said. "Including all the dirt on your overalls."

As we walked back to the cruiser, I was acutely aware

of the cold wet spot on my butt. Our escort, a burly cop about twice as tall as he needed to be, shook his head as we passed. A surge of heat rose up from my chest.

Just because I had the best, most handsome cop in the world at home to call my own didn't mean I was immune to the mockery of other officers of the law.

"Throw down a blanket in the cruiser," Chief Gillock called after us. "Something really stinks."

CHAPTER EIGHT

The recreation room in the Briars' community center was well appointed, at least based on what I could see of it through the crowd. There was a full wall of windows overlooking lush gardens, oak paneling on the wall opposite, and fancy chandeliers flickering overhead like old-time gas lamps. The carpet managed to be both attractive and sensible, and the folding chairs set up in front of a low stage had gel cushions that looked comfortable. Jilly said that Bridie complained about the cost of amenities but someone had made tasteful decisions about allocations.

"Why couldn't Lottie get herself elected?" I asked Bridie, leading her to a corner where Jilly and I could ask a few questions with less chance of being overheard. "She sounded like a good candidate for the board."

"She knew too much," Bridie said, trying not to stare at my muddy boots and pants... and failing. "No one wanted to give her any more power than she already had."

"What was there to know?" I tried to hold Keats between my boots so he wouldn't get trampled as people passed. They kept shoving me aside till I was the one who stomped a paw and made him yelp. "Sorry, buddy. At least it wasn't a work boot."

Bridie crooked her finger, and Jilly and I leaned in to listen. "The place looks pretty, girls, but there's so much going on under the surface. Treachery. Lies. Betrayal. And that's not even counting the magic."

"Gran, you know we don't believe in that stuff," Jilly said. "At least the magic part. Clover Grove thrives on treachery, lies and betrayal." Winking at me, she added, "No offence, Ivy. I know it's your hometown."

I laughed. "I love it warts and all."

"You may be in denial about magic," Bridie said, "but plenty of us believe. It's part of our culture."

"Can we just stick to legitimate motives?" Jilly said. "If this were about... *what you're saying*, it would have blown up long ago, right?"

"I suppose," Bridie conceded. "There are squabbles about magic but they always die down without anyone actually dying."

"Gran," Jilly warned. "The walls probably have ears here."

"Someone must have been really angry at Lottie to do something like this," I said. "Wouldn't that have gotten around?"

"Lottie had a knack for showing up in the wrong place at the right time. Yet despite what Cherise said, she didn't dole out gossip like the Mighties. She kept her cards close to the vest."

"Maybe she didn't really know anything," Jilly said. "Or didn't care as much about secrets as you think."

"If that were true, I guess we wouldn't be crammed into this room right now," Bridie said. "Although I still want to believe it was the swan. Or an accident."

"Keats and Percy believe Lottie left the Briars the hard way," I said.

"There's only one way, really," Bridie said. "Once you check in it's nearly impossible to leave otherwise. No one ever tells you that. They make it sound like a luxury cruise."

Jilly's whole body seemed to clench as Bridie stepped into historical territory. "I'm sure Aunt Shelley thought it was for the best, Gran. For your own safety."

"For *her* own safety, you mean," Bridie said.

"Well, you could have said no, right?"

"The boxes on the paperwork said yes or yes."

"Oh, Gran. You promised not to talk about all this if I visited. I'm happy to see you, but I don't want to spend our time reliving the past. You know I had nothing to do with any of it."

Bridie patted Jilly's arm and nodded. "I do. I guess I'm just upset about what's happened. I've felt trouble in my bones for a long time, and that's why I called you. It wasn't just about the swan."

"I figured," Jilly said. "Let's just salvage what we can from our visit while this gets sorted out."

I maneuvered my way back into the conversation. "Bridie, I meant what I said earlier about Keats having a nose for sleuthing. Percy has special gifts, too. If you know anything else about Lottie, maybe we can help the police get to the bottom of it faster."

"I'm not on the best terms with the Mighties right now, so I don't hear much. But even I can't help catching the drift now and then. Gossip is in the water, like a sewage problem."

"Is any of this sewage smelly enough that someone would have wanted Lottie gone?" I asked.

"I wouldn't have thought so. We've all got secrets so it

sort of nets out." Bridie pointed at two bald, paunchy men now standing on the stage. They looked similar except that one had a goatee. "The man with the beard is Vaughan Mills, board president, and the other is Ford Fletcher, vice president. Last I heard, Vaughan was having an affair with Ford's wife." Scanning the room, she flicked her index finger at a tall woman in a mint green suit with a matching striped scarf that looked like it was tied too tight. "Alba Fletcher. That's probably why Ford ran Vaughan down with his golf cart last month. Or maybe he just wanted to take over the board. Either way, it didn't help because Vaughan only broke a toe and continues with his official and unofficial activities."

"Oh my," Jilly said. "It *is* like Clover Grove."

"The smaller the pond the more savage the fish," Bridie said.

"What about Vaughan's wife?" I asked.

Bridie pointed to a sweet-looking woman in a motorized wheelchair. "That's Shirley Mills. She takes delight in reversing that chair into people and objects. There are bruises and dents all over the place."

"Well, if her husband's blatantly cheating, she must be furious," Jilly said. "Did Lottie know, too?"

"Oh yes. It was such common knowledge she didn't bother including it in her newsletter. She liked to do these anonymous teasers to keep people guessing. Called it 'Tarot Talk'."

"So Shirley, Vaughan, Ford and Alba can go on the suspect list," I said. "They may have been worried about being exposed."

"I wish more people worried about being exposed here," Bridie said. "I learned within a week of arrival to stay out of the romance arena." She smoothed her long hair and smiled. "Not that I haven't had opportunities."

"What else, Gran?" Jilly pressed.

"Well, pets are a constant source of tension. The rules allow one cat or one dog under twenty pounds, and they're only grandfathered for new residents. That gives rise to jealousy and resentment. Lottie probably knew about every petty quarrel, pardon my pun."

Keats gave a deep rumble that I felt rather than heard. He was still disgruntled at having to shelter between my calves. Adept as he was at negotiating clumsy feet and hooves, a room full of canes, walkers, wheelchairs and scooters added complexity and I was glad I'd left Percy behind at Bridie's.

Catching my eye, Keats flattened his ears. There was more bothering him than unpredictable devices. If I had to guess, I'd say Lottie's killer was in the room with us right now.

The thought sent a shiver down my back. It felt like a year since we'd left the farm on what I hoped was a vacation. Now here we were in the middle of yet another murder investigation. One I should probably avoid.

Keats shot me a look with his blue eye and I said, "What? I *could* stay out of it. Really."

"Pardon me?" Bridie said.

"Nothing. Sorry. Please go on. What other battles are brewing?"

Her lips pursed for a moment and she held up a finger to silence Jilly. "As I said, the issue of magic causes plenty of spats. Lottie liked to use tarot cards or her antique crystal ball for readings. Maybe someone didn't like what they heard and killed the messenger."

"Huh. Interesting," I said.

"Not interesting," Jilly countered.

Bridie wrung her hands until her bangles tinkled. "The more I think about it, the more I realize you girls need to keep your distance. Even helping with the swan is risky."

"She's right, Ivy. We should let the police do the heavy lifting." Jilly gave me a pleading look. "We're out of our depth here."

"It's so nice when family agree, isn't it?" Bridie said.

Before Jilly could answer, Chief Gillock joined the Briars' executive committee on stage.

"Good morning, everyone," he said. "I'm Andrew Gillock, the new chief of police in Strathmore County. I'm sorry to confirm what you've likely already heard. Today you lost a valued member of your community."

I wondered if he naturally projected like that or had dialed up the volume for the hard of hearing. Even so, there were mutterings of, "What did he say?"

"Charlotte Greenwich passed away in the pond this morning."

"It was that dang swan," Shirley Mills shouted. "You'd better wring its neck before it gets more of us."

Others chimed in with various suggestions of how to rid the Briars of the swan. Keats grumbled between my legs over the unfairness of the swan's being convicted without a trial.

Luckily Chief Gillock appeared to agree because he raised a hand to silence the room. "At the moment there's no evidence the swan is to blame. It's quite possible Miss Greenwich fell into the pond and drowned."

"She visited that pond every day, twice a day, to feed that swan." The speaker was Alba Fletcher, the woman in the mint green suit. "I highly doubt she just fell in today."

"Maybe she had a stroke," Elsie Cornwall said.

"Or heart failure," Alice Cheevers suggested.

"The surrounding turf is silty and unstable," the chief said. "Anyone could slip."

Casey Cox, the property manager, came up on the low stage, too. "I'm on this, folks. The swamp beyond the Briars has been encroaching on our little pond. It gets bigger and more boggy every year."

"Fill it in," someone muttered. I stood on tiptoe and saw Special Constable Doug leaning against the wall with a one-wheeled hoverboard clutched in his arms. That was an inspired way to get around the compound.

Bridie raised her hand. "My granddaughter's friend sank into the silt up to her knees this morning and we had to pull her out. Maybe Lottie had no one to help."

At least three dozen gray, white or bald heads turned our way and Keats bristled. Clearly no one was going to throw down a welcome mat for us.

"You three were the first to find Lottie," Cherise Heatherington said. "Maybe she didn't fall in on her own."

"Pardon me?" Bridie straightened and the words shot out. "Was that an accusation, Cherise? Please speak up so the chief can hear it."

Cherise adjusted her green sparkly glasses, unfazed. "You and Lottie had words recently. Is it a coincidence that your young visitors arrived just in time for her passing?"

The mumble between my shins turned into a low growl and I squeezed Keats quiet. Bridie had fallen silent under a similar squeeze from Jilly, so I raised my hand. "Mrs. Heatherington, I'm sure the chief can confirm that Lottie passed long before Jilly and I arrived this morning."

"I can't confirm anything at the moment," he said.

"Even if that were true," Cherise said, "you two got here in time to help Bridie hide the body."

"I highly doubt Mrs. Brighton is capable of doing as you're alleging," I said. "Miss Greenwich appeared to be considerably taller and more robust."

"We don't rely on brute strength around here," Cherise said. "That's what hexes are for."

A ruggedly handsome man who looked like an aging movie star jerked her backward. Rollie Heatherington, I presumed, judging by the unusually dark hairpiece. "Stay out of this, Cherise."

I tried to catch Chief Gillock's eye and failed. He was staring into the crowd, and his auburn eyebrows had soared after the word "hexes" hit him in the kisser.

Alba gave Cherise a cold stare. "Tread carefully, Cherise. We have a lovely community and many of us value our privacy. There's no reason to sling mud at the living, or the dead for that matter."

"Lottie Greenwich had detractors, but don't we all?" Alice Cheevers said. "For better or worse, she was one of us. Who knows who might be next?"

Now Officer Gillock spoke. "There's never been another drowning here and Mr. Cox is looking to improve safety measures." He turned to the board members. "I suggest fencing immediately."

Special Constable Doug raised his hand. "I move for fencing."

Vaughan shook his head. "That pond is our best view and fencing would ruin it. You don't get a vote, Doug. Motion denied anyway."

"Chief, we're not senile," Alba said. "Now that we know how hazardous the terrain is, we'll avoid it."

Casey Cox said to the police chief, "Welcome to my job. Trying to get agreement on anything is challenging."

"I'm sure we all agree to get rid of the swan," Ford Fletcher said. "I'll call pest control today."

There was a chorus of voices both in favor and against.

Chief Gillock raised his hand. "The swan stays until the investigation is complete," he said. "That's not open to a vote, either."

"What are you going to do, question him?" Vaughan said, snickering.

"I'll be studying him, yes," the chief said. "At the moment, that swan is our only witness."

"Except for Bridie Brighton," someone muttered. This time I couldn't place the voice but there were murmurs of agreement.

Keats looked up at me with a question in his eyes. "All right, fine," I whispered. "Obviously I can't stay out of this now. Jilly's family honor is at stake."

Cherise called out, "Or Bridie's guests with their suspicious timing."

Keats rose on his hind legs to shoot a blue-eyed glare at Cherise and while she probably couldn't see him, she backed off a couple of paces anyway.

"Add *our* honor to the equation, buddy," I muttered. "What we've got here is a homicidal holiday."

CHAPTER NINE

After Chief Gillock dispersed the crowd and returned to the pond, everyone reassembled in the courtyard and milled around. Walkers and wheelchairs collided like pinballs and hands reached out to steady others on canes. This day would end in more mishaps if someone didn't take charge. I waited for Vaughan to speak up, and when he didn't, I called out, "May I suggest we all take a moment of silence for Lottie Greenwich?"

"Lottie was never silent," Cherise said. "Her mouth is what probably got her in trouble. Or her newsletter."

"Cherise, stop. Just stop." The voice came from Bridie's friend, Alice Cheevers. "Lottie was one of us for more than a decade. Obviously we're all unnerved but being uncivilized won't help. We need to pull together in this crisis."

"It's bingo night," Shirley Mills called out. "And tomorrow was supposed to be our trip to town. Now we've lost our social convenor. We might never leave these walls again."

"Someone will step in, I'm sure," Alba said, glancing around. "A show of hands, please."

Not a single hand rose.

Correction. A single hand notched up jerkily.

It belonged to my best friend and was propelled by another heavily bejewelled and jangling hand. Jilly was being voluntold.

"Gran," she whispered. "We're only here for a few days."

"Or a few weeks," Bridie said. "We need you girls more than ever now."

"The farm needs us, too. We have guests arriving in a week. And Ivy will combust without her manure pile. So make the most of our few days and don't relegate us to bingo duty."

I raised my own hand. "I volunteer. My friend Jilly and I are only here for a few days but we know a thing or two about entertaining. We run an inn back home."

"Plus they're former executives," Bridie called. "My granddaughter owns a successful headhunting company in Boston."

"Owned," Jilly said. "Past tense. The sale closed last week."

Bridie looked horrified. "Tell me you're not going to live out your days in a barnyard, Jillian. What a waste of a good education."

Jilly laughed. "Runaway Inn is about more than live-stock. I'm a chef and a cooking instructor now, Gran, and I love my new life."

"Perhaps you could give us a cooking lesson," Alice said. "I'd love that."

"You're on," Jilly said. "And I've got a great idea for today. How about everyone contributes some ingredients from home and I'll make an early dinner. Potluck with a twist. We'll raise a glass to Lottie and raise our spirits at the same time."

Surprisingly, more than half the voices agreed. Once again, Jilly had used charm and food to soothe frayed nerves.

The idea caught enough fire that people dispersed. Bridie led us back inside the recreation center and then into the kitchen. Like the rest of the complex, it was well designed and equipped. Her eyes widened at the sight of two six-burner gas stoves.

"Two stoves and three dishwashers?" I said. "It's like a TV set, my friend."

"We have parties and banquets quite often," Bridie said. "Lottie had a flair for making occasions special." She forced a smile. "Thank you for volunteering to rally the troops, girls."

I glanced around to make sure we were alone. "It wasn't entirely selfless, Bridie. People were pointing fingers at all three of us *and* the swan. That's not right."

"They feel better having someone to blame," Bridie said. "Anyway, Chief Ginger seems to have a handle on things."

"We don't trust cops," I said, smiling at Keats, who smiled back with a sloppy pant.

"Don't trust cops?" She stared at me and then Jilly. "You're engaged to police officers."

"Did we miss the proposals?" I asked, waggling the bare fingers of my left hand. Jilly did the same.

"Well, you're as good as engaged," Bridie said.

"It ain't over till the bouquet's tossed," Jilly said, running her hand over the sleek stainless stove. "However, I'm willing to propose to this kitchen right now."

"Here's the thing, Bridie," I said. "Jilly and I come from

a corporate culture of distrust and self-reliance. I *do* trust the police to do the best they can. But I also trust Jilly, Keats and Percy to help me help the police when there's murder on the table. Our record is pretty impressive."

"No one's even confirmed Lottie was killed," Bridie said.

"In our world, it's safer to assume that from the get-go. It can buy valuable time to flush out clues before people get their stories locked down."

"Hence the potluck supper," Jilly said. "Gran, you and I will take charge in the kitchen, while Ivy works the crowd with Keats and Percy. Do you still have your cooking chops?"

"Like riding a bike," Bridie said. "Let's do our old family favorite, chicken pot pie, for starters. I know my mother's recipe by heart. Never had better, bless her sweet soul."

Jilly turned away from nostalgia to greet the first arrival. Elsie Cornwall had come back with a large package of frozen chicken and two huge leeks.

"Excellent choice, Elsie. It's like you read our minds," Jilly said.

"She did," Bridie said, smirking as she accepted the contributions.

Ignoring that, Jilly grabbed an apron off a hook and started opening cupboard doors. "We'll need butter, onions, flour, peas and carrots, for starters. I have a few other ideas to feed an army as well."

Elsie pulled out her phone and texted. "I've sent an SOS. What more can I do?"

"Show me around?" I asked. "It's best to stay out of Jilly's way when she's creating, and I'd love to know more about the Briars."

Elsie led me away and Keats circled behind, making sure we went exactly where he wanted us to go. If Elsie realized she was being herded, she didn't let on.

"I'm sorry you walked into a mess, Ivy," Elsie said. "Or should I say, 'waded.' This place is never without drama, but nothing like this." She paused and wrung her hands over the knob on her carved wooden cane. "Poor Lottie. She was very kind to me, you know. When I had surgery a few months back, she looked after my cat despite being on the anti-pet side of our voting members."

"It sounds like she was really dedicated to the community."

"That's how I saw it," Elsie said, letting Keats guide us through a lounge with leather couches and two fireplaces, and then down a hall with smaller meeting rooms and a library. There was even a good-sized auditorium for exercise classes and dancing.

Eventually we went outside to another beautifully landscaped courtyard that had a couple of hot tubs, a pool that was shaped like a teardrop, and several big sheds. Red and white wooden chairs were scattered around under matching, striped umbrellas. Though the day was gorgeous, the courtyard was empty. No one was in the mood for sunning after what had happened, I supposed.

"It seemed like opinion was divided on Lottie," I said.

"That's mainly because of her newsletter, I think." Elsie checked over her shoulder. "I suppose we were all afraid of Lottie's pen. She was a natural reporter and seemed to know things almost before they happened. She attributed that to tarot but you can't discount old-fashioned legwork."

"Seems like a lot of people claim to be psychic here," I said.

Elsie buttoned up her cardigan to her neck despite the

heat. "It's hard to know who to believe. All I can say is that Lottie was first on the scene of anything unusual. It kept her fitter than many."

"I heard she was aware of a romantic affair," I said.

"I'm afraid so, and it wasn't the first," Elsie said. "Lucky for me, my Carlisle is a man of integrity. Never gives me a moment's worry." She caught my eyes with a steady gaze. "In a tiny community, people do bend more rules. Still, there were bigger scandals to worry about."

"Oh? Like what?"

"The men and their silly golf carts, for starters. Vaughan Mills ran down a couple of people after drinking too much at the weekly poker games. Margo Sledge ended up on a walker and threatened to sue Casey Cox for not taking Vaughan off the road. Rollie Heatherington was another of Vaughan's hit-and-runs. Got a concussion and threatened to press charges."

"Oh my. I've had a hard knock to the head myself, so I get that."

"The strange thing is that Rollie came out of the hospital a nicer man, so Cherise made him stand down." Elsie unbuttoned her sweater again. "No one wants to go against Vaughan anyway. He holds the purse strings and makes decisions big and small. The votes are pretty much bogus, I'm afraid."

"What an interesting community," I said. "My small town is quirky, too."

Keats offered a mumble of agreement and herded us right around the pool. I wasn't sure what he wanted me to see but I did a mental inventory while keeping Elsie talking.

"The Briars is probably worse than most," Elsie said. "Because we can't come and go as we like. Every expedition needs to be supervised. Even hospital stays. I had a fulltime attendant after my surgery."

"Why is that?" I said, sticking my head into the second shed at Keats' urging. It was so dim I couldn't see much without turning on my phone light and piquing Elsie's curiosity with my own. "Everyone seems pretty healthy."

"If we still have our faculties, it's because Lottie ran a program for keeping our brains sharp. Music appreciation, debate club, crossword puzzles, you name it."

"Then why so much supervision?" I checked another shed and found it stuffed with life jackets, oars and paddles, fishing poles and nets. There were boats around here.

Elsie sat down in one of the deck chairs and leaned her cane against her knee. "Many families send people here when the circumstances at home are dangerous. Perhaps even criminal. It's meant to be a short-term solution, but as I'm sure Bridie's told you, few of us leave."

"So that's why security is so tight. Do the special constables manage to fend off intruders?"

"Larry's wonderful," she said. "I don't know where we'd be without him. Doug is another story. Still, it's felt very safe... until now."

I sat down across from her and asked the tough question. "Elsie, do you think someone from Lottie's past may have come after her?"

She looked down to avoid my eyes, only to find herself transfixed by the sheepdog stare. Keats caught her in the tractor beam of his blue eye and teased the words out of her.

"Maybe. Lottie's nephew was in trouble. On the outside. I only know because she forgot to erase her browser history on my computer when she was cat sitting. I never told a soul. As I said, she was kind to me."

"Did you ever talk to her about it?"

"I tried. Invited her for tea and walks to give her a chance to chat. Like I said, Lottie was sharp. She knew how to dodge and weave. Probably would have made a good secret agent."

Keats freed Elsie from his tractor beam—a signal that we'd done all we could for now. The potluck supper later would give us another chance to chat about Lottie's life, if not her death.

"Thanks for showing me around," I said, as we walked back inside. "The Briars is a beautiful place."

She shivered under her cardigan as the air conditioning hit us with an arctic blast.

"Sometimes it feels like a luxury prison," she said. "But safety first, I suppose. That's what my daughter says. I hope whoever did this—"

Her words snipped off abruptly as Vaughan Mills stepped out of a meeting room.

"Why so glum, Elsie?" he said. "There wasn't much love lost between you and Lottie, according to my wife. Shirley's always going on about the politics between you gals, and I can't keep up with who's getting along." Grinning at me, he added, "This place is like constant recess for grown-ups."

I wondered for a moment if Elsie had lied to me about being close to Lottie, but she said, "Lottie and I got along fine, Vaughan Mills, and I'd thank you not to feed the rumor mill. You're worse than the ladies." She took a little jab at him with her cane and he backed up. "Maybe you could stick to your own lane for a change. If you even know where that is."

His eyes widened as she stumped off, and before I could even think about trying to question him, he went into the meeting room again and slammed the door in my face.

"Let's not take that personally, buddy," I whispered, as Keats herded me back to the kitchen. "He's probably a little touchy about his driving record. We'll do some digging into his drunken poker games and seedy love life. But for now, let's go down and interrogate suspect number one."

CHAPTER TEN

Sleuthing had to wait until after I'd collected various things from Bridie's kitchen for Jilly's potluck preparations. On the way back to the rec center, I took a longer route and explored the community a little. It consisted of about 40 streets, all nearly identical. The center of town was the shopping hub, although Bridie said groceries came to the door. There was a bookstore, a salon, a barbershop, a pub, a thrift store and a pharmacy, among others. I could easily walk everywhere on foot, but many traveled by golf cart, scooter, or even bicycle.

Special Constable Doug cruised past me two or three times on his hoverboard. For a big man with some extra fluff, he was surprisingly adept at balancing on the one-wheeler.

"That'd be fun," I said to Percy and Keats, who walked beside me. "Wouldn't work on the terrain at home but I'd love to take a spin here."

Keats gave a ha-ha-ha that was decidedly at my expense.

"What? You don't think I can surf on one wheel? If that's a dare, sir, I accept it."

He steered me around the corner where we found police cruisers lined up in front of what must be Lottie's house. The red-headed chief was leaning against the railing of the low porch talking on the phone. When he saw me he turned his back so I kept walking, deliberately clanking the bags filled with pots and utensils. After a few yards, I felt his eyes on us and turned.

"Hey Chief," I called. "How goes the investigation?"

He came down the stairs and walked to the end of the driveway. "Pets on leash here, Ms. Galloway."

"Is that in the Briars bylaws?" I asked, coming back to meet him. "The president didn't complain about the dog earlier."

"It's in our county bylaws. And this property is in my county."

"What have you got against pets, Chief? Where I come from, that's a sign of dubious character."

He shook his head. "You're not on the farm anymore, Dorothy... I mean Ivy."

"Aw, you googled me," I said. "I'm flattered. But it seems like a waste of precious time that you could be using to figure out who murdered Lottie Greenwich."

"No one's said anything about murder, and I'd thank you not to alarm people."

"Everyone's talking about murder, Chief. You heard that. And my best friend's grandmother is top of their list of suspects, right after the swan."

"They put your name on that list, too," he said.

"Why on earth would I kill someone I'd never met?" I asked. "Do I look like a gun for hire?"

He scanned me from head to foot, and not in a salacious

way. I'd changed into clean overalls and my best sneakers. I figured I looked pretty good... for me.

"You look like someone who'd take unnecessary risks to protect those you love. Humans and animals."

"You can't believe everything you read online, Chief."

"True," he said. "Which is why I called my colleague in Clover Grove. Chief Harper. Perhaps you've met." His smirk told me he knew exactly how well Kellan and I knew each other. "He's the one who said the words, 'unnecessary risks.' Then he asked me to make sure you didn't take any on my watch."

My flush started round about my best sneakers and rushed to my face. "You had no right to call Kellan and—"

"Rat you out before you told him yourself?"

"I was going to. Very soon." I shifted a clattering bag from one hand to the other. "Now you've gone and worried him for no reason."

"Briars' security tipped me off about your history," he said. "I was just doing my job. Your job is running a farm and inn. Not interfering in my investigation."

"My mission in life is protecting animals, including this swan. He didn't kill Lottie. Unless he has fingers." I shrugged. "Maybe he has. I haven't had a look below the waterline."

Chief Gillock's auburn eyebrows scaled his pale, freckled forehead. "I won't engage in idle speculation."

"It's not idle speculation at all. I noticed bruising around the collar of Lottie's dress and since you're so diligent, I expect you did, too. She didn't go down without a fight and webbed feet don't leave marks like that."

"You're an expert on swans?" he asked.

"Not quite, but I intend to be. That's why Bridie Brighton invited us down here. So that I could get to know this swan and cajole him into a better mood. I heard Lottie brought him food morning and night, and most animals won't bite the hand that feeds them."

"Do swans bite?" he asked. "Or just beat things to death with their remarkable wingspan?"

"They don't have teeth, per se, but I understand a nip still hurts."

His arrogant attitude annoyed me and happily there was something I could do about that. Flicking my fingers, I let Keats work his sheepdog magic. He circled the chief and applied some teeth to a uniformed leg. Judging by the man's jump, the dog had gotten exactly the right amount of skin.

"Hey!" Chief Gillock's voice boomed but there was a satisfying hint of a squeal. "Harper might put up with your dog's antics but I will not."

He backed up the driveway slowly as Keats took dives at his boots. Meanwhile Percy swished sinuously around the chief's legs, trying either to trip him or leave his mark in orange fluff.

"Call these two off right now," Chief Gillock said. "Or I will have them seized."

"You won't," I said. "Ratting me out to my boyfriend cost you that chance. He's asked you to keep me from taking unnecessary risks and you know I'd do whatever it takes to rescue my pets." I snapped my fingers and Keats came right back. Percy did one last swish just to remind me he was a cat and took orders from no one, even me. "I'm sure Kellan will do the same to protect *your* lady when you visit our town."

"I don't expect that to happen anytime soon," he said. "Too many people die in Clover Grove and there's been a steady uptick since you moved home. Now it seems like you brought your bad luck to my jurisdiction."

"Another case of bad timing," I said. "Just remember that my inn is the perfect place for a romantic getaway. We offer a special honeymoon package."

Watching his face turn even redder than mine made me feel a whole lot better. Chief Gillock was easy to tease and that might come in handy.

I backed up, too, and nearly got clipped by a yellow Vespa. It was Special Constable Doug upping the ante on community policing. He had a vehicle for every occasion.

"Just stay out of my way, Ivy," the chief said. "Harper asked me to keep him posted. In case you didn't."

"Oh, I will. He'll be glad to know he's not the only one Keats herds like a sheep."

Chief Gillock shook his head. "I don't actually know what he sees in—ow!"

Keats had delivered another nip to protect my honor.

"Kellan's quite taken with my style sense," I said, strolling off in a rattle and clang of metal. "And my natural elegance."

I glanced over my shoulder and finally the officer found a grin. I didn't think he had it in him.

Because of that grin, I was going to make solving this case easier for him. I'd even give him the credit and a steep discount in the honeymoon suite if he didn't tattletale anymore.

"OF COURSE, I was going to tell you," I said, crouching in the shrubs well back from the swamp. "It only happened this morning."

"Ivy." Kellan sounded more exasperated than usual. "The last I heard from you, you'd decided to drive straight through the night because a car tailed you and there may or may not have been a body at the motel. Now there's a very real one, or so Chief Gillock says."

"Everything happened so fast, Kellan." I pressed down the bushes to make room for Keats. Percy had found himself a little nook with enough coverage to shield his marmalade fluff from prying eyes. "Between sinking into pond muck, the town hall meeting and helping set up for the potluck supper, this is my first real downtime."

"You didn't think I'd want to hear about this drowning from you directly?" He sounded hurt, which instantly sent chilly tendrils of shame from my chest into my limbs. My hands and feet tingled and my legs, folded under me, felt weak. If I had to run now, I wouldn't count on my chances of outpacing an irate swan.

Only Kellan could elicit that reaction, probably because I most feared his judgment. Generally I wasn't terribly concerned about what others thought of me, including my own family and especially the gossips of Clover Grove.

Kellan had a way of bringing me up sharp. When a mysterious death occurred, I preferred to go with the flow. That's how I ended up in trouble, but also how I uncovered valuable clues. Keats grumbled and I touched his ears to acknowledge his contributions. Going with the flow often meant following the pets' lead. Maybe my worst failing was forgetting that I was the human in the equation. I tried to stay as present in the moment as an animal, which meant I often forgot to "call home."

"I didn't think this was such a big deal, at first." Moving branches aside with my free hand, I wished I'd worn gloves. Edna had told me to carry my backpack go-kit 24/7. It was time I started thinking more like a prepper. "I mean, any death is a huge deal, obviously, but I didn't think it would impact us directly. So, Chief Gillock confirmed to you it was a murder?"

"He said enough that I'm worried about you being alone down there."

"I'm not alone. Jilly, Keats and Percy are with me. And Bridie, Jilly's gran."

"Gillock says Bridie was on the outs with Lottie and that people are accusing her of the crime."

"Which pretty much confirms she didn't do it, right? The first person named is never to blame. It's a decoy."

Kellan managed a laugh. "I didn't learn that theory in cop college. It must be something they teach in exec-turns-amateur-sleuth school." He waited a beat. "There *is* a school for that, right? Or are you totally self-taught?"

"Do you miss me?" I asked. "Because I sure miss you. Luckily I have a few pics of your smirk on my camera roll so I don't need to imagine your expression right now."

"Decoy," he said. "You know better than to appeal to my heart when I'm riding a wave of righteous anger."

"I'm just reminding you that we're on the same team, even if we're working long distance."

"That's what I'm worried about. Normally I can keep an eye on you and your doggie detective. I had to deputize a complete stranger with boyfriend duty."

"If it helps, he seems decent enough. I think I won him over with my rapier wit."

There was a pause at the other end and then, "How old is this guy?"

"Our age. He reminds me of you, actually. But it's early days. Let's see how he does with this case."

Another long pause. "Is he married?"

"I don't think so. He got all flushed when I suggested honeymooning at the farm."

"Suggested *what?*"

"Honeymooning." Keats' mouth dropped open in a pant of laughter, which alerted me to Kellan's misperception. "With *another* lucky lady, Kellan. Obviously he knows I'm taken. And if you have even the slightest worry, know that Chief Gillock eyes my clothes and my pets with disgust."

"That's how it all starts," Kellan said, laughing genuinely now. "Next thing you know all your sensible plans vanish and you're enchanted by farming."

I laughed, too. "You're overestimating my charms and I appreciate that. But you were always a secret animal lover, whether you knew it or not. Chief Gillock seems to hold them in contempt, which is why I'm worried about the fate of the swan."

"Gillock suspects the bird didn't kill this woman," Kellan said. "He might be kinder than you think, although I don't want him to be too kind if he reminds you of me. He does seem to have a head on his shoulders."

"The chief and I both noticed the bruising on her neck. Someone either strangled Lottie before drowning her or held her down to let the pond claim her."

"Isn't the place full of seniors? It takes strength to do something like that."

"These people aren't what you think," I said. "Or what I expected. They range from sixty to a hundred and lots are fit and able-bodied. A friend of Bridie's confirmed some are sent here by their families to protect them from danger in the world outside."

"What kind of danger?"

I watched the swan glide back and forth. Keats' and Percy's heads swiveled in the same slow arc. It was like the beautiful bird had cast a spell on them and they couldn't look away. Keats had never seemed quite so entranced before. Normally it was the other way around.

"You're not going to like it," I said. "Are you sure you want to know?"

"That's the whole point of this conversation, Ivy. I want to know everything so that I can assess the level of trouble you're in."

"Well, there's a woo-woo element. People either think they have magic powers, wish they had magic powers or are stuck in here because everyone knows they don't have magic powers."

"*What?*"

"I warned you. Woo-woo. But that's what Elsie and Bridie said, and before you suggest they're senile, Jilly said the same. You know she's a hundred percent sane."

There was silence at his end and I imagined he was churning fingers through dark hair. The mental image distracted me for a few seconds, which was the other reason I hadn't called him earlier. Thinking about Kellan distracted me more than it should considering we'd been dating eight months. That fizzy buzz should be wearing off by now, I figured. Keats would normally agree with me strongly and vocally, but he was still hypnotized by the swan's smooth glide.

At last Kellan said, "Jilly believes her gran has... magic powers?"

"No, the opposite. Bridie thinks she has psychic gifts but she gets it wrong all the time. She annoyed the wrong people back home with her prophetic misfires. That's why her daughter—Jilly's aunt—shut her in here. Shelley has enemies of her own, too, and the best way to get back at her would be to hurt Bridie. That part makes sense at least."

"Nothing about what you're saying makes sense," he

said. "In fact, the Briars is starting to sound like a facility for the delusional."

"Oh, I know. Maybe they are, but they seem normal in other ways. They love their pets and bingo and potlucks. If they're a little zany it's from being cooped up with the same people. There's drunk and disorderly conduct, gambling and flagrant affairs."

"In other words, typical small-town antics knocked up a notch."

"Exactly. I'm not really buying into this magic business. I haven't seen anything that gets anywhere close to Keats and Percy doing their thing." I smiled at the transfixed pets. "They're the only mind-readers I know."

"I'm glad to hear you're keeping a healthy skepticism," he said. "But what about the disappearing body at the motel? The two cars tailing you that managed to stay out of sight? Do you really think you lost them?"

He had a good point. "Those people were like pro spies in movies, so I honestly doubt we did. For all I know they might be here this very moment. Watching me."

"And what are you doing that's so interesting?"

"Just studying the swan. From a good distance. Tomorrow I'm going to a bird sanctuary to learn more."

"I like the sound of that," he said. "A nice safe bird sanctuary, where you can stay out of harm's way."

"There are alligators around these parts. How safe is that?"

The word was enough to startle Keats out of his trance and he whined.

"I can tell Keats isn't thrilled about meeting one of those."

"He's not thrilled about this case at all," I said. "Water, you know. There's a pond and a pool. Double whammy."

Now the dog shook, throwing off imaginary water and the swan's spell. His whine amped up to spur me on.

"Promise me you'll call at least twice a day, Ivy. Otherwise, I'll come down there. And if I come down there, I'm not here protecting your farm."

Ouch. Now he'd hit me where I lived. Literally.

"Is everything okay at home?" It was like I'd snapped out of *my* swan trance, too. "People pulling together?"

"So far so good," he said. "Cori says Edna's worried about the donkey thugs."

"Cori's your primary source of intel now?" I couldn't help grinning. A few months ago they could barely tolerate each other because he represented the law and she took delight in flouting it.

"We're not as dissimilar as you'd think. Or at least as I thought. There's a method in Cori's madness. The Rescue Mafia protects the innocent and punishes people who deserve to be punished. Maybe I'm a little jealous because I have to abide by the law and they get to be creative." The sigh he released almost blew my hair back despite the many miles between us. "Scratch the surface of some cops and you find a vigilante right underneath."

"Like this swan I'm surveilling," I said. "He's all calm on top and churning everything up underneath."

Kellan laughed. "I like that comparison. You sure it's a boy swan?"

"We haven't gotten that personal. I've taken some pics so they can tell me more at the sanctuary." I sent one off to Kellan, too, and heard the ping at his end. "There's your competition, good sir. Not a redheaded cop."

This time his laugh made me tingle for different reasons. "My only real competition has one blue eye."

"Like I've told you before, you have no competition.

Never have since tenth grade. I left my heart on ice when I went to college and you thawed it when I got home."

He was probably wasting that slow smile on the evidence locker, where he often went to get some privacy. Bunhead Betty, who sat at the front desk at the police station judging people like me, manned the gossip lines as skillfully as she did dispatch.

"So what are you going to do now?" he asked.

"Head back for the potluck," I said. "The conversation ought to be interesting."

"Don't let anyone hex you," he said. "Can Keats protect you from that?"

"There's cause to worry. This swan has him utterly transfixed. Percy, too. I'm not sure their superpowers are fully online."

"All the more reason to be cautious," Kellan said. "If you've got a tight community of people who think they can rely on magic, there are bound to be dustups."

"No argument there," I said. "It may be our most interesting case yet."

"Pardon me?"

"Right. Not my case at all. I'm just vacationing in a very thorny bush watching a swan."

I left him chuckling, which was my intent. But the truth was that I'd been watching something else for nearly a minute that looked very much like the muzzle of a shotgun.

CHAPTER ELEVEN

"Keats," I whispered. "Keats. Yoo-hoo. Earth to sheepdog. There's a situation here. Can you tear yourself away from Swan TV?"

The dog's ears flicked back and forth as if he were indeed trying to tune in to a particular station. Whether that was the swan's, the community's or something far beyond, I wasn't sure. I only knew that I needed him grounded beside me. Fast.

"There's a gun, buddy. It's not directed at us but the swan. Someone hoping to take out a suspect, and we can't allow that."

Another shudder passed over Keats from head to tail. I hadn't seen him so unsettled since his last bath, right before our trip. I had wanted him to look and smell nice for Jilly's gran, but it was a waste. We probably both smelled of swamp right now. Luckily, this wasn't on the scale of Huckleberry Swamp back home, with its fetid, leech-infested filth.

"Stay quiet, boys," I whispered. "We don't want to

startle the hunter and have the business end of that rifle shift our way. How are we going to play this?"

After a moment's reflection, I backed out of the bush, peered around and then got to my feet on the path. It seemed like nearly everyone was avoiding the pond, even though the police had finished their work here and were focused on Lottie's house.

"Bear with me, you two," I said. "Let's pretend I'm a regular person out for a walk with my pets, okay?"

Keats panted his agreement, now fully present. His tail and ears were at half-mast, proving he wasn't big on the owner of the rifle. Still, he didn't consider this a dire emergency.

Directing the dog and cat into the bush, I called out, "Keats! Percy! Boys, where are you? Don't go near the water, now. It could be dangerous."

A red baseball cap popped out of the shrubs about 10 yards away. The agent of doom turned out to be Special Constable Doug with a red-checked flannel hunting jacket over his uniform on a very warm day.

"Hey, Special Constable Doug," I called. "Whatcha doing?"

"Lunch break," he said, although it was midafternoon now. "Came down to enjoy the view."

"Through your viewfinder, you mean. Guns aren't exactly safe around seniors or pets. My dog and cat are wandering down here, actually. Have you seen them?"

He shook his head and scowled. "Pets aren't welcome here."

"And yet people have them."

"They cause tension in the community," he said. "I get more calls about poop infractions than anything else. I hope the board votes to let the current generation die off and then bans pets, period."

"That would be so hard on residents. Pets are so important for making people feel connected and content."

"Well, how about you connect yours to a leash right now, so they don't get shot?"

"How about you put your gun away so they don't get shot?" I pulled out my phone. "You heard Chief Gillock. He said to leave the swan alone until the police investigation is done. We could call him down to see if he's changed his mind, though."

Doug lowered the gun, trying to chill me with his icy blue eyes. "My first priority is the safety of residents here. If a swan is beating up our citizens, I can use whatever weapons I see fit to protect them."

I looked at the device hanging from his tool belt. "Including a crossbow? Seriously? Your citizens are getting run down by golf carts, Constable. Do you really think they can dodge flying arrows?"

His face took on a ruddy hue. "What are you talking about?"

"I heard some folks got squashed like flies by a drunk driver. I expect you know about that."

"Don't assume all you hear is true. Flustered people blurt things out. A good story is better than a true story."

"That part's true enough," I said, laughing. "I'm just passing along what I heard about potential litigation, but you know best."

"If I were you, I'd focus on keeping Bridie Brighton out of the news," he said. "Lottie Greenwich had a bone to pick with her."

"If you'd tell me what that was about, Jilly and I could sort it out with Bridie."

"Not my place," he said. "Like you said, there's a police investigation."

"If you care so much about the citizens, you'll let me do what I can to help. I bet you have your hands full with squabbles that aren't easy to solve."

"You got that right," he said. "Especially the ladies. What went on between Lottie and Bridie sounded like complete claptrap. Apparently, Bridie had a vision about Lottie and was going to expose her. And Lottie threatened to expose Bridie in return."

"What did Bridie have on Lottie?"

He shrugged. "Got me. Lottie didn't seem to hide much."

His blue eyes started darting back and forth. He was lying, so I'd have to offer something in return for the information. "I respect that you're protecting Lottie, Constable Doug. But I'm trying to protect Bridie and the swan. Perhaps I know something that would help you in your work. I'd be happy to share."

"What could you possibly know that I don't?"

I shrugged. "While you were busy hunting a protected species, someone may have borrowed your equipment."

Now I had his attention. He crunched through the bushes toward me, unaware that he was being subtly herded.

"You're obliged to tell me exactly what you saw. I am the law here."

"I'm fine with sharing the information directly with Chief Gillock. He's the law above the law. But if you want to elaborate on your earlier hint, I suppose I could make an allowance."

"Arnie," Doug said. "Lottie was hiding Arnie. I found

out about him on routine surveillance. He was watching me from her window. Scared the dickens out of me."

"A secret boyfriend?" I asked. "I've heard about that happening around here."

His shoulders convulsed and a burp of laughter escaped. "Arnie was an illicit love, all right, but of the four-legged variety. Outlawed in regulation."

"Cat or dog?" I asked.

"Something easier to hide. A ferret."

"Huh. I did not see that coming. So Bridie knew about Arnie. Was she the only one?"

"I think so. Lottie worked hard to keep it that way."

"Paid for your silence, you mean," I said.

"That wouldn't be ethical, now, would it?" he said. "Although sometimes in my line of work you need to cut a few corners to keep things running smoothly."

His eyes got shifty again, making me suspect he had a lucrative side hustle of extorting residents.

"I can appreciate that," I said. "So my only other question is... what's happening with the ferret now that Lottie's gone?"

His checkered shoulders rose and fell. "Not my problem. Dealing with unsanctioned animals is out of my purview."

"And yet you're down here fully armed to deal with an animal."

"That's different. It's wildlife. Besides, a ferret isn't going to kill our residents."

"You never know. My nephews' ferrets nip. Something like that could cause an infection and—"

He raised his hand. "Never mind. Arnie probably escaped during the police investigation. The doors were wide open when I rode by. You saw me checking on him."

"Did you tell the chief, at least?"

"I keep the secrets I agreed to keep. Only told you because you seem to know something of extreme value to me."

"Extreme," I said. "If you care about your Vespa, that is. It's the yellow one, right?"

"My Vespa?" He was moving so fast he didn't feel teeth on his pant leg, but Keats had a scrap of fabric hanging from his jaws. "It's the *only* one."

"So, when I was coming down here someone was ahead of me, pushing it. Then he booted that thing through a hedge off Bridie's street. Thought it would end in screams, but the bike roared off on the other side. Guess someone made a run for freedom."

Doug made a run for it, too. "Who was it?"

"Male, bald, paunchy," I called after him.

"That describes almost all the men," he called back.

"He had good command of the vehicle. Taking the curb was a bold move, so props for that. Then he cut through that hedge like a chainsaw. The motor gave a screech but—"

Doug was out of earshot now. Keats and I looked at each other and shared our first belly laugh since leaving Runaway Farm.

"We're getting our feet wet here, buddy," I said. "Hopefully not literally. Let's go and have a careful chat with the real star of this investigation."

With Doug gone, the swan's pace slowed from frenetic to merely rapid. His wings stayed up in what I took to be an aggressive display. If he were at ease, he'd be dipping his regal head under the water to dine on reeds and weeds.

"I get a masculine vibe," I said, noticing both my pets fell further and further behind as I neared the water's edge. The turf became increasingly boggy and I picked my way carefully to the rickety dock. Keats put on four white brakes and refused to join me. The dog that readily took on killers in Clover Grove had set his limit. Percy continued on with me, however, so I wasn't alone when I stood at the end of the ancient dock to meet the swan.

The big white bird circled, hit reverse with webbed feet I couldn't see in the murky water, and paused directly in front of the dock. He rocked gently and curved his elegant neck before pinning me with small eyes like black pearls.

"Greetings," I said. "I'm Ivy Galloway and this is Percy. The nervous nellie behind me is Keats. He's a brilliant dog with the heart of a warrior, but water is his undoing." There was an indignant mumble. "He can swim, but he'd rather keep his whites white and dry. I'm sure you can understand that."

The swan turned in a complete circle, as if displaying his finery.

"You're gorgeous," I said. "And I'd love to know more about what's happened since you arrived. Or even why you arrived. This can't be the pond of your dreams."

I scanned the water and that's when I noticed goldfish. These weren't the flashes of fire Bridie had mentioned. They were lifeless, mostly floating just below the surface. A couple of dozen at least.

The swan's pacing began again, as if to prove he felt as trapped as the human residents.

"I don't understand why you wouldn't move on, especially after what happened. The free food can't be a big enough incentive to stick around anymore. I'm sure you can find admirers anywhere who'd be willing to pay you in grain to adorn their shores."

The proud head dipped in what appeared to be resignation, even sadness, and his movements slowed. He let out a hoarse whistle that seemed to carry a note of sorrow. So mute swans were not mute after all.

"I'm sorry," I said. "Maybe I said the wrong thing. All I wanted to do was reassure you that I'll do my best to figure out what's going on here. I'm pretty good at getting to the bottom of mucky problems." The mumble behind me got more indignant. "We all are. I have a good team, including Jilly, whom you may have noticed earlier. I sense you're the innocent victim here and if you'll just give me a couple of days, I believe I can figure things out."

The bird's head snaked out and his beak opened in a hiss. I expected Percy to jump. Instead, the cat hissed back and raised a paw with claws splayed. Although the swan could easily have flicked my cat to the next county with one wing, he chose to reverse course. Percy offered a rather snippy meow that sounded like, "So there."

"Thanks, Percy," I said. "I'm sure the swan means us no harm. He's unhappy and we can't blame him for lashing out. Plus he doesn't know us or our skills." I took out my phone. "Mind if I snap a few photos, Mr. Swan? I'm going to a bird sanctuary to learn more about your species."

For the first time, the bird seemed to settle in what appeared to be a casual pose, wings settled. I took a few photos from different angles and then thanked him.

"I'll be back with a full report. Please take care of yourself in the meantime." I looked across the pond. "The area over there seems to have plenty of coverage. May I suggest you stay out of sight? I'll report the man with the gun but I don't have much faith he'll leave you in peace."

Almost like magic, the bird receded. With no apparent effort, he got further and further away. Keats finally dared to come forward. He gave a sharp bark as if to say, "Yeah. Go!"

"Don't bother," I said, turning. "It's beneath you."

We walked back to the road and then on to the recreation center.

"Boys, this place makes Sunny Acres look like sweet paradise, yet we almost met our maker there."

Keats mumbled agreement and I sighed.

"We'll prevail, I'm sure of it. But I don't need my palm read to know it's going to be one heck of a ride."

CHAPTER TWELVE

Vaughan Mills was immersed in a hot tub surrounded by churning bubbles when I tracked him down later. Four women sat in deck chairs in a semi-circle around him. The scene made me think of Hugh Hefner at his mansion, only the ladies were fully clothed in bright, tropical themed blouses and flowing linen skirts or slacks. Seeing us standing in the entrance to the courtyard, Elsie Cornwall and Alice Cheevers dangled their fingers to summon Keats, Percy or both. It didn't matter which pet because neither was getting anywhere near the churning geyser. Keats gave a rare bleat of protest to confirm the hot tub was more terrifying than anything he'd encountered before.

"Sorry ladies," I said. "My boys don't like water. Such a shame that the only vacation we're likely to get for years gives them heart palpitations."

Cherise Heatherington fanned her flushed face with what looked like one of Jilly's custom menus. It even had the Briars' logo on top. "I imagine we've all had heart palpitations today. It was such a shock. No one's ever died here before."

Vaughan laughed and then splashed around till he faced her directly. "Come on now, Cherise. People die here all the time."

"Of natural causes. The way the good Lord intended."

"Are you sure about that?" he said, still grinning.

Cherise's thin lips pursed. "Vaughan, really. You'll give the girl the wrong idea."

"I agree," said Alba Fletcher. She'd swapped her mint green suit in favor of a print blouse and another scarf with a fancy knot. I envied people who could work a scarf. Done right, it could really elevate an outfit.

"Ivy's come at a bad time, that's all," Elsie Cornwall said. "I already told her we have a lovely community. It's normally very peaceful here."

"Very peaceful," Alice echoed.

Vaughan's laugh turned into a snicker. "It's never peaceful here, ladies. Each morning I wait for my report from Shirley to see who's been naughty or nice. Maybe Lottie was too naughty."

"Vaughan!" Four female voices overlapped.

"It's nothing to joke about," said Alice Cheevers.

"I have to joke to stay sane," he said. "You ladies have no idea how tough it is being head of the board. Sometimes I think running the entire country would be easier."

Cherise rolled her eyes. "We need a second executive team to deal with you, Vaughan. I'd vote to take away your golf cart and poker chips."

Alba stared into the frothing water and pressed her lips together. Perhaps the rumors were true about her involvement with Vaughan. If so, she might be embarrassed for him.

His playboy smile vanished and his casual splashing stopped. "Now, you be careful, Cherise."

"Or what?" she said. "You don't have a card left to play, Vaughan."

Her tone was mildly threatening and the mascara dripping down her face in the steam made her positively ghoulish.

Elsie knotted her hands over the knob on her cane and squeezed till the knuckles whitened. "Please stop, you two. Ivy will think we're terrible."

"Not at all," I said. "I'm the youngest of six kids, and I own sixty head of livestock. There's always a rumble going on somewhere. I do hope the turmoil here is resolved quickly so that Jilly can have a really good visit with her grandmother."

The rough water between the five subsided and the look they exchanged said no one was on team Bridie.

"Now that was a nonstop hen fight," Vaughan said. "Lottie and Bridie were always pecking at each other."

"I hope Bridie has a good alibi," Cherise said. "Because they had quite a spat in The Silver Spoon last week. Overheard by many, though I missed it myself."

"Is that the cute little café in the main square?" I asked.

She nodded. "They were still at it in the thrift store, arguing over used books on spells and hexes. I heard it was spellbinding."

Elsie was the only one who didn't giggle at that.

"Don't go there, ladies," Vaughan said. "Ivy doesn't need to hear about your strange notions."

"It doesn't faze me that some of you believe in magic," I said. "I've seen a few strange things in my time."

Cherise patted the skin under her eyes with a tissue to blot the makeup pooling there. "Some say the swan is bewitched. That it's one of our former residents come back in winged form to get revenge on Lottie."

"If so, I pity the bird," Alba Fletcher said. "There's probably an army of vengeful spirits trying to get under those feathers.

"None of us got off scot-free in Lottie's newsletter," Vaughan said.

"I dreaded every issue," Alice admitted. "Knowing it was going to make feathers fly."

"Some loved it for the same reason," Cherise said.

I suspected she was one of them, although it was hard to believe she hadn't been featured sometimes.

"It's best to put the newsletter to rest with Lottie," Elsie said. "There's so little real news here."

"Except for today," Alice said. "And there's no one to write an obituary. Lottie did very well with those."

"That's true," Elsie said. "I always looked forward to the obits." Realizing how that sounded, she added, "Not the deaths, obviously, just the tributes and life stories."

Vaughan rose from the water and I turned my head in case he wasn't wearing trunks.

"Obituaries are important," he said. "I'll call for volunteers to replace Lottie at tonight's dinner."

"No one's going to volunteer to be next to drown," Cherise said.

"It wouldn't happen the same way twice, I'm sure," Elsie said.

Alba offered a grim smile. "The next vengeful spirit might inhabit another animal."

"We only get raccoons in here," Alice said. "That would be a sad way to go."

I had to cover my mouth at that, and Keats didn't even bother to hide his mumble of laughter.

"Ladies, stop your nattering," Vaughan said. "It's time for dinner and I want to be first in line."

"You're always first in line," Cherise said, grumbling as she rose.

"It's a perk I deserve for putting up with the palaver," he said, heading inside with a towel wrapped around his waist.

No one seemed to notice I stayed behind for a much-needed break. Dragging a chair as far as possible from the hot tub and pool, I sat down for a minute and patted my lap for Percy. Keats refused to settle, and it wasn't because of the water. There were things to monitor inside, it seemed.

"Just let me text Kellan about Doug and his rifle," I said. "It's the kind of thing he'd want to know."

A few minutes later, Jilly texted to summon me for dinner and I headed inside. Normally I'd be starving by now but fatigue and the day's events had dulled my prodigious appetite. If anything could revive it, it was the sight of the buffet Jilly had laid out on end-to-end tables in the recreation room. The platters of food looked gorgeous and smelled delicious.

Faced with this feast, people forgot they'd accused Jilly of murder only hours ago. Now they surrounded her with heaping plates and accolades.

My best friend was flushed from the hot kitchen and the color made her look more like her old self. Bridie had perked up, too. She'd changed into another bohemian dress, twisted her hair into a bun and swapped out her many jewels. She looked ready to take on her frenemies. It was a good front, but internal politics would surely wear her down. Maybe we could take her home to Runaway Farm for a break when all this was resolved.

That was a prickly subject to broach with Jilly later. In the meantime, I'd use the cover of dinner to ask more questions and maybe even poke around some of the smaller rooms I'd passed earlier.

My plan fizzled with the arrival of Chief Gillock and his team. A silence fell over the crowd. He apologized for interrupting dinner, but he was ready to "start some conversations."

I glanced at Jilly and we walked over to the chief together.

"Join us for dinner first, Chief," she said.

He shook his head, while his officers stared eagerly at the table. "We need to press on. There are lots of interviews ahead."

"I understand," Jilly said. "But keep in mind these are seniors and some probably haven't had a bite all day."

Casey Cox came up behind us. "I agree with her, Chief. I'm worried about everyone's welfare. A shock like this could have downstream effects." His brown eyes widened at his wording, and he added quickly, "I just mean my father and I care deeply about our community. Please give people time to eat and then sleep. You can continue tomorrow."

The chief let Jilly lead him to the buffet table and put a plate in his hand. I watched from the doorway, and when the chatter resumed and cutlery clinked on china, I slipped away with Keats and Percy.

Out front, at least three dozen golf carts sat with keys in their ignitions. "No one would mind if I borrowed one of these for a few minutes, right? Hop in, boys."

The wind in my face was refreshing as I pelted through the streets to Lottie Greenwich's house. The yellow hazard tape was still up but the lights were off and the vehicles gone. Everyone was down at the rec center enjoying the buffet. There would never be a better moment.

I drove the golf cart into a parkette across the street that was full of those flowering trees with the cloying smell. Shorter bushes offered plenty of cover and I tucked the golf cart inside. It was dusk now, and as our feet touched the pavement, the streetlights came on suddenly. Maybe Kellan had a camera on me and would blast a warning over a loudspeaker.

"Let's not let our imaginations run away with us," I said, as we crossed quickly. "We'll nip in, catch the ferret and dash. And by we, I mean *me*. I'm counting on you two to locate him but you will not touch a single hair on his head, understood?"

Keats looked up and gave a mumble that sounded like, "What fun is that?"

"Investigations aren't supposed to be fun." I fell back when we reached the other side. As usual, the pets took the lead in situations like this. My instincts were good and theirs a million times better. "But we can take a quick look around while we're there. In case the police missed something."

They often did miss things and not because they were sloppy. Kellan and his team were far from that. But they couldn't possibly pick up details that a very smart dog with refined senses might consider useful. Percy's unquenchable curiosity had thrown plenty of clues into my path as well. Often quite literally.

One thing I could usually count on was their finding a way inside. Keats led me around the back of the house and used his nose to search for a spare key. Meanwhile, Percy jumped onto windowsills to look for breaches. Since I hadn't had a wink of sleep the night before, I was grateful this turned out to be straightforward. Keats promptly went into a point. I slipped on rubber gloves I'd lifted from the rec center kitchen and used one index finger to poke into the gaping mouth of a foot-long stone fish that sat by a burbling fountain. Pinching the key, I walked to the house. It was almost *too* easy. Easy made me suspicious.

Standing in the kitchen, I got my bearings. The layout of the house was identical to Bridie's, which made getting around in the darkness much easier.

There was a notable difference in décor, however. A flash of my phone light in the living room revealed Lottie's passion for the mystical. The square coffee table held several decks of tarot cards, an array of crystals, and a huge book with gold lettering that read, Everyday Spells for Everyday Magic. There was also an old pocket watch and a pendant with topaz that gleamed with the warmth of Keats' brown eye. I must have stared at it for a few seconds too long because Keats nudged my hand.

"Right, thanks, buddy. How about you boys use your everyday magic to ferret out the ferret? I'll take a few pictures in case something comes in handy later."

There were two side tables flanking a Victorian style velvet settee. The table closest to me had a spread of tarot cards. I wondered if Lottie had laid them out yesterday to see what the day held. The cards had gold edges and elaborate illustrations that looked hand-drawn. I snapped a photo quickly and forced myself to turn away. The darkness was making my fatigue worse and eroding my common sense. I had a strong desire to take off the gloves and touch everything. It was all so pretty, especially the stones.

Keats mumbled something from the dining room.

"Coming," I answered.

The narrow antique desk I passed on the way held a

glass globe about the size of a baseball. The light was even lower here yet the orb gave off a chilly glow that reminded me of Keats' blue eye. I didn't need to look far to compare, because the dog had come back into the room with his belly nearly touching the rug. I suspected Arnie, the ferret, had preceded him.

Percy's fluffy tail lashed as he stalked toward the TV stand. Along the bottom shelf sat a couple of dozen DVDs and they tipped over with a clatter before either of my pets reached it.

"Arnie," I said. "We come in peace. I'm sure you've realized something's greatly amiss. Lottie's gone, I'm afraid. I'd like you to stay with me, at least temporarily. I'll find your things and we'll go."

The ferret didn't emerge, so I got down on my hands and knees and flicked on my light.

"There will always be a place for you at my farm, Arnie, but the cat and dog come with the package. Consider yourself warned."

A pointy face with piercing eyes and small round ears peered out from behind the toppled DVDs. I stretched out my hand cautiously, hoping he'd step onto my palm. Arnie had other ideas. He poked his nose into my sleeve and shot inside. I couldn't help squealing as he navigated the turn of my armpit and wriggled down the front of my T-shirt to settle around my waist. I'd need to be careful not to squish him.

Keats whined and I got to my feet. "Ferret aboard. Mission accomplished. I suppose we should get going."

The dog circled and tried herding me back into the kitchen after Percy.

"Just give me a minute, buddy. I want to take a quick

look at that crystal ball. Do you think those things are rigged?"

He whined again as I picked it up but didn't make any sudden moves in case I dropped it.

"I know, but we should be okay for a little longer. Everyone's distracted with Jilly's feast."

I cradled the crystal ball carefully in both gloved hands and stared at it. At first, all I saw was a swirl of fog but then my own face came into focus. The reflection wasn't flattering. I'd aged 10 years in a single day.

"I look awful," I said. "That's what I get for peeping."

Still, I didn't put the ball back on its ornate filigree stand. It felt warm through the rubber gloves and a light buzz of energy traveled up my arms. Now I was more alert.

Spinning the orb, I checked the bottom. "It must have a battery. Or maybe it's solar powered."

Other shapes seemed to swirl inside and for a second I saw Runaway Farm. It was like a little movie playing inside. Edna Evans was running ahead of Drama Llama, knees pumping, while the thug donkeys followed. Pulling up the rear was Clippers, the miniature horse. A giggle slipped from my lips and this time Keats delivered a sharp yip to bring my brain back online.

"Whew! I must be totally woozy. I see things moving in there, like the swan flapping. Isn't that strange?"

"Very."

The voice startled me so much that the crystal ball lifted right out of my hands and if my reflexes hadn't sharpened suddenly, I would have broken this unique, kitschy piece. Instead, I slapped my right hand over it and clamped it down into my left palm.

The adrenaline shooting through my limbs dulled the

buzz I'd felt emanating from it earlier. Now it was just regular glass. Even the blue light had faded. I supposed it had used up its battery life, although I couldn't see anyplace for a battery in the smooth surface.

My breath evened out because I knew the voice. It had already rebuked me once or twice today, and I knew I could expect more. The overhead light came on, and a strong flashlight for good measure.

"Why hello, Chief Gillock," I said, gently setting the crystal ball on its stand. "Finished dinner already?"

"I barely got started when I noticed you were missing," he said. "Your beau warned me you were elusive. He didn't mention light-fingered."

"Oh, please. I wasn't going to steal this." I gave the crystal ball a last pat. "Although it is fun. Do you remember Magic 8 balls? As kids we'd ask ours if Mom would be in a bad mood after work. Every single day it said 'without a doubt,' like it had jammed. Unfortunately, it wasn't wrong."

He stared at me for a moment as if pondering my sanity. "I meant the golf cart you just lifted. Did you also take Doug Farrow's Vespa today?"

"Pretty sure Vaughan Mills took the Vespa. I'm the one who told Doug about it. As for the golf cart, I was merely borrowing a ride and plan to return it before dinner's over."

"Ivy, you can't just barge into a crime scene and manhandle things. Gloves or no gloves. Given your connections, I assume you know proper protocol."

"Of course, but this was a critical matter and I didn't think you and your men could handle it properly."

His chin came up, and it really was an imposing jawline. "You think you can handle police work better than I can?"

"This job was outside your purview and squarely within mine," I said.

"As what? A farmer?"

"Actually, yes."

His eyes dropped to my waist and then he reared back when he saw Arnie moving around under my overalls.

"Are you all right?" he asked.

"Bit of an upset stomach," I said. "Why?"

He gestured to my waist. "That isn't... I mean, you must feel very uncomfortable."

"I do, actually. I didn't expect Arnie to be so wiggly."

"Arnie?"

"Lottie's ferret. He ran up my sleeve and this seemed like the best way to keep tabs on him till I found his cage."

"A ferret. Oh." The relief in his voice was palpable. "There's no cage."

I looked at Keats and his paw came up. "There's a cage. My dog can find it."

"I don't need your dog to help my investigation."

"I'm sure you'll successfully solve the mystery of Lottie's death, Chief. But it sounds like you didn't even know she had a pet till now. So maybe you could put pride aside and accept our help. Hopefully Kellan also mentioned I have specialized skills that come in handy."

"He said you could probably help sort things out with the swan."

"That's it?" It was disappointing that Chief Harper hadn't sold my skills harder, but I supposed *boyfriend* Kellan just wanted to keep me safe. Especially when I was so far from home. If he heard the swan hiss, however, he might think twice about recommending me for bird wrangling.

"That's it," the chief said, crossing his arms. "We were

both of the professional opinion that you should keep your distance from this case. You're well aware that it may not have been an accidental drowning or a swan attack. Everyone needs to be cautious right now. Yet here you were, gazing into a crystal ball. What was so mesmerizing?"

I made a sweeping gesture. "It's not just the crystal ball, Chief. It's *all* mesmerizing, don't you think? Either Lottie really enjoyed mystical collectibles, or she believed she was a—"

Nothing came out so he supplied, "A fortune teller?"

"It sure looks that way. Doesn't that intrigue you?"

"Not really, because I doubt it has any relevance to the case." Turning, he ushered me into the kitchen. He flicked a switch there and the overhead light showed an average kitchen without mystical elements. "Miss Greenwich had strained relationships with a number of the residents, including and perhaps especially Mrs. Brighton."

"Apparently they both claimed to be the better psychic," I said. "There may have been some ego at stake but it doesn't sound like motive for murder, does it?"

He shrugged. "Till the autopsy's done, I'm not using that word."

"Well, we are," I said, gesturing to my pets.

"I heard you talking to them. I didn't hear them talk back."

I signaled to Keats who was sniffing around the back door. "Right now, he's about to tell us where to find the ferret cage, unless I'm much mistaken." The dog shoved a rug aside to scratch at the hardwood floor. "It must be in the basement."

Chief Gillock smirked. "There is no basement."

"Check for a crawl space, then. Keats doesn't lie."

Shooing the dog away, the chief knelt to rap on the

floorboards. There was a hollow sound and after a few moments he found the notch to open a trap door. Sitting back on his heels, he shone his light inside and his expression would have been comical if not for the bobbing of his Adam's apple. Clearly the crawl space held more than a ferret cage, but as I walked toward him, he lowered the door.

"Oh, come on," I said. "My dog found it."

"I'll hand over the cage, fair and square. But you'll need to leave the rest with me." He directed a big palm and said, "Stay, Ivy. Stay."

"Insulting, Chief Gillock. Insulting and unnecessary."

"I'm sorry about that, but it's for your own good." He opened the trapdoor and took some photos before leaning inside to pull out the cage. "And before you get any big ideas, I'll be clearing out this crawl space personally tonight."

"Fine. Whatever." Keats and Percy were taking a good look inside. In fact, as he handed me the cage and a container of what looked like kibble, Percy jumped right in.

I walked over and the chief lowered the trapdoor. Then he cupped his hand. "I'll take the house key."

Sighing, I reached into my pocket and Arnie slithered over to my other side. The chief looked a little queasy about my undulating midriff. That made me miss Kellan even more. My boyfriend not only found my way with animals tolerable but adorable. The man before me was similar in many ways, yet he found me bizarre and possibly repulsive. The thought made me laugh out loud and Keats joined in with a happy pant.

"What's so funny?" the chief asked, waggling the fingers of his right hand. His left still held the trapdoor open a few inches.

I dropped the key into his palm and said, "That you've been had by a cat."

"What do you mean?"

Percy exploded from the crawl space with a bit more flash than necessary, but Chief Gillock's man scream was a night-brightener every bit as good as a crystal ball.

CHAPTER THIRTEEN

C hief Gillock wasn't the only one screaming at the Briars that night. A much shriller sound ripped out of Bridie Brighton when she witnessed Arnie doing somersaults under my overalls.

All her supposed magical powers apparently hadn't prepared her for an alien invasion inside a houseguest. And when the ferret's sleek head popped out of my collar Jilly added her voice to the din. Keats enjoyed every second of the hubbub but Percy retired to Jilly's bed to catch some shuteye.

"That thing cannot stay here," Bridie said. "I will not have rodents in the house, Ivy. Honestly, the dog and the cat are pushing me past the point of comfort. I don't know how you two live with such a menagerie." She pulled her eyes away from Arnie and looked at her granddaughter. "You weren't raised that way."

"True," Jilly said, smiling. "I was raised to live in a sterile high-rise and wheel and deal in people, not pets. But then I saw the light and I've never looked back."

She reached out and Arnie scampered across her arm

like a drawbridge and nestled in the loose golden curls on her shoulder. A year ago, my friend would have taken weeks to adjust to a critter like Arnie. Now she absorbed him into our lives—and even her hair—in under a minute.

"That's not what we wanted for you," Bridie said. "Your mother and I had big dreams."

"Gran, stop." Jilly's voice left no room for argument. "We're not taking that trip down memory lane. Like I said, I'm happy at Runaway Farm. Cooking is my calling. I hope you saw that tonight."

Bridie looked determined to continue her lament, so I intervened. "Speaking of seeing the light, I held my first crystal ball tonight."

"What?" Bridie and Jilly spoke in unison and it was nice to hear them agree, if only in surprise.

"I heard about Arnie, Lottie's ferret, from Constable Doug earlier. He said you knew about it, Bridie, and were threatening to expose her."

Her brow furrowed. "I suspected she had an illicit pet because she was covered in brown hair sometimes. But I would never rat someone out for... well, keeping a rat. Lottie and I clashed about tarot interpretations, but I wouldn't sink so low as to part her from a pet."

"Doug was wrong about your threat, but right about the ferret. I figured Arnie would evade the police, so I went over to rescue him. Keats and Percy rounded him up with no trouble, and while they did, I checked out Lottie's place. There was a pretty crystal ball."

Bridie nodded. "It's an antique. The finest quality. I've never been able to see a darn thing in it and trust me, I've tried. I don't think Lottie could either, although she pretended otherwise."

Tipping her head, Jilly asked, "Did *you* see something, Ivy?"

I shrugged. "I thought so, but it was probably an optical illusion. I'm so tired I could pass out on my feet."

"What did you see?" she asked, stroking Arnie with one finger. "I bet it was the farm."

"Yeah. Edna was getting chased around the camelid pasture by Drama and the thugs. And Clippers."

"Clippers? What would he be doing out there?"

"He wouldn't be. That's how I know I was delirious."

"What else did you see?" Bridie asked.

"The swan. He was flapping like crazy, ready to attack someone. I nearly dropped the crystal ball. That's when Chief Gillock came in."

"Is the ball okay?" Bridie said. "I'd love to acquire it if there's an estate sale."

Ignoring that, Jilly asked, "And what about Chief Gillock? Did he give you a hard time for trespassing?"

"Oh yeah. But then Keats revealed something the chief didn't know about."

"What?" Bridie was curious enough to come a little closer to Arnie.

I shrugged. "He wouldn't let me see. Keats and Percy got a good look and a sniff, though."

"That's okay, then," Jilly said. "They'll know what to look for."

Bridie stared at her granddaughter. "Jilly, really. You don't believe these two pets can help solve Lottie's murder?"

"I bet Arnie knows something, too," Jilly said. "And the swan even more. It'll take Ivy's brilliant mind to put all the pieces together, but I have full confidence she will. In the meantime, Gran, you and I need to keep people busy and distracted. I spoke to the chief at dinner and he said we could go into town tomorrow, as long as Constable Doug comes along."

I looked at Keats and shook my head. "I doubt anyone's the safer with Doug on duty. What happened to the other cop? The nicer one?"

"Larry Helms?" Bridie said. "He got injured on duty and Casey sent him home. Doug's pulling a double."

"You know who we really need on the job?" I asked.

"Edna," Jilly said, without losing a beat. "And Gertie, too. Seniors guarding seniors."

"Who are these women?" Bridie asked.

"Edna is our nosy neighbor who's saved my bacon—and my pig—a few times. Her hobby is preparing for the end of the world, a passion she shares with Gertie. We have plenty of friends in Clover Grove, but they're the ones we count on most."

"More than your boyfriends?" Bridie asked, with a sly smile. "Officers of the law, both of them?"

I gave her a sly smile back. "Oh, we count on them, too, when we want to follow protocol. When we don't, our prepper friends have our back. Keats and Percy are the first line of defense, of course."

"It sounds like quite a network." Bridie sounded wistful, and it was all I could do not to invite her home to the farm then and there. "You never really know who your friends are at the Briars."

I opened the door to Arnie's cage and Jilly stuck her hand inside. The ferret scooted down her arm and then dropped into the cage. I closed the door behind him.

"Sleep tight, little guy," I said. "First thing tomorrow, I'm going to find out who Bridie's true friends are, which is the first step toward finding out who Lottie's true friends *weren't*."

Arnie stared out at Bridie with beady eyes, as if trying to tell her something. No one understood the message, least of all his new hostess.

"How exactly do you intend to do that, Ivy?" she asked.

"Old-fashioned HR skills," I said. "Conversation that isn't as casual as it seems. It's one of the few gifts from my old job. Believe it or not, listening carefully even helps with animals."

She shook her head skeptically and then herded us to our bedrooms with less finesse than a certain sheepdog. "I know you're well intended, Ivy, but this all sounds like hogwash."

Jilly turned quickly. "Gran, you be nice. We came a long way to help you. Ivy is suspending her disbelief about *your* hogwash, so you can do the same for her."

"You were a sweet little girl," Bridie said, giving her a none-too-gentle push into a guest room. "Now you're..."

"Tough," I said. "Tough as nails and the best friend anyone could ask for."

"I wonder how I turned out this way," Jilly said, turning to her grandmother. "I think we could pin it to an exact day."

"That must have been your warrior birthday," I said. "We should celebrate it every year." I gave Bridie a look that drew on the grim reaper of the old days. "We're all tired. And for the record, my mom always points out how sweet I was, too. The day I swung a baseball bat at a criminal in an alley changed all that. And Jilly was right behind me."

Whatever Bridie wanted to say lodged in her throat and

she stared at me, probably sensing she couldn't get to Jilly except through me and my army. That changed the stakes.

"Goodnight, girls," she said at last. "It's wonderful to have you here."

It was enough of a retreat that Keats gently herded Bridie toward Jilly, whose arms opened to offer another hug.

Sometimes it took a murder and a sheepdog to chase old demons into the cage where they belonged.

I WAS UP and out of the house at dawn the next day, eager to make my rounds and also give Jilly and her grandmother some privacy to catch up.

Keats and Percy trotted down the street ahead of me and automatically turned toward the pond.

"Wait, boys," I said. "We'll get there, but let's be sensible for a change and wait till it's light before getting too adventurous." I signaled them to head for the main square instead. "Besides, I feel jet-lagged and desperate for coffee. Maybe that café opens early."

The Silver Spoon was not only open but crowded when we arrived. All the seats inside were taken and most on the patio. Hands rose in greeting and I noticed many people looked a little friendlier than they had the day before. Jilly's potluck dinner had thawed some hearts, it seemed, and Percy and Keats got to work on the rest. I went inside to get my coffee and they wove among the seats, doing their ambassador thing. Percy accepted an offer to jump into Elsie Cornwall's lap, bringing a smile like sunshine.

Keats cast a wider net and I watched his reactions through the window. His ears flicked as he took a measure on character. No one impressed him greatly, but there were no alarm bells, either.

With a large cup of black coffee in my hand, I went outside and took the empty seat next to Elsie. We were on the edge of the patio, giving us a bit of privacy.

"Have you learned anything more about what happened?" she asked, getting straight to the point. "I've heard you're nearly as good as the police at figuring out mysteries." Percy flexed his claws into her leg and she gave a little gasp. "Make that *just* as good."

I laughed. "I have my moments but this one's a stumper. Some say Bridie and Lottie weren't getting along, yet Bridie says things were basically fine between them."

Elsie ran her hand over the cat and his purr loosened her tongue. "There was a big dustup a few weeks ago over a tarot card reading and it kept simmering. Many of us read the cards, you know, and they're subject to inter-pretation."

"What was the big deal about that particular reading?"

She glanced around carefully before speaking. "Someone tried at least half a dozen of us to get a forecast on a delicate personal situation."

"Romantic?"

"I'm afraid so. She was afraid her husband had a lady friend and Lottie's tarot spread showed betrayal."

"And Bridie's said the opposite?"

Elsie nodded. "Naturally, the woman wanted to believe Bridie, even though Lottie's track record was far more accurate."

I leaned a little closer and whispered, "Was this Shirley Mills? Vaughan's wife? He seems like a bit of a player."

She gave a little sigh. "Very much so. It wouldn't be the first time he's strayed, but this seemed to bother her more.

Maybe it felt more serious, and it's difficult to split up, here. You can never really escape your ex."

I glanced around, too, and saw the parties in question were out of earshot. "Do you think he would have left Shirley for Alba? Or that Alba would have left Ford?"

"Hard to say. Alba's been unhappy for years, and Vaughan has influence."

"Might Shirley have been angry enough at Lottie to... well, kill the messenger?"

"I can't imagine so. We've all had bad readings. Some come to pass, many don't."

"I suppose Shirley may have been angry enough to remove Lottie from the equation, but did she have the strength?"

Elsie lifted her hand from Percy and shook off orange fluff, watching as it caught a breeze and floated over to land in Alba Fletcher's lap. "Ford Fletcher may have been the bigger threat. He wouldn't want to lose Alba, especially not to Vaughan."

"Wronged spouses are a good place to start," I said. "I'm sure the police will have that angle covered. I like to look at less obvious motives first."

"All I can say is that Lottie started to look harried recently. She was always independent but she withdrew even more. It seemed like she was always looking over her shoulder. I did wonder if Vaughan or Ford had been giving her a hard time over her predictions. Perhaps it was something worse."

"Worse how?"

Elsie resumed patting Percy with one hand while buttoning and unbuttoning her yellow cotton cardigan with the other. The thread must have been heavy-duty to hold up under the habit.

"Maybe an outsider? As I mentioned, she had a nephew in trouble somewhere. It's difficult to get in and out of here, but it has happened." She watched Alba flick the orange fluff away with disgust. "Honestly, that seems more likely at this point, Ivy."

I was pretty sure Vaughan Mills had left the Briars through a breach in the fencing yesterday on Special Constable Doug's Vespa. If he could get out, enemies could surely get in.

"They should probably beef up security here," I said. "I'm surprised Vaughan isn't more worried on behalf of all of you."

"I'm sure they will when Larry gets back. There's only Doug now and he has his hands full."

Not so full that he wouldn't take a break to go swan hunting.

Keats came to collect me. Hands reached out to pat him and he ducked under each one. The ambassador role had worn thin and it was better suited to Percy's temperament anyway. This sheepdog wanted to be doing, not schmoozing, and the glint in his blue eye told me we had better places to be right now.

I bid Elsie goodbye and followed the pets down the sidewalk, feeling the weight of many eyes. Between the swan's antics, our arrival and Lottie's demise, life had gotten a lot more interesting for the Briars' residents recently. I couldn't help thinking sheer boredom was behind many of their skirmishes.

We took a twisty way down to the pond in case anyone decided to follow. I checked over my shoulders often for scooters, wheelchairs and the more fleet-footed. Turned out everyone preferred to stay at the café and speculate about what we were doing rather than do the work of finding out. It was probably more fun that way.

I expected to be alone with the swan but Keats went into a point before we stepped off the pavement onto the trail. His ears were forward and his tail neutral, so I wasn't particularly worried. Then my eyes lit on a woman with an elegant silver bun sitting on one of the park benches. She was staring out at the water with her back to me. I wondered how she could be so comfortable being there alone. Even I was nervous, and I had a furry crime-detection system.

"Good morning," she called out without turning. "Beautiful day."

Maybe she'd picked up on my footsteps or Keats' pant. With his tongue lolling so early, it was going to be a humid day.

"Gorgeous," I said, scanning for the swan as I walked toward her. The big bird emerged suddenly from the bushes at the far side, like the sun breaking through clouds. "Oh, good. I worried it was gone."

"He," she said. "Use masculine pronouns." She sounded like a prim schoolmarm. "This is Zeus, and he's very much a male."

"Zeus? Well, that's a good fit."

"I can't take credit for naming him," she said.

"Lottie chose the name?"

She shook her head. "Lottie called him Swanny, which he didn't appreciate. Undignified for a magnificent creature like him."

"Ah. So he told you himself." By now I was just two yards away from her. I stopped and waited for permission to approach. "You have a kinship."

Eyeing me through glasses with round, gold-rimmed

frames, she took her time before answering. "I've always understood animals. Based on what I've heard, you're the same."

"Often I do," I said. "Although they don't tell me their names." I glanced at Keats and Percy. "I hope these two don't mind what I chose."

She flicked her right hand and the sun danced off a massive diamond set among even more diamonds. "You'd know. They simply wouldn't respond." Finally she turned and smiled at me. "Besides, who could be offended by being named after two great romantic poets?"

I laughed. "Did they tell you their names, too?"

"The rumor mill took care of that," she said. "I don't mix much around here, but I do read the newsletter. Lottie announced your impending arrival in the latest edition." Sighing, she added, "The final edition, as it turns out. Poor Lottie. She wasn't always likeable but I believe she had our best interests at heart."

The swan had picked up his pace, gliding about five yards and then turning to repeat. In fact, it was so precise it almost looked like a mechanical swan on a track. A carnival ride for small children. His head turned quickly and I felt his eyes upon me. Perhaps dignified Zeus didn't appreciate being compared to a fun park character.

"He's a swan of strong opinions and I sense he'd like to share them with you," she said. "He didn't come out of the bushes until you arrived."

"Yesterday I told him I wanted to help, but I don't really speak swan yet." I gestured to my pets, who were still hanging back. "Sometimes these two play go-between but they don't like water."

"No one should trust *this* water," she said. "Our beautiful goldfish have died. I can't imagine why he'd want to stay here, even though we feed him."

"All the goldfish died?"

She nodded. "I believe so. The landscapers clear the pond often but I've seen no signs of life. Then the swan showed up."

"And he's been unhappy from the start?" I asked.

"Angry. Aggressive. Chases people he doesn't like, particularly men. People used to row around the pond but no one dares now." Patting the seat beside her, she added, "I'm Videa Dumasse, one of the few you didn't meet at your potluck supper. Some of us either can't or won't mix. I prize my peace of mind over fitting in."

"Me too," I said, joining her. "That wasn't always the case. I got conked on the head rescuing this dog last year and woke up a rebel."

Videa laughed. "Then you were always a rebel inside. You just woke up." She patted my arm and it felt like the big diamond pinged me with a jolt as strong as caffeine. "Most people never do, so congratulations."

"Life has been interesting since then." I looked over my shoulder at Keats, who sat with his tail coiled around his white paws, muzzle swiveling at the same pace as the swan's movements. "One adventure after another."

"That's what happens when you accept your calling. Not all of us are lucky enough to fulfill our potential."

Her eyes blinked rapidly behind the round glasses and I wondered if she was fighting tears.

"You don't want to be here," I said.

"No one really wants to be here." Her voice sounded far away. "Most of us came because we weren't safe outside."

"I heard that from others. And that some of you have

special abilities."

She shrugged. "Whether we do or not, if others think so we can become targets."

"Being different is dangerous," I said.

"Being safe is dangerous, too," she said. "We're physically safe here—at least we were, until what happened to Lottie—but our mental health suffers. We're like birds in a cage." Turning, she offered a twisted smile. "Sorry to sound so negative. That's just my opinion."

"How long has it been?"

"A few years. My son asked me to come after I got on the wrong side of someone in my hometown. He was worried for me."

"Was it... was it related to magic?" Just speaking the word aloud to a stranger made me uncomfortable. Not because I didn't want to believe. I was willing to be convinced such a thing existed. But for the moment, my work boots were planted firmly on the ground and it seemed like I shouldn't presume to say much about something I couldn't understand.

Her eyes were sharp behind the spectacles. "Whether or not magic is real, the threats around it can be. I would have taken on the risk myself but as a mother, you don't have that luxury. So I made my son's life easier by moving here."

"Maybe you can leave when things cool off," I said.

"Perhaps. People rarely do, though. Memories are long and grudges passed down through the generations. Mostly we live out our days in safety." Her fingers rose in air quotes around the last word. "And whatever they pipe in here keeps us alive long past what's sensible." Percy climbed over the back of the bench and invited himself into her lap. He especially enjoyed being patted by a bejeweled hand.

"There's no point in living beyond a hundred just because you can. Yet many here do, and in good health."

"That's so interesting. It can't be that bad here if people live longer than average."

Her lips formed a little pucker and I wondered exactly how old she was. I would have guessed about 70 but now suspected a well-preserved 80. "Maybe I'm just feeling low over what happened to Lottie. Sometimes I'm lonely despite being crowded."

"I get that," I said. "I'm the last of six kids and since moving back to my hometown the whole family is underfoot. I have more freedom, yet I sometimes feel trapped."

"By their expectations. By their opinions of who you are and should be."

"Thank goodness for my animals. And Jilly. And Kellan, my boyfriend." Glancing at her big ring, I said, "You aren't married?"

She angled the big rock to the sun and one of the facets shot out a beam that almost blinded me. "Not anymore. My husband and I separated and he ran into some bad luck. Fatal luck. That was the last straw before I moved here." Percy gave a purr-meow to prompt that ring to resume stroking. "I hoped we'd reconcile but it wasn't to be."

We watched the swan in silence for a time, before I had another idea. "Jilly and I are spearheading a culture revival project in our town. Maybe we can think of events that would engage you more. Guest speakers on interesting subjects, for example."

"Guests are discouraged," she said. "Bridie had to push hard to get you two past the board. What swayed them was your animal expertise."

That got me on my feet. "Then I guess I'd better deliver. If I can't figure out what's troubling Zeus, the board might close down to guests even more and you need fresh blood around here." I looked over at the place I'd discovered Lottie and added, "Not literally."

The swan had expanded his route to include that spot. At each turn, he snapped around sharply with wings half-raised. He seemed more agitated than yesterday.

Snapping my fingers, I summoned Percy, who left the big diamond reluctantly. Keats, on the other hand, swished his tail in relief over being released from the hypnotic spell of the swan's movements.

"Thanks for the chat," I said. "See you both soon."

"Ivy," she called after me. "Do be careful. It might be more dangerous for you now outside our walls, too."

"Why do you say that?"

"I just have a strange feeling that enemies are circling. There are worse threats than swans."

"Good thing I have my crew," I said, gesturing to the pets now racing ahead. "I may not be able to tap into mystic frequencies, but they can."

"Oh, you can too." Her smile transformed her into a beautiful woman. "I daresay you know that."

I shrugged as I turned. "This trip has made me question a lot of things."

"Question constantly, and then question some more. You won't get clear answers, though, so don't expect them."

"Like a crystal ball," I said. "Or a Magic 8 ball, in my world."

"Or even a fortune cookie. Yours says 'Destined for great things.'"

I stepped into a mulchy spot that soaked over the laces of my boots, which had only just dried. "And also, 'Beware of potholes.'"

I left her laughing and considered that a victory.

CHAPTER FOURTEEN

"I'm farmsick," I told Keats, as the gates of the Briar Estates closed behind us. Percy couldn't join us on the trip to the waterfowl sanctuary because he'd be a hard sell to the manager. It would be tough enough to get Keats inside, but at least the dog would demonstrate his obedience on command. Percy was more likely to do the opposite. Just because. Still, I felt a little bereft without him and Jilly.

Bracing himself on the dash, Keats swished his tail quite merrily. The sheepdog Sherlock was enjoying this vacation far more than I was. Still, my spirits lifted as we put some miles between us and the Briars. It wasn't the holiday resort I'd imagined. There wasn't even a beach.

"I know you'll disagree with me, buddy, but I think a body of water is important for mental health. That's why the Briars' residents are so attached to their pond even though it's become toxic. First the goldfish died, then a disgruntled swan arrived, and now someone has passed away. We need to cleanse it of bad juju."

Keats not only dropped his tail but let it curl under his

body. He wasn't going to volunteer to help change the vibe of a glorified swamp.

"We should talk to the property manager about it. Casey probably doesn't realize why it's important. Otherwise, he'd pressure the board to rehabilitate it. I bet there are pond experts around and the Briars drops a pretty penny on landscaping everything else."

The dog turned away slowly to make sure I registered his negativity. There were few subjects Keats refused to weigh in on, but pond health appeared to be one of them.

"I'm sorry, buddy, but I'm thinking of going forward with a pond project at home, too. It's only a matter of time before Cori drops mallards on us and they won't be happy in a kiddie pool."

Now Keats grumbled something.

"Build it and they will come? Exactly." He glared at me as I deliberately spun his comment in a positive way. "Don't worry. The swan isn't joining us. I wish he could, because a stint at Runaway Farm would do him good."

Keats turned back to the road and ended the conversation. After a mile or two, his tail rose and a weight lifted off both of us. We were both feeling trapped at the Briars and after a decade of corporate misery, my tolerance for confinement was low. That's why I spent so much time in the pastures and meadows back home and wanted to expand the farm even more. Edna knew I had designs on her property one day. She could sell it to me, live rent-free, and use the money to build the premier bunker in North America.

Keats mumbled a question.

"No, I don't have the money for that, but we live an abundant life, my friend. I have faith that it's coming. That's why I'm open to whatever Cori dumps on us. Each time she does, my world seems to expand. My ark doesn't sink. In fact, it becomes more buoyant than ever."

His next mumble was non-committal. It was easy for me to say yes to all comers, but as canine farm manager, it kept his paws full. And while he liked being busy, he also wanted time to pursue the various mysteries scattered in our path. That was his recreation. In short, my dog was better at work-life balance than me.

The thought prompted me to call Kellan, the one who suffered most when I got caught up in my projects.

I didn't need to tell him I was driving. He had a good ear for engines.

"Careful with those shifts," he said, as I put him on hands-free. We both worried that my previous abuse of the transmission would herald the truck's early demise. It would be one death we didn't need to investigate. "You've run away from the Briars, I take it."

"I had to submit to grilling to get a day pass," I said. "It's no wonder people feel trapped there. I'd implode in no time."

"Good," he said. "That means you'll come home soon."

Warmth filled me from the bottom up, starting with my swamp-soaked toes. "I can't wait. This isn't a fun girls' getaway. Turns out murder doesn't take a vacation. At least, not for me."

"Or me," he said. "It's a good thing we understand that about each other."

The warmth reached my face and my inner sun came out in a huge smile. It amazed me that our bond seemed to grow deeper with every phone call, every walk at the farm, every strange experience we tackled together.

"I love you, too," he said.

I laughed. "You knew that's what I was thinking? My dog's obviously not the only psychic in my life."

"There's such a thing as a pregnant pause," he said.

"Well, you certainly delivered," I said. "And you're right, absence has made this heart grow fonder. I miss you. I miss your police work. And with Jilly so distracted, my team needs more players." Keats turned his blue eye on me, so I added, "No offence, buddy. It's good to have backup, right?"

I filled Kellan in on my visit to Lottie's house and he didn't even lecture me until I whined about Chief Gillock refusing to tell me what he found in the crawl space.

"Gillock doesn't owe you any information about what he found, Ivy. I'm way more flexible about that sort of thing than I should be. I only do it because I've seen the value of your unique gifts." Keats stared at the phone now and Kellan added, "You too, Keats."

The dog gave a happy pant and resumed navigation.

"If he shared what he knows it might speed things along. My primary mission is to deal with the swan but it overlaps with what happened to Lottie. I'm sure of it."

"You may be right, but he's bound by a code and doesn't realize you might be able to figure out what happened faster than he can. I did tell him, you know."

"Really? That's so sweet."

He laughed. "Supporting your sleuthing and delivering goat babies scored me more points with you than anything else."

"True. Women who look for romance in flowers and chocolate are missing out."

A comfortable silence fell between us. This man made me feel seen and safe, even at a great distance. For him, I would try to be more cautious, because I very much wanted a future together.

"What are you thinking?" he asked.

"You need to ask? Where are your psychic powers now?"

"Maybe I just want to hear it."

"Well, if you must know, I was picturing us paddling in a canoe."

"A canoe! That I didn't expect."

"You know I've been thinking that we need a pond at the farm. One that's full of rushes and frogs and waterfowl. It would be so soothing to paddle around in there."

"Sounds nice," Kellan said. "Although I assume you're getting a dirty look right now? I can't picture Keats sitting in the middle of that canoe."

"He's in a snit over the idea. I guess it's something you and I can enjoy alone."

"I'm all for it, then," he said. "When your dad's treasure trove is liquidated, he might donate enough to get the work done."

My smile faded. "I don't want *that* money. Even though he came by it honestly, it feels tainted by crime. I'd rather earn it myself somehow."

"I understand how you feel, but using the funds to help rescue animals might wash the dirt right off that gold. What's more, it's something your grandmother, Polly, would have endorsed fully when she left it for her descendants."

Keats turned and cocked his head. Kellan's argument had merit.

"I guess it's something to consider if the offer comes my way," I said. "For all we know, Calvin could take off to a desert island."

"Then he wouldn't need money at all, would he?"

That made me laugh. "You've got all the answers today, Chief. And I'm hoping you might dig up a few more."

"Uh-oh. I'm not big on asking Gillock for more."

"Actually, I don't want him to know what I'm doing."

"Even worse," Kellan said.

"It's about the Briars' residents. I keep hearing they've been sent here by family, or had to escape trouble of a criminal kind in their old lives. It's like a witness protection facility."

"Ivy, it's a seniors community. Is it possible they've... well, forgotten the details? Or are dramatizing them?"

"They're not senile, if that's what you mean. Everyone I've met is very sharp and they seem to be living long, healthy lives. Plus Jilly says the same thing, remember?"

"Fine. Send me the names you're curious about and I'll do some checking," he said. "Anything else?"

"Doug Farrow, the community cop. I want to know his story. After the swan hunter incident, he's at the top of my suspect list. I'm pretty sure he's taking kickbacks, for starters."

"I'll look into Doug, too. Is that all?"

"You'll swing by the farm and check on everything?"

"Every night, like I promised. But I wouldn't know a sick animal if I saw one."

"I'm more worried about the humans. With Mom, Gertie and Edna sharing space all day long, it's bound to come to fisticuffs at some point."

"Asher sounds like a better man for that job," Kellan said. "His charm is being wasted on the petty crimes we've been seeing lately. Without you around, things have gotten quiet."

"I don't *cause* crime, merely end up embroiled in it." I

took the exit to the waterfowl sanctuary. "How's Asher doing, anyway?"

"Pining, actually. I think Jilly's put him on ice."

His voice was cautious, no doubt because the territory between my brother and my best friend was potentially hazardous for both of us.

"This thing with her gran sent her into a spiral of doubt and regret," I said. "Asher got caught up in it, but I bet everything turns around when we fix the swan issue. And the murder issue, insofar as they overlap. That murky pond holds secrets."

"Then I guess I'd better see what I can do to help on my end. We don't want an irate swan and a dead body coming between a once-happy couple."

"There's my romantic," I said.

"It's self-interest too," he said. "Asher is a better cop with Jilly in his life. More focused and determined. He wants to be worthy of her."

"So how about we get them married off in my orchard this fall? I keep picturing a wedding among red apples and orange leaves."

"Sounds very pretty," he said. "Maybe you'll catch the bouquet."

My face ignited and I almost steered off the road. "I'd try my best, but I do have three single sisters who aren't pushovers." I waited a beat. "Didn't my mom suggest you go for one of her nicer daughters?"

He laughed. "None of your sisters is all sugar and spice. Dahlia made sure you could hold your own in the world. But I have no doubt whatsoever that I snagged the best Galloway girl—the tallest, smartest and kindest of a fine quintet."

"All right then. If you're quite sure, I'll pummel my

own sisters to get that bouquet. Keats and the rest of the ark will help. It'll be the wedding they talk about for a hundred years in hill country."

His laugh rang out in the truck and chased away a lot of my anxiety and homesickness.

"Let's see if we can pull this thing off," he said. "Solving murders might be easier than matchmaking. Come home soon, Ivy."

"I can't wait," I said, driving under a huge sign shaped like a duck with lettering that read, Stillson Waterfowl Sanctuary. "This vacation stuff is for the birds."

CHAPTER FIFTEEN

A flock of Canada geese surrounded the truck. In the passenger seat, Keats was so excited he stood on his hind legs and hopped in a full circle. I couldn't remember seeing his circus dog act since the day I rescued him. He'd performed many other stunts, but the tricks he learned before my time were mostly beneath him now.

Unless there was a flock of geese beneath him. Then all bets were off.

"Keats, may I have a word? I know how much you enjoy herding our feathered friends, but it won't fly here."

He didn't even roll his eyes at the pun. His sheepdog heart was tripping over itself and both paws tried to work the latch. It was a relief that he hadn't already figured out how to come and go as he liked. Maybe he had and was just too worked up to execute.

Finally he whined in frustration and I crossed my arms. "Buddy, we go nowhere till we've had this talk."

He hopped back around and stayed up, front paws hanging. I tried to hold back a grin and failed.

"Do not try to charm me, Keats. I'm being serious. This is a no-herd zone. There will be injured and sick birds that need to be treated with kid gloves. I won't have us kicked out before we get the information we need to help Zeus. So... do I have your agreement? Or would you prefer to wait in the truck?"

The truck wasn't really an option, however. It was a warm day and I couldn't leave him for more than a few minutes, even in the shade.

He gave a resigned whimper. It would take a lot of willpower, but he'd restrain himself.

"Just close your eyes and think about homicide," I said. "There are more important things at stake today than geese. But if you're very good I may get you some geese to herd at home. For your new pond."

His lip lifted in a rare sneer at the word pond.

"Don't show me those teeth, or you'll find yourself in a lifejacket," I said, getting out of the truck. "There's one in the back."

I made broad sweeping gestures to shoo the geese before releasing the dog. The birds took one look at him and waddled off.

"One problem down, one to go," I said, as we walked to the weather-beaten wood hut that looked like an office.

A white-haired man in coveralls came out at the first knock. I introduced myself and Keats, who sat politely at my side with his ears not only up but forward. He aimed to please, and after a long moment of evaluating the dog, the man smiled.

"Are you going to be able to hold yourself back?" he asked Keats, in a charming English accent. "This place is feathery temptation for any dog."

Before I could answer, Keats mumbled his own assurances, and the man laughed. "No one else would believe you, but I will."

Keats raised one white paw and offered to shake. I hadn't seen him do *that* in a long time, either.

The man knelt and solemnly took the paw. They had some sort of silent communion and then he nodded. "All right then, my tuxedoed friend. I have your word as a gentleman and I'll trust you. My name is Amos, by the way."

He stood and offered me the same hand. "And you, young lady... can I trust you not to cause mayhem?"

I gave him a big smile. "Of course. Why?"

"Because old men use Google, too," he said. "I check out anyone who comes to visit and while your heart's obviously in the right place, you sure do get into trouble."

"That I do, Amos. Like I mentioned, I'm on a special mission to solve a swan situation at a gated community."

"Why don't I come over and grab him for you?" he said. "It wouldn't be my first swan rescue."

"Grab him? Grab him how? He's ferocious."

He led me along a gravel path. "Just a typical cob. That's a male swan, by the way. The female is a pen. Both tend to be crusty at this time of year. It's breeding season."

"He's a lonely bachelor, it seems."

His snowy head tilted. "More likely a widower, I'm afraid. Singles tend to flock up until they meet the one, at which point they basically mate for life." He gave me a sad smile. "If they lose a mate, they'll grieve for quite some time —maybe forever. Your cob's behavior sounds consistent with that."

"How tragic." My hand moved over my heart. "Do you think that's it?"

"Happens often enough, unfortunately. Some stop

eating and literally pine to death. But if we could convince him to pair up with a new pen, he'd come around. I've seen worse challenges. Most swans here have been snagged in fishing tackle or hit by a boat."

"That's terrible. A big white bird should be easy to miss."

"You'd think. Although to be fair I've seen swans take on boaters by choice. They don't know their limitations. One of our cobs lost his foot to a small motor. I call him Sid Vicious, and his wife is Nancy. He manages fine in our pond, but he can't live in the wild anymore."

Amos stopped beside the first of several ponds I could see ahead. The water was calm and blue, despite being full of more species of birds than I'd ever seen.

"No swans here?" I asked.

"They rejected this one," he said. "Swans need the right conditions during nesting season and they'll defend their territory to the death."

"And yet you volunteered to come over and grab our troublemaker? Just like that?"

"Sure. The trick is to hug them close until they stop fighting. Protect your eyes and expect a few bruises."

Keats whimpered and I touched his ears. "I was hoping for peaceful negotiation rather than eviction. I just need to understand what he wants. There must be a reason he landed in the little pond at the Briars all alone."

"That pond's not so little," he said. "It's dammed up where you are but there's over thirty miles of wetland beyond."

Keats shuddered. This sounded too much like Huckleberry Swamp back home for his liking.

"Maybe his mate is out there in trouble," I said.

"Unlikely," Amos said, walking on. "They bond so

fiercely that he'd choose to die beside her no matter what happened."

"This is sounding like a love story gone terribly wrong," I said.

We rounded a bend and I gasped. Swimming toward us at warp speed were two stunning swans with wings raised.

"Walk the dog back," Amos said. "They're used to me and wouldn't mind you. The dog is the threat in their eyes."

Now I saw why. Behind them trailed eight fluffy grey cygnets that didn't look long out of the egg. Turning, I dropped Keats' leash and said, "Fall back, please." He hesitated to leave me in the company of dangerous warriors, so I added, "Neither of us wants to end up in the drink today. I'll be fine."

That was enough to sway him and he literally backed up, with his muzzle swiveling between me and the swans. When the birds slowed their roll, he sat on his haunches, still on high alert.

"He's a good one," said Amos. "Listens well."

"Very protective, though, so this is hard for him."

"It's okay. The cob's stood down and the pen's circling back."

The regal bird was hardly at ease, however. He came close to the shoreline and stared at me. I lowered my eyes and then offered a little bow. "Thank you," I said. "For not killing my dog."

Raising my eyes, I saw his feathers fold, like a Victorian lady snapping her fan shut for dramatic effect.

"Nice touch," Amos said. "He trusts you as much as a protective papa can." He gave a little laugh. "Don't turn your back though. They like a sneak attack."

"I've learned that the hard way with animals at my

hobby farm," I said. "My tailbone has barely recovered from a goat assault two weeks ago."

"Have you thought about taking in rescue swans? I'm connected with sanctuaries all over the country."

Keats answered for me with an assertive mumble that carried.

"That's a no from the sheepdog," I said. "I don't have a pond, yet."

"If you're considering hosting swans, they need a hundred yards of water for a running takeoff and prefer it shallow for optimal grazing."

"Wouldn't they just fly away then? And for that matter, why hasn't the one at the Briars done just that?"

"I'm assuming he can't," Amos said. "Maybe he's injured, but more likely he's been deliberately grounded by humans."

"Grounded *how*?"

He gestured to the swan couple in front of us. "I've clipped their guard feathers to keep them here because they wouldn't survive in the real wild."

"Does it hurt them?" I asked.

"Done right, no. I cut five primary flight feathers out of one wing. That's enough to keep them from liftoff until their next molt. Rinse and repeat annually."

I pulled out my phone and scrolled through the photos. "How do I know if he's been clipped?"

He accepted the phone I offered and then shrugged. "You'll need to get a full wingspread to see. Done correctly, it'll look like a comb with teeth missing."

"I see. So it's not inhumane?"

"Clipping can be in the best interests of the bird. I'm not a big fan of pinioning, however."

"I've never heard that word."

"People who raise swans for sale remove a joint in the wing so that they never even learn to fly. They twirl around until they give up. Their pond is all they know."

"What a shame that some swans never experience flight at all."

"Obviously, as a rescuer, I prefer to let swans be swans. I ground injured birds till they recover and send them on their way." A smile lit up his face. "Some come back in spring to nest here. Best of both worlds, as they can raise their young safely. We've done a lot to support the swan population."

"Are they all mute swans?" I asked.

"You'll see," he said, motioning for me to walk on.

I did the same with Keats, keeping a wary eye on the family until we were well past.

Over the next two hours we strolled past pond after pond, each big enough to offer a breeding pair sufficient territory to call home. It seemed that they were content to share with other waterfowl, just not their white-feathered brethren.

Most of the ponds contained mute swans, but there were two pairs of larger trumpeter swans with black beaks, and a striking pair of black swans.

"I've never seen black swans," I said. "Now I want two ponds so I can have black and white." I grinned at Keats. "A perfect match for my dog."

"Black swans prefer a warmer climate so they wouldn't love your winters," he said. "Doesn't mean you can't do it. Just takes more work."

"I'm no stranger to work, but I've also learned that so many creatures just arrive that there's no need to go out of my way to find more."

Amos crossed his arms. "So, what are you going to do

about your swan predicament at the retirement community?"

My smile faded. "Well, first I need to figure out his flight information. If he can fly, why is he staying? If he *can't* fly, how did he get there? He couldn't have strolled in."

"Don't be so sure. There are dams and water beyond. Many a swan has portaged a mile to get where it wants to go. They're very determined."

I stared at the pair of black swans contentedly dipping their heads to pull reeds. "Do they ever become, well, tame?"

He shook his head. "Not particularly, but I don't encourage it, either. Our birds aren't pond ornaments. Personally, I'd never fully trust a cob. He's just doing what his genes tell him to do, and I can't fault him for that. One of my rescuer friends let his guard down and got a broken nose as a reminder."

"Duly noted," I said, as Keats shivered beside me. "I'll study the Briars' feathered guest and figure out what's bothering him. Seeing your swans proves he's either unwell or unhappy. He doesn't have the ease and confidence of your birds. He swims back and forth constantly when I'm there and apparently hides in the bush when I'm not."

"Send me more footage and I'll help interpret," he said. "First thing to do is figure out if he's injured or bound in some way by fishing tackle. If all else fails, I'll extract him and see how he fares here. I can find him a new lady if that's what ails him."

My heart lifted as we walked back to the parking area. "I love second chance love stories. I hope it's as simple as that."

"It's rarely as simple as that with swans, but stay positive."

I laughed. "Optimism is in my genes, apparently. It gets clipped often and grows back, like flight feathers."

"That's a wonderful trait to have," Amos said. "Your cob is in good hands."

I let Keats into the truck and turned. "I hope so. If he's chosen to come to the Briars, there must be a good reason. He's a beautiful puzzle to be solved."

Amos offered his hand to help me climb into the truck and I accepted it. I might be a fiercely independent farmer, but gallantry from the right source was always welcome.

"There's a job here for you if you decide to become a snowbird," he said.

Rolling down the window, I shook my head. "I'm no fan of our winters but chances are good I'll go down with my ark someday."

"Ivy," he said, sounding more serious now. "Get yourself a good lifejacket. I sense you're going to need it."

"Brought one with me," I said, putting the truck in reverse. Once we were on the road I added, "We'd better stock up on flotation devices for Edna's bunker. Do zombies swim, buddy?"

His mumble told me in no uncertain terms that if the apocalypse featured swimming zombies, I was on my own.

CHAPTER SIXTEEN

I drove from the waterfowl sanctuary directly to Clarington, the closest town to the Briars, where Jilly was co-hosting a group outing alongside Special Constable Doug. Normally, Constable Larry was the daytime chaperone, but he was still sidelined with his injury. Luckily the yellow Vespa had turned up after Vaughan's joyride, because Doug needed it today. As I looked for a parking spot, he shot across an intersection on a red light in hot pursuit of Shirley Mills, who was going like stink in her motorized wheelchair. They both had some moves and I was disappointed to miss how the chase ended.

"We've got our work cut out for us, too," I told Keats as we got out of the truck. "I want to know how these folks use their day pass. They have money to burn and the town has apparently grown on the strength of the Briars and other communities like it." I looked around. "There's security staff on every street corner. Bizarre."

Texting Jilly, I headed for the tall monument in the center of town where we'd agreed to meet. On the way, however, I noticed Vaughan Mills leaving a store called

Haute Baubles with a bag in his hand. He pulled out what appeared to be a small blue velvet case, slipped it into his pocket, and then ditched the bag in a trash can.

Keats gave me a look and I nodded. "I'm curious about that, too, buddy. Shall we shop for jewels?"

A bell tinkled over the door as we walked into the small store. There was only one long glass display case, and as I peered inside, a woman came out of the back room. It was a bit of a shock to see black curls after spending so much time among silver locks.

She took her time scanning my overalls and then grimaced. Flying waterfowl had used me for target practice at the sanctuary and I probably didn't smell too fresh, either. Luckily, I'd worn a baseball cap, which I removed now and shook out my hair.

"Welcome to Clarington," the salesclerk said. Her smile didn't meet her eyes, which were as black as the onyx brooch in the case at my fingertips. "I believe you're new in town." She leaned over the case to stare at Keats. "Dogs aren't permitted in the store. Perhaps you missed the sign."

"I saw it." I flashed a smile carefully calibrated to match hers. "I figured you'd make an exception for my certified therapy dog. I wouldn't dare leave him outside where he could be stolen, even if I had remembered to bring his leash."

"Dogs don't get stolen in Clarington," she said. "This town has a big heart. And a lot of security. He'll be perfectly safe out front."

I glanced out the window and shook my head. "There are scooters and wheelchairs zooming around and he could be struck. If you're that concerned, we should move on. I'd been hoping to find a hostess gift here, but I'm sure there are other places where therapy dogs are welcome."

Her smile amped up a notch and mine did the same. When in doubt, mirroring was always the way to go. The salesclerk waved manicured fingertips over the display case as if she'd become a game show host. "Do take a look. What do you think she'd like?"

I stared into the case and deliberately ran my index finger across the glass. The nail was chipped and dirty. No matter how hard I scrubbed, I couldn't quite erase the evidence of farm chores. Normally I'd be a little embarrassed to flaunt my lifestyle in a store like this, but her attitude irked me. She'd clearly decided based on my dog and appearance that I was a poor prospect for a sale. The silk shammy she pulled out to buff my fingerprints away confirmed she wouldn't get one, either.

"Lovely work," I said, tapping the glass a few times to give her something to polish. "Are these originals?"

She gave an almost imperceptible nod. "My aunt is the designer. Every piece is one of a kind so no one will ever show up wearing the same thing."

"What do you have in my price range?" I asked. "I wouldn't want to spend more than five hundred, but I still want it to be nice."

Her smile instantly became more sincere. The farmer was now a contender.

"May I ask your host's age?" she said. "That will help me narrow it down."

"Late seventies, I think. She lives at the Briars, so I want to make sure it really stands out from everything else you've sold."

"As I said, each piece is unique," she said. "Some more special than others, of course."

I ran my finger along the glass again, noticing for the first time how thick the callouses were. There was a grass stain on my knuckle from weeds I'd pulled the morning we left. The salesclerk noticed it too because her orange shammy twitched like a flare.

Glancing down at Keats for help, I followed his gaze and then tapped an empty spot near the end of a top row. "What was sitting there? I feel like I just missed something amazing."

She took a quick swish at the glass. "It was a heart locket that's been here a long time. The right person eventually comes along."

"Sort of like placing a rescue animal in the right home," I said.

Her onyx eyes were cold. "Perhaps. I wouldn't know."

"Well, that heart is going to look lovely on Shirley Mills, but it wouldn't make the right hostess gift. Too romantic."

Her lids dropped over her eyes. One ruby red fingernail traced the glass, leaving no trace of a smudge. "I never discuss client purchases. Discretion is part of the package here at Haute Baubles."

"Of course. I won't say a thing to Vaughan or his wife. But you can be sure I'll be looking out for that locket."

Her red nail hung over the glass like a fat drop of blood. It trembled just enough to confirm my suspicions. Vaughan had purchased the locket for someone other than Shirley, and the clerk was worried the farmer had loose lips.

"Do you see something your host might like?" she asked, before pressing her lips together in a thin scarlet line.

"I'm not sure. But I do see something my best friend would adore." I tapped the case over a ring with three green stones. "May I try that on?"

She flipped back her glossy black curls. "Those are real emeralds."

"I assumed so. Green is my friend's signature color. This is perfect for her."

"Madam," she said, "this is well out of your price range."

"It's probably well within her boyfriend's, though. I'll try it on for size."

Sighing, she unlocked the case and pulled out the little box. "I don't think it will fit you. Your hands look quite... large."

"They are, actually. Perfect for wrangling sheep or delivering baby goats."

She winced as she bent to collect a bottle of rubbing alcohol from under the counter. After carefully wiping down the ring, she offered it to me between pinched fingers. I had to tug a little to get it, and then slipped it onto my left ring finger. Unfortunately, she was right. It lodged at my knuckle, and while I hadn't applied much pressure, it tingled where it sat. I held out my hand and angled it to catch the sun's rays. It not only looked stunning but *felt* stunning. This was Jilly's ring. I was quite sure of it.

Reaching for my phone, I snapped a couple of photos to send to Asher if the time came. Then I eased the ring off and took my sweet time about returning it. All the while, the clerk cupped her hands underneath in case it slipped into the pocket of my overalls and rode home to farm country in shame.

She doused the ring in rubbing alcohol before replacing it in its box and locked it safely away from my grubby hands.

"Any chance you could put that on hold for a few days?" I asked.

"Only with a significant deposit," she said, with a smirk. "We have so many eager clients who might want it today."

No one else had even peeked into the window while I was there, so I shrugged. "I guess if the ring is truly meant for my friend, it'll still be here when I come back."

She mirrored my shrug, giving me a taste of my own medicine. "What about your host?"

"These baubles might be a little too haute for her. But thanks so much for your time."

Keats gave a good shake before leaving and sent dirt, dust and feathers into the sunbeams. They swirled for a moment and coalesced into a shape reminiscent of a dog. A longer and lower breed, like a corgi, perhaps. It was like seeing a shape in a cloud—there one minute and gone the next.

I blinked a few times and then shook my head. Keats gave me a strange look with his eerie blue eye and I wondered if he saw the dusty specter, too.

"What's wrong?" the salesclerk called.

"Did you or your aunt ever own a dog?"

The swish of black curls left no room for doubt. "Never. We have allergies. In fact, I'm still finding dog hair years later from the previous owner's stupid, fat wiener dog."

"Interesting," I said, opening the door.

"Why is that interesting?" she called, flicking her hair back.

I flicked my hair back, too. "I think my dog picked up on it, that's all."

If he did, he was happy to leave the phantom dachshund behind and trot briskly up the street with purpose. Clarington hadn't given up all its secrets to us yet.

CHAPTER SEVENTEEN

Elsie was sitting outside a café near the monument in the middle of town. I thought about stopping to chat, but Jilly was still waiting. I waved instead but Elsie didn't notice. In fact, she was on her phone and dabbing at her eyes with napkins. Even her mauve hair seemed limp and dejected.

"I hope she's okay," I said. "Probably a call from home, wherever that is. I bet those chats bring up a lot of sad memories."

Special Constable Doug whipped by at the next corner, no doubt trying to keep track of his many charges. Some residents appeared to have bolted like toddlers with no concern at all for their safety. Or Constable Doug's for that matter. With his speed and sharp turns, he'd end up smacking into a stop sign, just like my mother.

"I miss Mom," I told Keats, as we hurried across the square to where Jilly was sitting on a bench surrounded by other residents.

Keats was hard to surprise but I pulled it off now.

"I know, right? I never thought I'd say that, either. But

it's true. I miss her. And everyone else, especially Kellan. But in this moment, I miss Mom."

He mumbled, as if pressing me to dig a little deeper for reasons.

"I'm not sure why. Maybe it was seeing Elsie back there crying. Maybe it was hearing from Videa earlier about how much it hurts to leave your loved ones behind." I twisted my hair into a ponytail and sighed. "I mean, I prefer it when Mom stays at her apartment but I wouldn't want to move too far from her again. Or my brother and sisters for that matter. Jilly, Edna and Gertie may be my besties, but it seems like my family's growing on me. Like fungus."

The next mumble just reiterated what I already knew: Keats loved all of them. They were my pack, and as a result, his pack.

"I guess we should travel more often, buddy, if it brings on epiphanies like that."

His tail swished an affirmative. Keats wasn't troubled at all with homesickness. He pretty much lived in the moment.

"What's wrong?" Jilly asked, as we joined them. "You look like you've seen a ghost."

"Worse," I said. "I just realized I miss my mother."

Jilly laughed out loud. It was the first time I'd heard the full-on, rollicking Blackwood laugh since... well, I couldn't remember when. Probably before her grandmother started calling weeks ago. The Briars hadn't revived her, but the real Jilly was still in there, waiting to get out.

"Tell me more," she said.

I fanned my face with my hand. "I'm hoping it'll pass. The heat's getting to me."

"It's not the heat, dear, but the humidity," Alice Cheevers said, as the group got up to give us the grand tour.

No one seemed to notice that our unofficial tour guide wore a fur coat. Keats hadn't been here before but it seemed like he already had a destination in mind.

"Good thing we'll be back in farm country before summer arrives or I'd burst into flames." Looking around, I asked, "Anyone know where Vaughan is?"

"Anyone know where anyone is?" Bridie asked. "People split like balls on a pool table when the bus doors opened." She smiled down at Keats, whose tail was still swishing. "Like dogs at an off-leash park."

"Vaughan always ends up at the casino," Cherise Heathcrington said. "With Ford Fletcher."

"And Rollie," Alice said. "Your husband."

Cherise glared at her. "Rollie doesn't gamble. He just goes along for the company."

"I'm surprised there's a casino in a town as small as Clarington," I said.

"They'd put a casino in the middle of the Briars if they could," Cherise said. "Any way to part seniors from their pensions."

"Some people have gotten in over their heads, I'm afraid," Alice said. "But no one ever gets evicted over late fees. The money always comes."

"From family?" I asked.

"From the people who want us to be happy here." Alice gave a grim smile. "Gambling is an addiction. The kind that got some people sent here in the first place."

I fell back from the rest of the group and Bridie joined me. She was wearing another roomy peasant dress, accessorized with bangles and beads. Her style was dated but probably comfortable, especially in the heat. Overalls weren't a wise subtropical choice.

When I was sure no one was listening, I turned to

Bridie and said, "Isn't it weird that Vaughan, holder of the Briars' purse strings, is a fan of casinos?"

"Ivy, you've been on the planet long enough to know how politics work," she said. "A condo board is just small pond politics. Vaughan greased enough palms to get elected and he's as dirty as they come."

"I haven't been around long enough to expect things like that in a seniors community, Bridie."

"They probably happen in many seniors communities to one degree or another," she said. "We're probably worse than some and better than others. I'm not sure. The Briars is all I've known for a long time. It's my home for better or worse."

"Do you actually like living there?" I asked.

"I like the weather," she said. "And my friends, such as they are. I lost a few in the tarot debacle, as I'm sure you've heard."

"It seems like this psychic stuff just causes trouble. Like gambling."

"That's a good analogy," she said. "It's a form of gambling. Banking on a future we can't control." She stared at Jilly's back and sighed. "When I came here, I thought I knew everything. Now I'm riddled with doubts. People smell that, you know."

"Yeah, I guess. Dogs do, too. All emotions, really. That comes in handy sometimes."

"I'm glad Jilly has friends like you," Bridie said, crossing her arms as if feeling a sudden chill. "It's a relief knowing she's protected."

I caught her elbow. "Protected from what, exactly? Is someone after her?"

"I don't think so. Not now, anyway."

"Bridie." I gave her arm a little shake and the bangles

rang out. "This isn't something to joke about. Jilly and I have gotten into some challenging situations back home."

"Oh, I know. Don't think I haven't tried to question her about them. As far as I can tell, they have nothing to do with our family. Our history. But of course, it's impossible to get two words out of that girl."

Keats was trotting along beside Jilly now, touching her dangling hand with his nose now and then. I don't think she noticed, but that didn't stop him from trying to boost her spirits.

"This visit might bring you closer together," I said. "It's a start."

"I hope you're right. I adore both my granddaughters and the hardest thing about being here is not seeing them. My daughters on the other hand..." She glanced at me and rolled her eyes. "Such drama!"

Keats left Jilly and circled the crowd to bring everyone up sharp in front of a tavern called The Thirsty Fish. Two heavy oak doors opened and Special Constable Doug emerged pulling Vaughan Mills behind him. I was surprised to see Vaughan follow so meekly. But as soon as his feet hit the sidewalk, he gave a couple of sharp twists and wriggled out of Doug's grasp. Then he hopped on the yellow Vespa and booted off. Ford and Rollie came out just in time to hear his yell of triumph and doubled over, laughing.

Doug didn't give up the fight. He seized a bicycle from an old woman's hands, mounted it on the run with the ease of a cowboy, and disappeared around a corner in pursuit of his target.

I looked at Bridie and she laughed, too. "Boys will be boys. At any age."

I didn't bother telling her that Vaughan was my number

one suspect in Lottie's death. Not only was he taking bribes and having an affair, he was probably cooking the books so he could gamble away the condo fees. I wondered if Lottie Greenwich had found a way to check the paper trail and expose him.

Doug zipped by again, panting hard as he searched for Vaughan. He had slipped to second position on the suspect list. In fact, he was starting to look more like the hero he wanted to be.

"Don't fret, Ivy," Bridie said. "Vaughan just loves giving Doug a run for his money when he gets the chance. You'll find them sharing a pint at the pub back home tonight, mark my words."

"So they're not even serious?" I asked.

"Just serious enough. Doug is doing his job and Vaughan is playing maverick. Sometimes it feels like a sitcom."

"Only in a sitcom no one dies," I said.

"And swans just swim around and look pretty," she added.

"You can't count on wildlife," I said.

"You can't count on anything, really. Not even the sun coming up in the east. You just need to put on your best bangles and get ready to fight if you need to."

"You remind me of my mom," I said, laughing.

"Is that a good thing or not?"

"Good. Mostly." We strolled down a pretty street that wasn't so different from Clover Grove. There were similar quaint stores offering similar wares, only with a tropical theme. "Maybe you can visit someday and meet her."

"Ivy, I'd love nothing more than to visit Runaway Farm. See if you can talk my granddaughter into busting me out of here." She drew in a deep breath. "I'd like to attend—"

She paused and I fully expected her to say Jilly's wedding.

Instead, she blurted, "Edna's seminar."

"Seminar? What seminar?"

"Jilly said Edna's planning to teach people how to prepare for... Well, you know."

"The apocalypse?"

"Exactly. And I'd like to learn more."

"That's the first I've heard of any seminars."

"It's by invitation only," Bridie said. "Apparently you need to pass a series of survival tests just to get in." She straightened her shoulders. "It may look like I lead a cushy life, but I try to stay fit and now I'm motivated. I like to think I'd do well in an apocalypse."

"Not afraid of zombies?"

"Hardly. They're too stupid to pose much of a threat." Looking around to make sure Jilly was still out of range, she said, "It's the witches you need to watch out for. They'll survive anything. Even another big bang."

"A bunker probably wouldn't do you much good if *that's* what you're worried about."

"Edna has lots in her arsenal, from what I hear. You can take anything down if you go about it the right way."

I couldn't help laughing and Jilly turned to stare at us. It felt like I'd put a boot over the line in the family squabble, but on the other hand, Jilly had told Bridie about Edna's supposed seminar before I knew about it.

"Never you mind," Bridie said, raising her voice a little. "Jilly and I will work things out just fine. I've learned a few things about dealing with witches and granddaughters in the past few years."

"I heard that," Jilly called.

"I sure hope so, sweetheart," Bridie called back. "It was lobbed right at you."

I slipped away to join Alice and Cherise, leaving Keats to tie another canine love knot around Jilly and Bridie. It probably wouldn't hold them today. Not yet. But I had faith that with persistence, he could squeeze those two back into each other's hearts for good.

CHAPTER EIGHTEEN

Jilly had decided to throw a cocktail party in the recreation center when we got back. The Briars' folk were on a freedom high and she wanted to keep the good feelings flowing for as long as possible. Enough people had tossed money into a kitty that she'd been able to buy some fun and fancy liqueurs. Having worked her way through college as a bartender, she knew her way around a blender and the dream kitchen had three good ones. She got them roaring and then sent me out to serve umbrella drinks in the pool area.

I was worried everyone would be so tired they'd end up tipsy and tipping into the pool, but most seemed to hold their booze better than I could. One peachy concoction was enough to make my head spin in the late afternoon heat, and my interrogation skills declined with every sip.

"Blender drinks are the enemy of the amateur sleuth," I told Keats. "This would be the ideal time to pick some brains but I have the finesse of a sledgehammer."

He mumbled his agreement but wasn't inclined to work the crowd anyway. As I mingled, he stuck close to my heels.

Very close. Sufficiently so that I eventually realized he was trying to tell me something, and it wasn't to grab myself another peach beach breeze, or whatever Jilly had called it. In fact, the hackles along his spine had risen and his ears alternated up and down separately, as if he were trying to hear two things at once. I carried the empty tray back to Jilly and told her I needed to go down to the pond and check on the swan.

She took her finger off the blender button and stared at the dog. "You're not going down there without me. Not when Keats looks like that."

Relief surged through me and cleared away the peach buzz. "Party's over, then."

When the bar closed, people quickly dispersed, with so many hugs for Jilly that I had to do most of the cleanup. By the time I made my way out to the equipment shed near the pool, Keats was pacing and agitated. Percy was puffed, too.

"What are we looking for?" Jilly said, following me into the shed.

"Protection." I aimed my phone light around the dim interior. "From what I'm not sure."

In the end, we settled for hip waders, rain gear, a fishing net and other odds and ends. The oars and paddles I saw the other day were missing now, so they'd probably been left with the watercraft.

I stuffed everything I could into two big duffel bags we also found there. Then we stopped at my truck, which was still parked outside, to collect lifejackets. Percy was perched on the hood, waiting for us. Bridie had let him outside when she got home, as I'd asked. Hoisting our gear, Jilly and I started walking after Keats, who led us to a trail that turned out to be a shortcut to the pond.

"So, you're planning on wading in there?" she asked, as

we walked over the grass to the water. "If you'd mentioned that earlier I might have suggested another peach beach breeze for courage."

"I just want to get a closer look at the swan, like the guy at the sanctuary asked," I said. "He wants to know if Zeus is wounded, and if his wings are clipped."

"That's a yes to the wading?" she said. "I notice you brought enough gear for all, but three of us are planning to keep paws on dry land."

I grinned at her. "Jilly, my friend, it's a beautiful night for a boat ride, don't you think? Look at that sunset. It's as peachy as your umbrella drinks."

"I don't see a boat, Ivy. And if you've packed an inflatable, just know that I don't consider that an option. I'll stand guard from here."

"Videa said people went rowing, so there must be a boat at the far end, where we haven't explored. Let's check if it's seaworthy."

She followed me, sharing a grumbled conversation with Keats that I deliberately tuned out. Eventually she raised her voice. "What if the bird *is* wounded?"

"Amos said the toughest part is grabbing the swan, but then they calm right down when you hug them close. You can make sure Keats and Percy are safe while I do the hugging."

"We only have an hour or two of light left. This couldn't wait till morning?"

"Keats said no. You saw his message."

She squelched after me over increasingly swampy turf. "What will we do with the swan once we've caught him? Is there a plan?"

"I've got the name of a good avian vet," I said.

"So you'll stick the bird in the duffel bag and hope Doug lets us out for a drive?"

"Maybe I'll steal his Vespa and see if he's fixed the breach in the fence. I think the straps of the duffel bag will go over my shoulders."

"Ivy!"

I turned to grin at her. "Kidding, Jilly. Both the avian vet and Amos make house calls. All we're doing is assessing the situation. We've handled much worse together."

"I'm not so sure of that. We have no idea what's in that water. Why did all the goldfish die?"

"Good question. But I doubt the swan would stick around if the water were too toxic. Amos said this swamp extends for miles and Zeus could find a way out if he chose. My theory is that he's hiding something in the bushes. Like an injured bride. Did you know they mate for life and that a bereaved swan can literally pine to death?"

"That's so sad," she said, taking the distraction I threw out as bait. "We don't want him pining to death if there's anything we can do about it."

"Exactly. Our visit will not end with his swan song. Amos says he can give Zeus a safe, clean pond, a pretty winged lass, and a happily ever after. Since he's still eating the grain Videa leaves out, he hasn't given up on life just yet."

I watched for the big bird as we circled the pond. Normally he emerged right away when I arrived, but not this time. Maybe he was sicker than he seemed.

When we reached the far end, we found a second dock that was relatively new and stable. Along one side of it, a canoe, a double kayak and a silver rowboat rocked idly on gentle ripples.

"Score!" I said. "We even have a choice, Jilly."

"If there's a 'we' there's no choice," she said. "I would only consider the rowboat."

"The kayak or canoe would be easier to maneuver in the bush," I said. "The boat might get stuck and I'd have to jump out and push."

"Then we'd better gear up. Honestly. I can't imagine these seniors kayaking out into the marsh."

"I wouldn't put it past them. You saw how they moved in town. Many are quite spry."

"Well, it isn't safe for them, for us and especially not the pets."

Keats tried to mumble something, but his teeth were chattering too hard from terror.

"Buddy, you don't have to come," I said, unzipping the first duffel bag. "You and Percy can hang right here and wait for us."

"We can't leave them and go very far," Jilly said. "There's a murderer around, in case you've forgotten."

"Good point. Maybe I should run them back to Bridie's."

"Or maybe we just shouldn't go very far. Leave the real search and rescue to Amos."

I looked at Keats and he tried to still his trembling. He was determined to come with us no matter what it cost him. "All right," I said. "We'll stay within shooting distance from the dock."

"I'd prefer another turn of phrase, but okay," she said.

Both of us stepped into the hip waders, which turned out to be chest waders that were evidently sized for large men. We tightened the straps over our shoulders but there was nothing we could do about the huge boots attached to them. Then we layered on lifejackets and big yellow slickers.

Jilly groaned. "I suppose we'll be taking up scuba diving at some point?"

"We'd need pro training for scuba. And skydiving. Maybe that's part of Edna's survival seminar no one told me about."

"She didn't tell you?" Jilly said. "That's strange. I assumed you knew."

"Bridie said it's by invitation only. So perhaps mine got lost in the mail between our properties."

"I'm sure it's an oversight, and I wouldn't worry about it," Jilly said. "What's next?"

What came next was likely to be the hardest part of our expedition. Getting Keats into a coat at any time was difficult, and with all the extra padding, I could barely bend over or move my arms. I really should have led with his lifejacket.

"Let's keep this simple, buddy. How about you skip your coat ritual of pretending you're dead? The energy I spend fighting you is energy I need for rowing."

I was sure he'd see the sense in that, but he collapsed onto his side and stared into the distance, tongue hanging out so far it touched the dock.

"I can't watch this," Jilly said. "I'll take care of Percy."

By all rights, the cat should have been the one protesting our aquatic expedition. Instead he stepped forward like a marmalade soldier and let Jilly puff and grunt over him till he was strapped into the tiny pink lifejacket that was meant for a Chihuahua. In fact, I could hear a loud purr as I worked around the limp dog.

"Look at Percy, Keats," I said. "He's sucking it up like a champ. And in case you didn't notice, he's feline. They're basically allergic to water."

The strike continued. The dog's blue eye closed. With

my rubber handicap, I was going to pass out and lose the battle by default.

There were clumping footsteps and Jilly bent over the prone dog, too. "Get up, you," she said. "Or feel the thump of oversized rubber on your derriere."

The blue eye opened. He knew she wouldn't but our sweaty faces must have made an impression. After a heavy sigh, he pushed himself onto his belly and then into a wobbly stand.

It was enough to allow the two of us to wrestle him into the lifejacket. Then I groped in the front pocket of my overalls and came up with his leash. At this he gave an indignant yip, but I was adamant. I only wished I had brought Percy's harness, too.

"Let's grab the rope off the kayak," Jilly said. "We can loop it through Percy's lifejacket."

"You're brilliant," I said.

Untying the kayak, I hauled it onto the bank, and unknotted the rope. Jilly took care of Percy while I got into the rowboat and slipped the heavy wooden oars into place. Keats finally found his inner hero and jumped in without my asking. He moved to the prow and stood with white paws propped up, just as he would on the dashboard of the truck. The trembling abated once he accepted his role as skipper.

Relegated to the seat at the back, Jilly tried to get Percy settled on her lap, but he couldn't get a grip on the waders or rain slicker. Finally he perched beside her on the seat and she clutched the rope tightly.

"Let's get this over with," she said, brushing back stray curls with her free hand. "I'm boiling in this gear. It feels like the Amazon jungle."

"Looks like it, too," I said, trying to get the oars to work in tandem.

"You have rowed a boat before, right?" she asked.

"Not to my knowledge. We're short on lakes in Clover Grove. But how hard could it be?"

She groaned again. "Famous last words."

I spun the boat once and then straightened out and finally headed into the brush where Zeus usually lurked. There was a beautiful sunset lighting up the pond but the foliage became so dense with vines and hanging moss that it was very dim.

"Good thing a swan is a living beacon," I said. "But keep your phone ready in case we need the light."

Before long, the heavy brush started slowing us down. Branches seemed to reach out and grab at us. Jilly crooked up her elbow to protect her eyes.

"Hey, there he is!" I said, spotting the swan floating on the far side of a pool that was about 10 yards long and twice as wide. He was quite still, which suggested his webbed feet were massaging the water just right to hold position. His wings were half up and his orange peak pointed in our direction.

"He looks fine," Jilly said. "What now? There's no point trying to capture him if he's chilling in his own private clearing. He must have wanted some privacy from the prying eyes of the Briars." After a beat she added, "Don't we all?"

I glanced over my shoulder at Keats and saw his ears were down and his tail puffed.

"I don't think Zeus is chilling," I said. "In fact, I get the sense that he was waiting for us to find him."

Jilly's eyes jumped from Keats to Percy, who was puffed

around his lifejacket. "Well, something's going on. No question about that."

"And now the boat is stuck. I should have brought a machete," I said. "Edna probably covers this in her apocalyptic survival course, to which I wasn't invited."

My friend actually laughed, which broke some of the tension that was as thick as the humid air and hanging moss. "You're not going to let that go, are you?"

"Did I mention seeing her trying to outrun Drama Llama in Lottie's crystal ball? Her legs were really pumping."

"A delicious fantasy," she said. "Now, how are we going to get out of this bind? By the time we go back for tools it'll be pitch black in here."

Keats mumbled what sounded like an urgent command to press on.

"I don't see a way through, buddy," I said. "And Zeus, you're not being much help, just sitting there like an ornament. You could at least show us the way."

The answer came from an unexpected source. Our smallest expedition member simply leapt off the seat onto a hanging bough, pulling the rope out of Jilly's hand. The tree was long dead but looked alive in an otherworldly way because it was covered with green moss and vines.

"Percy, no!" Jilly's voice was shrill as she grabbed for the rope. "Come back here right now."

As always, the cat had a mind of his own. The bright neon pink of his lifejacket bobbed along the bough and when I managed to spin the boat a little with one oar, I saw we could force our way through and follow him.

The real problem came after we penetrated the clearing and Percy reached the end of his bough. He was much higher now and his piteous meows made it clear he was afraid to jump down into the rowboat either for fear of missing his mark or dangling from his rope if it snagged.

"I'll catch you,' Percy," I said. Settling the oars in the boat, I stood carefully and raised my arms toward the cat. There was a yard-long gap between us and I doubt either of us relished his descent.

Jilly and Keats both gave mumbles of protest, and the former said, "Bad idea, Ivy. If Percy jumps on you, he's just going to slide off the slicker and it won't end well. And if you take off the slicker, you'll get scratched up."

"Better idea," I said. "I'll prop the oar against the bough. The wood is rough enough that he should be able to get a grip with his claws and come down. He's a master climber."

It sounded reasonable, and the cat seemed game, but no sooner had he begun his descent than ripples rocked the boat just enough to shove the oar off the branch. Now I was clutching it with Percy dangling above me. I tried to hold the oar steady but despite my best efforts, it swung out and Percy dropped into the water with it.

Jilly screamed, Keats yelped and Percy yowled. I saved my breath to jump over the side while Jilly and Keats braced themselves.

At least the water was warm. It was about five feet deep, although the silt under my hip waders felt ready to suck me to the earth's core. I swished my arms through the water to keep afloat and rotated till I saw Percy clinging to the floating oar. He didn't waste any more breath on protests, but those still in the boat did enough vocalizing for all of us.

"We're fine," I said. "Totally fine. Keats, calm down. I can practically walk over to get Percy and hand him to you. The bigger question is how will I get back in the boat?"

"One problem at a time," Jilly said. "Save my cat baby."

I managed to lift the oar enough that she could grab it without joining me, and Percy scrambled back on board. Jilly pulled in the oar and I looked around for my own ticket out. No way could I risk tipping all of them into the rather pungent pond. Keats would never forgive me.

He peered over the side and mumbled something that sounded like, "You're on your own, here."

"I know." I floundered and flopped. All the gear had seemed like a great idea back on shore, but it was a decided hindrance now. "Wait. I've got an idea. The trunk of the tree Percy used has knobby bits where the branches broke off. Like little stairs. I can climb up and get into the boat from there. Jilly, can you shove the boat a little closer?"

"You're going to climb that tree in rubber boots?"

"Piece of cake," I said, wallowing over to the tree trunk. "It's not the worst thing I've faced. Not by a long shot."

It wasn't the best thing I'd faced, either. The knobs that had seemed substantial barely accommodated the boot tips. But once I was able to grab the bough Percy had used, things went much better. Soon I was a few inches over the boat, which Jilly had maneuvered into position.

My landing left much to be desired, but we didn't capsize. There would be bruises on my arms and back, and probably on Keats' soul, which I firmly believed he had.

"You okay?" Jilly asked, as I panted in the space between the two front seats.

"Sure, except for feeling like a flipped turtle." I scrabbled around till I could get a grip on the seat and then pulled myself up. "What a fabulous workout. It's a good thing farming keeps me fit."

"I'm glad you still have your sense of humor," she said, tucking Percy into her rain slicker. "Mine drowned back there."

"All good," I said, slipping the oars back in place. "Now where's the swan?"

I glanced out over the clearing and that's when I saw it...

The worst thing I'd faced.

Ever.

Hands down.

CHAPTER NINETEEN

"Promise me you won't scream, Jilly," I said, beckoning Keats to come closer. "Because maybe, if we're very quiet, it won't notice us."

"The swan?" she asked. "He's been watching the whole time. Although now it seems like he's looking at—oh. *Oh, no.* Tell me that's a log."

"Only if a log has bulbous eyes and teeth."

"Ivy... I can't. I really can't." Her voice was low and hoarse and Keats, now between my feet, made a keening sound.

"Quiet, you two. Alligators don't see that well. They're like snakes and respond to vibrations."

"They can see well enough to chase golfers," Jilly said. "I've watched those videos."

"Maybe those were crocodiles," I said. "They're far more vicious, from what I read."

"So you read up on this?"

"Just a little. Just in case." I fumbled with the oars and tried to get them moving. "Gators tend to be mild mannered unless they have a nest around."

Jilly tried to smother a moan. "What do we do if it catches us?"

"First, it can't while we're in the boat."

"But if it did?"

"Beat on its snout and eyes as hard as you can. Those are the sensitive parts. Whatever you do, don't play dead."

As I angled the boat, her head swiveled to track the gator. "I wish I hadn't asked."

"But see how useful I'd be in Edna's survival course? Gators and crocs will run rampant after the apocalypse. Dinosaurs might make a return."

"There's a time for joking and a time for fleeing," she said. "Rule number one in the survival course."

"We're good if we all stay in the boat." I set the oar against the tree and shoved hard to free us. "No way can it climb up the slippery side with those stubby little legs."

"I think I'm going to wet myself," Jilly said.

"Good thing you're wearing chest waders," I said, as we finally broke free of the vegetation.

"How is that a good thing? I'll be soaking in my own urine."

"It's great for the skin—an ingredient of specialty moisturizers. You're going to come out of this looking years younger."

"My feet, maybe."

"Then you can start your next career as a foot model."

There was a pause and then a small snort. "Ivy, do not make me laugh. Vibrations, remember. This is a very dangerous situation, particularly for the pets."

"And the swan, I would think. Why on earth is he hanging around with that thing?"

"How about we discuss swan motivations back on the shore? Maybe the bird will follow and the gator won't."

That's not how it worked out, though. The swan stayed right where he was, on the other side of the clearing. The gator, on the other hand, moved toward the boat, a floating log about eight feet long. It moved with such ease that it barely caused a ripple. Keats couldn't see it, lodged as he was between my shins. But he knew, and his growl was deep enough to send plenty of vibrations.

"Keep it down, buddy. At least make that thing work for it." I pushed strands of wet hair out of my eyes. "I know I'm supposed to love all creatures great and small, but some are harder than others, I must admit."

"If you even think about rescuing an alligator, it'll blow fifteen years of friendship right out of the proverbial water," Jilly said. "I wish it no harm but I don't care to make its acquaintance."

"Me either." I spun the boat slowly and gently in the clearing. "My own reptilian brain balks at reptiles."

"What are you doing, Ivy?" Jilly's voice had a jarring note. "You're heading the wrong way!"

"Just moving back far enough to row up a good head of steam. We'll rocket through the bush and beat the gator back to the dock. Then we call for backup."

"That's the best idea you've had all day," she said. "Standing by with my phone."

I used the oar to do a full circle with my eyes jumping back and forth between the alligator and the swan. Zeus' head swiveled, always turning in the same direction. His orange bill turned away from the gator. That couldn't be a coincidence. There was something else he wanted us to see, I was sure of it. He deserved a chance to show us before we beat it out of there.

Giving a quarter turn, the swan raised his wings higher, and arched his neck.

That's when I noticed the other object in the water. Not a missing mate, as I had anticipated. Not a family of sweet cygnets. Not even an alligator bride or groom.

It was bright and striped, and drifted just beneath the murky surface.

A dress.

A dress that was still on its owner, who floated face down.

Keats' growling grew louder, competing with Jilly's protests as I rowed closer.

"No choice, Jilly," I said. "Please hand me your phone and then look away. You don't want to see this, take my word for it."

Jilly took my word for a lot of things but there was no way she wasn't going to see with her own eyes why I was moving further *into* the marsh and allowing the alligator to move between us and safe harbor.

I thought about standing to get a better angle but nixed the idea. That had already ended badly once. Although it had ended better than it could have, all things considered. Instead, I just let the boat carry us close enough to take a few photos.

"How awful," Jilly croaked. "Do you know who it is?"

"Judging by the brown hair and what people wore in town today, I'm going to say Alice Cheevers."

"Oh no, poor Alice. She was lovely."

Percy poked his head out of her slicker and she tucked it back in. Meanwhile, Keats started growling again.

There was nothing more we could do at this point, so once Jilly's phone was back in her hand, I turned the boat and moved far enough away to avoid disturbing the body.

"Got it, Zeus," I called to the swan. "You can come out, now. We'll send the cops."

The swan didn't follow us, though. Perhaps he was protecting the body from the alligator, or just marking the spot until the authorities arrived.

Jilly called 911, explaining our predicament in a brisk, matter-of-fact voice. You would have thought she was placing an order for takeout, rather than sharing grisly details of another death. When the chips were down, Jilly Blackwood always rose to the occasion, even if there was a gator nipping at her hip waders.

As soon as she hung up, I aimed the boat at the sparsest section of bush and really leaned into the oars, picking up speed with each pull.

"Duck," Jilly said, as the branches tore at our hair and poked at our eyes.

Once we were in the thick of it, I lifted the oars and let momentum carry us through. It was only a few yards till we were in the open water of the pond. For a second I thought we were truly free, until an eight-foot log cruised out of the bush after us. A V formed on the darkening water.

I glanced over my shoulder to locate the dock and refine my navigation. "Thank goodness someone's already waiting for us. That was fast."

The dock was shrouded in shadows, but I could tell the person was a woman. It must be one of the residents.

"Please get back," I called out. "Way back. There's an alligator following us."

"Not anymore," the woman called back. She didn't sound as old as any resident here. Maybe Chief Gillock had deployed a female officer. "You're good now."

I turned and she was right. The alligator had turned its V around, creating a little vortex, and was heading back into the bush.

"How could she see that?" I asked Jilly. "It's too dark."

Jilly didn't answer for a long moment. Shadows had fallen over her face, too, so I couldn't make out her expression. However, I felt tension gathering around her like storm clouds.

"What is it?" I asked. "Nothing can be worse than an alligator and a dead body, Jilly. Can it?"

A few seconds passed before Keats stuck his head out from behind the shelter of my rubber boots. Percy poked his head out of Jilly's slicker again and this time she didn't shove him back.

"Not worse than that," she said at last. "Just a different kind of torment."

I kept rowing, although now I sensed she'd like me to slow down. "Who is it? You must recognize the voice."

She gave a quick nod. Her left hand reached for Percy's head, and her right for Keats. He immediately moved under her fingertips. Like Jilly, when duty called, Keats always served.

Once she'd gotten herself grounded while still gliding over the water, she said, "Janelle. It's Janelle."

CHAPTER TWENTY

S o many names had flown by since we left the farm that it took me a second to figure out exactly who stood on the dock.

"Your cousin Janelle?" I asked. "The one who basically broke up your family?"

"Yes," Jilly said. "That Janelle."

"It wasn't my fault," the woman on the dock said, confirming both her identity and how well sound carried over the water at night.

"It *was* her fault," Jilly muttered. "Just by being her."

"Which isn't my fault," Janelle said. "Just like you being you isn't yours."

"Ladies." I angled the oars to slow our approach. "We have bigger fish to fry right now. The cops are on their way and this discussion had better wait." I looked over my shoulder at Janelle's shadowy form and then at Jilly. "Can we agree to leave this until the animals are safe, Jilly? I need your help. What if the gator comes after them?"

"It won't," Janelle said. "There's easier hunting out there."

"I hope you don't mean Zeus," I said.

"Zeus?" Janelle said. "Oh, that must be the swan."

"That's right. I'm bringing the boat into the dock, Janelle. I'm Ivy, by the way—Jilly's best friend. And just to be clear, no matter what, I'm on her side."

"Understood," Janelle said.

"Then if you don't mind, I'm going to need your help. As soon as the boat is hitched, I'll grab my dog and ask you to give me a hand to get out. Next is Jilly, with the cat."

"She's not helping me out," Jilly said.

"Oh, come on, Jilly. It's been nearly twenty years," Janelle said.

"Feels like yesterday, and I'm still furious. So, you can help Ivy and then Ivy can help me."

"Works for me," I said, "as long as Keats is okay with Janelle holding him. No paw touches the ground until we're back at Bridie's. Got it, everyone? Then you guys can hash things out over a stiff drink. I know I need one."

Keats appraised Janelle with his cool blue eye, and his muzzle lifted to take in her essence. After a second or two, his ears—still under Jilly's fingertips—came forward. Then his tail lifted.

"Traitor," Jilly muttered.

"Oh, you know how Keats is," I said. "Loves my mom just because we're related. Janelle is your kin."

"Was," Jilly said. "Once upon a time."

Janelle let that go, which probably took some effort.

"Remember the plan," I said. "With that alligator cruising around, I'm not getting out of this boat until I have a promise from both of you to put my pets' safety first."

"Agreed," they said at once. Their voices not only over-lapped, but came back as an echo a second later, sounding eerily alike.

Jilly must have noticed too, because she let out a grunt of disgust as I tossed the rope to Janelle and let her tie up the boat. Then Janelle held out her hand to me. Now that we were parked right under her, I could see that Janelle and Jilly had more in common than melodious voices. The woman on the dock wore heels and a simple, elegant dress. Her hair, while darker than Jilly's, cascaded over her shoulders in the same loose curls and her eyes, in the dim light from the phone, seemed to be the same emerald green. They also shared Bridie's classic features, if not her boho style.

Scooping up Keats with my left hand, I accepted Janelle's with my right and gasped at her touch.

"What?" Jilly said.

"Nothing," I said. "Just a little jumpy, that's all."

How could I explain to my best friend that the cousin she obviously loathed gave off a small but noticeable electrical charge? My nerves were already jangling from what had happened in the swamp, so I was prepared to think I'd imagined it. In fact, I deliberately chose to believe that.

"Nice to meet you, Ivy," Janelle said. "And you, too, Keats. I've heard all about the wonder dog and it's an honor."

"Oh please," Jilly said.

"Well, she's right about that," I said. "But only that, I'm sure."

Normally Keats didn't waste energy wagging, let alone when being carried by a stranger, but the white tuft of his tail slapped against Janelle's chic dress.

"Traitor," Jilly muttered again as I helped her out of the boat.

Keats leaned over Janelle's arm and touched Jilly's

cheek with his nose, murmuring assurances no doubt, that she would always be his first love, after me.

Jilly backed away, perhaps to avoid being sucked into her cousin's orbit as Keats clearly had been. When Percy struggled to get out of her slicker, she pushed his head down and buttoned up.

Only while watching Jilly in the light of the phone hanging from her hand, did I realize how we must look to an outsider in our swamp gear. My friend's hair had swelled into a frizzy dome, her makeup was running and there was a smudge of sludge on one cheek. And on top of everything else, she looked utterly spent. Janelle was the last straw. What my friend might have been able to handle with grace a few weeks ago was too much after the gator and the second body.

No doubt I looked far worse than Jilly, but I wasn't burned out yet. Often, when we got caught up in adventure, I still had 60 faces waiting for me to feed and bed them. The responsibilities of the farm weighed on me constantly. Tonight, after we'd dealt with the police, I could kick back with an adult beverage and call my boyfriend. Almost like a regular person.

Keats gazed at me and whined. I took him from Janelle and thanked her. "Don't worry buddy," I whispered. "I would never give it up. It's worth every prematurely gray hair."

"The farm?" Janelle asked, as if overhearing my thoughts.

"Yeah. I was just thinking about all the work we didn't need to do tonight. To Keats it isn't work at all."

The sirens in the distance stopped, no doubt as Special Constable Doug grilled the police at the gate before admission. Not long after, cars pulled up onto the grass and Chief Gillock ran over.

"What on earth?" he asked, directing a powerful flashlight from my head to my boots.

"Can you just go out and deal with Alice, Chief Gillock?" I said. "The swan is probably still marking the spot. And there's an alligator out there."

"There's more than one gator, I can promise you that," he said. "We need to set up before we get started." He used the light to point from me to Jilly and back. "Follow me, ladies. We'll talk in the car."

"In case you haven't noticed, I had a dip in the pond earlier," I said. "Can I change out of my wet clothes first? I'm worried about leeches."

"You took a dip in a swamp full of gators?" He shook his head. "You really are city girls."

"It wasn't a choice," I said. "My cat fell off the oar and... Well, never mind. I didn't know about the gators yet."

"Always assume there are gators," he said. "And please explain why your cat was—" The words seemed to die in his mouth as his light landed on Janelle. "Oh."

Shielding her eyes from the beam, Janelle smiled. "Hello, Chief. I'm Janelle Brighton, Bridie's other granddaughter. It would be lovely if the girls could go home and freshen up before chatting."

"I need to know what we're heading into," he said, although his voice moderated.

"As I understand it, they were just looking for the swan and found him with the deceased."

Chief Gillock probably didn't realize he was staring, but the light held steady on Janelle. She looked like a glamorous movie star, especially in present company. No doubt her dress was covered in pawprints and dog hair but he wasn't close enough to see that.

"Girls! Girls! Are you all right?" Bridie came running across the park from our usual entrance.

"Gran, we're fine." Jilly and Janelle spoke together, and then glared at each other. In that moment, I saw that Janelle was equally furious at Jilly, despite her appeasing words earlier.

Keats gave a low, sad mumble and I pressed my face into his fur. "Don't worry about Jilly," I whispered. "She'll be okay. Crazy things happen with family but it can all work out. Look at mine."

When I lifted my head, Janelle was staring at me. With all the hubbub of officers unloading equipment, she couldn't have overheard me.

"I got here as soon as I could," Bridie said. "That dang ferret escaped from the cage and chewed a hole through my window screen. I caught him just in time." Her eyes danced from Jilly to Janelle and back, and I suspected she was grateful to Arnie for giving her a chance to arrive late for the cousins' reunion. "Picking him up in my bare hands was a dreadful ordeal, Ivy. Those little bones... and the wiggling. I've used a bit of wire to rig the cage."

"Thanks, Bridie," I said. "I know from experience that having so many guests is stressful." Especially when they didn't get along, I added silently. This reunion would have been awkward in the best of circumstances, and the murder —plural, most likely—added complexity. However, experience had also shown me that a challenge like this could bring perspective and maybe even pave the way to reconciliation. It had happened with my mom and then my absentee father. I wouldn't wish a murder on anyone, but I could honestly say solving mysteries together gave the

Galloways more peace. Maybe it would work out for these three as well.

"I'm staying in the recreation center," Janelle said. "There's a guest suite."

Jilly let out an audible sigh of relief.

Staring around at the police, Bridie patted down her frizzy hair. "I don't know why anyone would choose to live in the tropics. It's impossible to have nice hair. Jillian, yours looks terrible, and Ivy... Well, I don't know what to say. And those outfits. Really."

"There are more pressing matters than bad hair, Gran," Jilly said. "Ivy believes you lost a friend tonight."

"No speculation," the chief said, as he started directing his officers to set up lights and inflate dinghies. "Ivy, you'll need to come back out to show us what you found."

I clutched Keats closer. "Really? Do I have to?"

Janelle stepped in front of me and faced the chief. "Is that really necessary, Chief Gillock? You've got a whole fleet set up here. Ivy and my cousin have been through quite a lot this evening."

"And over the past few days," Bridie chimed in. "It's been one thing after another."

The chief tried to peer around Janelle and then gave up. A strange expression came over his face as he stared at her. His eyes widened and his jaw slackened. He looked a little dazed. If I didn't know better about a cop's ability to compartmentalize, I'd say he was falling under Janelle's spell. Keats gave a ha-ha-ha of agreement.

In fact, all the male officers were staring in Janelle's direction, as if she were a collectible. Like the winning puck from a playoff game. I had been at enough crime scenes to know that cops were usually laser focused on the job at hand. Asher was a notable exception, because he had trouble paying attention to anything when Jilly was in the vicinity. My friend had always had a powerful allure for men. Perhaps this was something else that ran in the family, along with emerald eyes.

"All right, we'll take a look on our own," the chief said. "As long as you'll stay put in the squad car until we've recovered the body."

"Chief, please be reasonable," Janelle said. "Can't you see that Ivy is shivering? She's in shock."

I hadn't even noticed I was shivering until she pointed it out. "I'm okay," I said. "I'll stay here till you find her. The swan is still on guard and with those lights, you won't be able to miss the striped dress. I hope you brought a chain-saw, though, because the vegetation is savage."

"We're well equipped to handle the situation." He pulled his eyes away from Janelle. "What I really want to know is why you and Miss Blackwood would venture out there after I specifically asked you—nay, *ordered you*—to stay out of this investigation."

"We were just checking on the swan's health and welfare," I said. "On the advice of a waterfowl specialist. When we discovered something you needed to know about we called you on the spot."

"Chief?" Janelle raised a manicured index finger. He looked back at her reluctantly, his brown eyes landing above, below and offside. It was as if he sensed he couldn't look right at her without being mesmerized. "It seems like Ivy and Jilly have done everyone a huge favor, especially the poor woman in question. Wouldn't you say? Now her story can be told."

He lost the battle and stared at her again. "I suppose. But it's frustrating to have people deliberately flout protocol. Someone from out of state. A cowboy."

I laughed, and others joined me, even Jilly.

"I am a cowboy, quite literally," I said. "I own it."

"Here's what I suggest, Chief," Janelle continued. "Ivy and Jilly can walk home with Gran and I'll go up to the rec center and help Vaughan collect everyone else. I'm sure you'll want to debrief the residents."

"Okay. Sounds good." The chief was seemingly oblivious to the fact that he was taking orders from Janelle.

"Perfect," she said. "I look forward to seeing you there soon." Gesturing to the dinghies at the shore, she added, "Safe voyage."

"Thank you," he said, turning to head down to the inflatable boats.

Keats gave another pant-laugh from my arms and Janelle wagged a finger at him. "Never mind," she said. "Get them shipped out before we let our guard down."

One of the officers shoved the boat off and then jumped in to join the chief, who managed to stand with his arms crossed without so much as a wobble. I could tell by the set of his jaw that he was in full command again and wasn't surprised when his gaze fell on me once more. Perhaps Janelle's magnetic appeal only worked at close range.

"Ivy, will you be giving a full report to Chief Harper about this, or shall I?"

"Got it covered," I called. "Shower, whiskey and full report to Kellan. Can I look forward to *your* full report later as well?"

"No." He raised his voice to be heard over the small motor. "But I'll have more questions for you."

Keats mumbled something insolent and I answered, "He's not Kellan, buddy. We have to play by different rules here."

"You mean, you have to play by *some* rules here," Jilly

said, smiling. "That will only make victory sweeter when you piece things together like you always do."

"Like Cori said, it's good for sheepdogs like us to keep busy and challenged," I said.

"She said I was a Jack Russell," Jilly said. "I still resent that."

"An astute observation," Janelle muttered. "Whoever this Cori is."

I gave Janelle a warning look. "Thank you so much for your help. We're off to do just as you ordered."

"Fine." She sounded like a sullen teen instead of a siren now.

Jilly and I shuffled across the grass in our hip waders, arms linked.

"Don't you want to get out of those things now?" I asked her. "Or did you really wet yourself?"

"Better to play it safe. What's your excuse?"

"I don't know what else might be in there," I said. "No need to invite public ridicule."

"My friend, you've changed," she said.

"Just for now," I said, as Keats squirmed in my arms. When we reached the road, I finally let him down and he pranced with his show horse strut. Like me, he cherished his freedom. "I'll go back to letting it all hang out when we get home."

CHAPTER TWENTY-ONE

Sleep pretty much eluded me that night. The bed in Bridie's spare room was perfectly comfortable but I hadn't managed to find more than a few hours of shuteye since our arrival. My perpetually busy brain seemed to be on overdrive here. It was always hyperactive while working on a case, but in Clover Grove, I had my infrastructure to calm me down—my routine, my chores, and my therapeutic manure pile. By now, I'd have eaten a few slices of pie at Mandy's Country Store to build stamina.

"That's what's missing," I said to Keats as I dressed at dawn. "Pie."

Percy had chosen to grace Jilly with his presence overnight, so I skulked out of the house with Keats. I didn't have a particular mission in mind. I just needed to be moving.

Keats led me toward the center of town, and hopefully pie.

"If the café is open I'll see what's available," I said. "Maybe the sugar will get my brain working properly because I don't even know what our next steps are, buddy."

The dog picked up the pace, which encouraged me. Maybe the next steps were more apparent to him.

When we reached The Silver Spoon café, it was barely six a.m. but every seat inside and out was taken, while others perched on walkers and wheelchairs. I wasn't the only one trying to solve the puzzle of who killed not only Lottie, but Alice Cheevers. Both women had floated away with bruises on their necks, but because Chief Gillock hadn't shared that detail publicly, some continued to blame Zeus, who didn't have fingers to strangle anyone. I stood on the sidelines with Keats, watching as two men flapped their arms, no doubt demonstrating exactly how a swan might take down a woman—a woman who had seemed well liked. Lottie's list of detractors was long, but no one had complained to me about Alice.

"Maybe we should keep walking," I told Keats. "I don't really want to hear people dissing Zeus, but there's not a thing I can say without getting in trouble with one of the chiefs. For the record, two chiefs are not better than one."

My conversation with Kellan the night before had been strained. The second victim had sucked away his humor, and he had asked me to consider leaving the Briar Estates and going to a hotel with Jilly, Bridie and Janelle. I dismissed the idea, as he knew I would. There was no way I'd abandon the swan when he was being convicted in the court of public opinion. On top of that, spending time in a hotel with the warring Blackwood and Brighton clan held little appeal. Their differences were best worked out through action toward a common purpose. Teams that worked together grew together. That was another valuable thing I'd learned at Flordale Corp, and put into real world practice with my own family. Solving this mystery might exorcise some old demons.

"There are no demons, obviously," I said. "But I do think Janelle has a little something extra going on. Maybe she has some siren blood. Jilly's no slouch in that department either. She used to hold sway over a roomful of business titans so aggressive they'd pick your bones bare in ten seconds, like piranhas. The cousins have more in common than either wants to admit."

Keats mumbled his agreement. What's more, he offered a half-hearted point in the direction of the patio. Like me, he wanted to avoid the place, but he also felt a duty to report something that didn't quite belong among the sea of silver hair. Janelle's brunette curls appeared when the crowd around her shifted. Every senior at her table had a mister in front of his name. The women seemed better able to resist her considerable charms.

"Okay, fine," I said. "We'll go in."

Janelle raised her hand to beckon us over, but I signaled that I needed to fuel up first. Inside, relief washed over me when I saw not one but three pies in the glass display case. I didn't know how I'd missed them the day before. Perhaps we'd be further along with the investigation if I hadn't.

The elderly woman behind the counter squinted at me when I asked for two pieces of pie on one plate. Cutting two slivers, she put them on separate plates. I gave her a nice smile and asked for a slice of the third pie. "Let's make it a trifecta," I said. "No need to dirty another plate."

She carved a sliver out of the last pie and set it on a third plate. "Don't you even want to know the flavor?" she asked.

I shook my head. "All pie is good pie."

She pushed the three plates toward me. "It's a bit much for this time of the day, isn't it?"

I studied the mingy offerings. "Not nearly enough, actually. But we'll start there."

After paying her, I used a fork to shove all the pie onto one plate. Together they made up a single slice at Mandy's store.

"Thanks," I said. "I couldn't manage three plates and the coffee, but this works."

I dropped a couple of coins into the tip jar, flashed more teeth and then pushed open the door with my elbow. Keats was waiting right outside, but then he pranced ahead of me to Janelle's table. She was wearing a simple white dress that looked like a million bucks, light makeup and no jewelry at all.

That anyone would choose a white dress on a regular day astounded me. One thing I knew for sure was that the only white dress I'd ever wear would be at my wedding. And even that was chancy in my grimy life.

"Gentlemen," she said. "It's been great chatting but I need to catch up with Ivy. How about we all meet by the pool this afternoon?"

They dispersed promptly, if regretfully, and I took the vacant seat beside her where I could still watch the action. Keats sat on alert beside me, like a tuxedoed statue.

"He doesn't look very happy," she said. "What's wrong?"

"Something's off. Bad vibe, I guess," I said. "He's read the crowd and wants to move on."

He mumbled an affirmative. There was nothing to see here.

"I know about his special skills," she said, lowering her voice. "In the sleuthing department. Yours, too."

"They don't work as well here as back home," I said. "I overestimated my value."

"You've only been here, what... three days? Did you expect to accomplish miracles in such a short time?"

I smiled at Keats and his mouth opened in a proud pant.

"Yes, actually. In a situation like this, it's all about speed. The longer it's left to fester, the more complicated it gets. Consider what happened to poor Alice. If I'd worked faster, maybe she'd be alive right now."

"Ivy, you're being way too hard on yourself," she said. "The Briars is a unique environment. Nothing like Clover Grove, I'm sure. Personally, I'm always happy to visit and even happier to leave."

I sighed. "It just feels like I'm missing something obvious."

"That's because these folks are experts at hiding things. You need to be to survive. Maybe I can help. I mean, if it's okay with Jilly. I do know my way around the place."

"I noticed. It's like you cast a spell over people. Male people especially."

"No spells required." She wiggled fingers at some of her fans. "It helps to have a captive audience. I mean, literally captive. Plus I've worked in hospitality for years."

"Hotels?" I asked.

Her green eyes darted everywhere. She definitely didn't have Jilly's stillness and focus.

"High-end resorts, mostly," she said. "Mountains, deserts, seaside, you name it. I've seen the world that way. New faces, new places and jobs on demand. Plus you never need to worry about room and board."

"Sounds a bit like the carnie life... always rolling on."

"I did that for awhile as a teen, too," she said. "Had my own fortune teller booth. After a couple of nights sleeping outside, I decided there had to be a better way." She sat back and sighed. "I ended up running into the same people at resorts. Old carnies never die, they just find work as bartenders or waiters or car jockeys. I've been in customer service for a decade."

"That explains your handling skills," I said. "Jilly and I trained in HR so we're good with people, but you left us in the dust last night."

"That would have gone far differently if *I'd* been the one in the water with the alligators. You've got guts, Ivy." She pointed at the untouched pie in front of me. "Better eat up so Keats can roll."

I picked up my fork and poked it. "Maybe it'll taste better than it looks."

"It didn't," she said, gesturing to an empty plate. "Mediocre at best. I consider myself something of a pie connoisseur."

"Me too!" I felt disloyal to Jilly for my enthusiasm. For finding anything in common with her cousin, in fact. Now I knew exactly how she'd felt last month when she was caught between Asher and me after our dad came back. In fact, it was far worse for her because my brother was her boyfriend, whereas Janelle was someone I would likely never see again after this week. It was a shame, really, because I already liked her and Keats did, too. Janelle passed the sniff test for us, but something had gone epically wrong between the cousins long ago. The way before me was clear. Jilly would tolerate Janelle helping with the case because it was for the greater good, but we couldn't get too palsy unless something between them changed.

I chewed a mouthful and felt pie-sick for Mandy's wonderful concoctions. All pie was *not* good pie, as it turned out.

"How'd the meeting go last night?" I asked. "Did you learn anything interesting?"

She shook her head. "They're baffled and scared, although many put up a good front. No one seemed to have a clue what's going on."

"Not even Special Constable Doug?" I asked, around another mouthful of mediocre. "He's still on my suspect list."

"Dougie's all talk," she said. "I highly doubt he has the cojones for... you know."

"That's what I always think. Until it turns out someone does."

"True enough. I've been surprised and disappointed plenty of times, too. But Doug? I don't see it."

"What about Vaughan?" I asked. "He's got motives right up to the goatee. Both men have swindled the residents and Lottie definitely knew about some of it."

"I've known Vaughan a long time, and I suppose it's possible." She gestured discreetly to Shirley Mills, sitting in her wheelchair with Cherise and others. "No matter what stunts he pulls, he takes very good care of Shirley. That's what keeps him from utter buffoon status. He loves his wife."

"Men who love their wives still kill," I said. "Ask me how I know."

She was still scanning the crowd and I noticed she'd fallen into a rhythm with Keats, heads pivoting back and forth. "So what's on for today?"

"I'd really love to get a look in the property office," I said. "Check out the personnel files and board documentation. The chief may have taken everything into evidence though."

"Why don't we give it a try?" she said. "People are distracted here. I'll stand watch and you slip in."

Keats pumped his paws and urged us on with eager mumbles. "That's a yes from my co-pilot," I said.

As we left our table, a woman's voice called out to Janelle. "Honey, can I have a minute?"

It was Alba, Vaughan's supposed girlfriend. She was sitting alone now, in her mint green suit again with the precisely knotted scarf.

"Of course," Janelle said. "What can I do for you, Alba?"

"First, I speak for everyone in asking if you have any special insights about our dear friend Alice. If anyone would know, it would be you."

I stared at Janelle and she gave me a bland smile. "My fortune telling days are behind me, ladies. I called so many things wrong that it got embarrassing."

"But you were absolutely right last time," Alba said. "Do you remember?"

"I do." Janelle's smile was dazzling, which was probably half the battle in hoaxing people into thinking these things were real. "I said you'd have a little granddaughter by the time I saw you again."

Alba clapped her hands. "Yes, and I couldn't be more thrilled. Now I'd like to know if you see a future for me with a certain gentleman friend. He's quite charming but he makes big promises I'm not sure I should trust."

"Oh Alba, I don't like making predictions about relationships," Janelle said. "In the end everything works out exactly as fate intends."

"Please, honey? There's a lot at stake, and you know how this community talks. If he doesn't have the goods to back up his words, I'd rather move on."

Janelle leaned forward a little. "All right. If you're sure you want to know..."

"I do. Take my locket."

I hadn't even noticed the heart-shaped locket tucked under Alba's scarf. She unhooked the clasp and offered it to Janelle. It was similar in style to other pieces I saw at Haute Baubles. Had Vaughan presented it to her only yesterday?

Janelle shook her head and simply touched the back of Alba's hand and closed her eyes. They popped open again quickly and she used a teaspoon to push the locket that now sat on the table back over to Alba. If the older woman saw anything strange about that, she didn't let on.

"Well? Is it a match?"

Janelle swallowed hard before speaking. "Alba, I know you've really enjoyed this interlude, but I think you know without my telling you that you wouldn't be happy in that situation for long. If you really can't work things out with Ford, you'd be better to find someone else who deserves a fine woman like you."

Alba's face collapsed. "Oh. Oh my."

Reaching across the table, Janelle took the woman's hand and squeezed. "Now, here's the good news. If and when that happens, I can introduce you to someone else."

Taking the locket, Alba examined it. "This wasn't meant for me. I'll return it." Sighing, she slipped it into her purse. "Do you know other fine men? I've already met everyone here."

Giving her an enigmatic smile, Janelle stood up. "We'll talk when the time comes."

Another voice called out, "Janny? Over here, please."

"Elsie, I can't today," she said. "Ivy and I are going for a walk."

"I'm sure Ivy won't mind," Elsie said. "It'll just take a minute."

I shrugged and then nodded. In fact, I was intrigued to watch Janelle work her carnie wiles on these ladies. She wasn't charging them, and if she'd convinced Alba to leave Vaughan to Shirley, that could only increase peace in the community. Bridie had probably filled her in on all the gossip already so she knew which cards to play.

Elsie got up from her table and beckoned for us to follow her out of the café. Leaning heavily on her cane, she stumped right around the thrift store. There was an old bench behind it, and after getting herself settled, Elsie opened a large leather bag and carefully removed a blue velvet sack. "I inherited this recently and I'd like to know if it works."

She set the object on the bench and then eased it out of the bag. It was a crystal ball, and judging by the ornate, filigree stand she set it on, that treasure had been on Lottie's desk until very recently.

Janelle reached out to touch the glass. "Elsie, you don't want to keep this around. Objects always carry the imprint of former owners and I'm quite sure you'll be sad whenever you touch it. I certainly am right now."

I moved in a little closer. "Elsie, did that belong to Lottie Greenwich?"

Her brows came together in defiance. "What if it did? She'd want me to have it."

"It's still evidence," I said. "Chief Gillock wouldn't be happy that you touched it."

I couldn't tell her exactly how I knew that, but Keats gave a snuffle of amusement.

"I only went in because of Arnie," Elsie said. "Lottie's

pet. She had given me a key for that very reason." Her face fell. "I couldn't find him, though."

"I bet the police took care of everything," I said. "But you should probably put the crystal ball back. It's the kind of thing they'll miss. You wouldn't want them searching door to door for it."

Now her sparse eyebrows rose under her mauve hair. "I'll take it back right now. I couldn't get it to work anyway. All I see is mist."

"Me too," Janelle said.

At least she wasn't conning the old woman with fake predictions.

Elsie started to tuck the crystal ball away but she was flustered now and it rolled out of her hands. Lunging forward, I caught it before it slipped off the bench.

"Oh, thank goodness," she said. "If I'd broken it, I'm sure Lottie would have haunted me for the rest of my days."

"You wouldn't want that, trust me," Janelle said. "It wouldn't be *your* life anymore."

I was only half-listening to them, because as I held the ball between tingling hands, the misty interior cleared and I saw the distinct image of a swan. Smiling, I tilted the ball this way and that and the swan seemed to float around on clear, glassy waters. This lucky swan had much nicer digs than poor Zeus and his murky swamp. Maybe that was where he would end up one day. Holding the ball closer to my nose, I noticed a reflection in the water. It looked like a large building with turrets, but then ripples erased the image and there was only mist again.

"Did you see something?" Elsie asked, leaning forward to take the crystal ball.

I shook my head. "I thought I did for a second but I'm seriously sleep deprived."

After leaving Elsie behind, we walked toward the property office behind the recreation center.

"Looks like we lost our window of opportunity," I said, as Keats lost steam beside me. The dog on a mission had called off the plan and was disgruntled about it, too. "People must be around by now."

"I'm sorry," Janelle said. "I should have known that would happen. It always does and people are extra rattled today."

"They don't seem as rattled as they should be," I said. "It's like a reason to gather and chatter."

Her busy eyes came back to land on me. "Remember what I said earlier. They're experts at hiding things, so don't believe what you see."

"Anyway, you did well," I said. "Hopefully, Alba will end her affair with Vaughan. That guy is no great catch."

"Try to put yourself in their shoes. There's a very small pool here, and with options so limited they end up recycling thrift store goods."

I couldn't help laughing. "At least your grandmother doesn't get caught up in all that."

"Not anymore. Bridie Brighton was a hot ticket in her day, though. Much too hot for my grandfather to handle." She clicked along briskly in taupe sandals that showed off a perfect pedicure. Her shoe game was impeccable. Better even than my mother's, and that was saying something.

Just as we reached the recreation center, Casey Cox and Doug Farrow came down the front stairs. Both men waved when they saw Janelle, though their smiles faded quickly. If the residents were good at hiding their worries, these two were not.

"How *are* you, guys?" Janelle said. "What a terrible week you've had."

"Terrible," Casey agreed. "My father is beside himself. He knew both of these women for years before he retired. I had a heck of a time stopping him from coming down here in person today. He's not well, though, and more stress wouldn't help."

"Your dad is a sweet man," Janelle said. "Tell him I sent my best."

"Guaranteed to perk him up." Casey stared at her in the same way all the cops had the night before. "How long are you staying?"

"As long as it takes for things to settle down. Gran needs my support." She paused and added, "*Our* support."

Doug shook off her spell first and turned fierce blue eyes on me. "You rode in on your high horse with big promises to deal with this swan. Now it's killed someone else. That's on you." There was a low growl at his feet and Doug looked down to meet an equally fierce stare. "And now your dog's threatening me."

Janelle touched his arm. "Doug, calm down. I know how hard you work to keep people safe here. It's understandable you'd take this the hardest."

Casey blinked a few times and said, "I'm taking it hard too, believe me. Aside from worrying about our current residents, I'm concerned about our reputation and future. Who will want to move here after this?"

"The Briars will never lack for business," she assured him. "No need to worry about that. Just focus on finding out who did this and all will be fine."

"We already know who did it," Doug said. He released the first button of his uniform as if he were about to choke. "What's white and white and white all over?"

"It wasn't the swan, Doug," Janelle said. "The more you focus on that, the more clues you'll miss. Where's your partner, Larry? I haven't seen him since I got here, and you could use an extra pair of hands."

"Out with a head injury," Doug said. "I found him lying on the tennis court beside my new hoverboard. He was always itching to try it, but it takes a certain finesse."

"Didn't stop me from trying it, too," Casey said, pointing to a cut near his eye. "Banged myself up good."

"It does look fun," Janelle said. "What a shame about Larry, though."

"He'll be back soon," Casey said. "In the meantime, just do your best, Doug. We're all in this together. Management, security, residents... it's one big family at the Briars."

"Exactly," Janelle said. "Good luck with your work today, gentlemen. I hope we'll see you tonight. My cousin's doing this black tie thing to cheer people up."

"I brought a suit for the memorial service," Casey said. "So I'm all set."

They walked away together toward the property office, leaving Keats and me at loose ends for a mission.

Janelle showed me a little garden I hadn't seen before, and the sight of dozens of tall lilies in various colors brought some peace to my heart. It reminded me of Clover Grove gardens, and many sweet dates with Kellan.

After a moment or two, Janelle said, "Now, tell me what you saw in the crystal ball."

"Nothing," I said. "Well, just the swan, who's always on my mind. I should run down and see how he's doing."

"Is that all? You practically touched it with your nose."

Now I was the one with shifty eyes. "Well, for a second I thought I saw a reflection in the water. A building with turrets. I wondered if that's where he'll end up one day."

"A building with turrets? Are you sure it was Zeus and not another just like him?"

"Mute swans look pretty much the same, I guess."

Janelle stared at me for a second. Her heels brought her almost to my height, which meant she had a few inches on Jilly. "How interesting. That crystal ball revealed nothing to Elsie or me, yet you saw a swan outside the Strathmore Hotel."

"The Strathmore Hotel? Your gran mentioned it but I've never been there."

"I know every decent hotel in the state," she said. "Especially the Strathmore. Spent a year serving rum punch to drunken execs on corporate getaways. How about we run over there and take a look?"

"I don't believe in crystal balls, Janelle."

"There's nothing to believe. You saw a mental image of a swan at a place you've probably seen online. The Strathmore's quite old and quite famous. I doubt this is the first time your unconscious mind has made some handy connections for you. Even a hardcore cop will say the same."

"I suppose. When you put it that way."

"Plus, I hear how you and your dog go on." She gave me a grin. "Everyone hears how you and your dog go on."

"Hey. Careful," I said. "I go on like that with my cat, too."

Now she laughed. "Well, do you believe what your dog tells you? I dare you to say no in front of him because he'll call you out as a liar."

"That's different," I said. "He's using his sheepdog senses to pick up on things I can't."

"What's he suggesting now?" she asked. "I'm no expert at reading canines."

Keats wasn't waiting around to tell me anything. He was leading us out of the garden.

"Let's get the truck from Bridie's," I said. "You're about to take a little drive down memory lane."

"I still have the same car for the ride and it's parked right here at security. This is going to be a blast."

"Perfect," I said. "But you've forgotten two things vitally important to any mission."

"Oh? What's that?"

Pulling out my phone, I grinned at her. "Jilly and Percy."

CHAPTER TWENTY-TWO

"Have you ever heard the expression, 'age before beauty'?" Bridie asked, from the back seat of Janelle's beat-up old bronze hatchback.

"Of course," I said. "That's why I offered you the front seat, Bridie."

She had chosen instead to clamber into the back of the two-door car. Maybe she wanted to keep close tabs on Jilly lest her granddaughters turn to fisticuffs on the open highway.

"I didn't realize we'd get stuck with the pets."

"I asked Keats to sit with me," I said. "For some reason he thinks Jilly offers more comfortable seating."

"But why the cat?" she asked. "I've never seen one shed as much as Percy and orange is no one's favorite color."

"Gran, my car is basically orange," Janelle said. "Don't diss your ride."

Bridie lobbed another question at me. "Why did the cat even need to come? It's not normal to take cats everywhere."

"Two reasons," I said. "First, it's a bad idea to leave a cat alone with a rodent who manages to escape his cage despite our herculean efforts. Second, I'm not normal."

"She's proud of that, Gran," Jilly said. "I'm proud of her, too."

Bridie sniffed. "I know all about what it's like to be different, Jillian, but there's no need to attract attention to it by driving cats to swanky hotels."

Bridie was turning out to be bohemian in fashion more than personality. She was surprisingly proper for someone whose jewelry jingled with every step. If she was interested in Edna's survival course, however, there was another side to her that didn't show at the Briars.

"The Strathmore isn't that swanky," Janelle said. "It's fifty years past its prime and coasts on reputation. They treated their staff poorly and I moved on in pretty short order."

"Big surprise," Jilly muttered.

Janelle's knuckles whitened on the steering wheel. "I usually stayed within an easy drive of the Briars and visited Gran often."

The unspoken accusation was loud and clear: Jilly had moved to Boston and essentially ditched her grandmother for 15 years.

"I would have visited Gran, too, if she'd stayed in Wyldwood Springs," Jilly said.

"Doubtful," Janelle said.

"It's not my fault she had to move down here." Jilly's voice rose and Keats mumbled something calming. I hoped Bridie would intervene so that I didn't have to. My best friend had bravely defused many awkward situations among the Galloways and it might be time to return the favor.

"It's not my fault either," Janelle said. "Do you think I wanted that to happen?"

Jilly waited a beat. "I think you didn't try hard enough to stop it."

"I was fifteen, Jilly. It was an accident. And I didn't have anyone to help me figure out a good solution."

"Girls, girls," Bridie said, at last. "Please don't blame each other. Blame me."

Janelle glanced at Bridie in the rearview mirror. "It wasn't your fault either, Gran."

"Yes, it was," Jilly said. "She could have handled it better. Handled *them* better. Done *something*."

"That's not fair," Janelle said.

"It is fair," Bridie said. "I should have intervened between your mothers." Her sigh was loud enough to compete with the drone of the old motor. "If I'd raised them well, they could have negotiated their way through the situation and helped you do the same. Now, no one's been speaking for years and I take the blame for that. It's tragic, girls. We only have each other."

"Not true," Jilly said. "I have Ivy. And lots of great friends in Clover Grove. Not to mention Keats, Percy and sixty farm animals."

"Plus a boyfriend who worships the ground you walk on," I added.

There was a brief silence and then Janelle said, "I have my car. We've become very close. And a first-class shoe collection in storage units."

Everyone laughed. Jilly's was a grudging snort, but it was a tiny chink in her armor and everyone knew it. Janelle had pointed out rather gracefully that no matter how hard things were for Jilly, her life hadn't been easy, either. She'd never had Jilly's success or income. This car was her best friend, and perhaps sometimes her home.

I took the opportunity to shift the tone. "You know what you need, Janelle? A dog."

"A dog? With my nomadic lifestyle? I don't think so. No resort would put me up with a dog in tow."

"Don't be so sure," I said. "There are lots of pet-friendly hotels these days, especially in our part of the country. We booked one on the way here that sounds right up your alley."

Before she could answer, Jilly chimed in. "We didn't get to stay there because we got tailed."

"Tailed?" For the first time Janelle sounded surprised. She stared at Bridie in the mirror again. "Is that why you asked me to come?"

"You asked her to come when I'm here?" Jilly said. "On purpose?"

There was a decided grumble in the back seat. Keats had had enough of this tension among people he liked. After some shuffling and grunting, he settled on Bridie's lap, while Percy repaired to Jilly's.

"I don't want a dog in my lap." That's what Bridie's mouth said but her fingers told a different story. Keats curled into a tight ball with his ears fetchingly available and Bridie couldn't resist the invitation. His brown eye infused her with warmth, whether she wanted it or not. I knew she did. She was a kind woman and seeing her granddaughters at loggerheads when she felt responsible must hurt.

"He goes where he's needed," I said. "I'm sure he'd do a stint in Janelle's lap if she didn't have her hands so full trying to handle this car."

"What do you mean?" Janelle said. "It drives like a dream."

I'd never had a rougher ride and that was saying something in view of my own driving exploits. At least my truck had springs and power steering. It didn't help that the side road she'd turned onto was pocked with potholes that pounded my tailbone, which still hadn't fully recovered from being butted by a large, irritable goat.

"I admire your fortitude," I said. "And, as an outsider, I just want to say I also admire how both you and Jilly came down here to protect Bridie when she was in need. If you have nothing else in common, there's that."

They both started to protest and I spoke over them. "Of course you *do* have a lot in common. Your voices, your features, your curly hair, your capacity to handle people, and—Jilly, forgive me—your sense of humor."

"Let's talk about integrity," Jilly said.

"I don't know about the past," I said. "I can only comment on what I see now. And both of you care about Bridie, which is a starting point. If you're interested in a starting point."

"I'm not, actually, because—" Jilly's next word was cut off as Janelle hit a big pothole, accidentally on purpose. "Would you mind?"

"Mind knocking some sense into you?" Janelle said, hitting another pothole. "No, I would not."

"Janelle, there's collateral damage here," I said. "Your gran, my pets and my butt. Tell your automotive bestie to stand down on those craters."

"Sorry." Glancing into the back seat, she said, "And I'm sorry to you, Jilly. I am interested in starting over and I'm not afraid to say so. Years of rolling from place to place, job to job, boyfriend to boyfriend, finally showed me how to take personal accountability. I made mistakes and I'm willing to make amends."

I held my breath, hoping Jilly would accept the olive branch. The silence went on so long that Janelle lifted her foot off the gas to give her time but in a few yards, we reached the driveway to the Strathmore Hotel. Talk of reconciliation would have to wait.

"That's the one," I said, staring up as she pulled the old beater into a parking spot. "The building I saw in the crystal ball."

"The crystal ball?" Jilly said. "What are you talking about? I thought you googled the place."

"I did, after seeing it in Lottie's crystal ball." I shrugged. "Who knows where the image came from? I knew about the hotel and researched the area before we left the farm. The point is, it seemed like there may be a clue here."

"So you've put me through all this for a vision from a crystal ball?" Jilly deliberately kneed the back of my seat.

"Basically, yeah," I said. "I've put you through worse in pursuit of the truth."

The next thump from the back was almost as hard. She wasn't so sure.

"Oh, come on," I said. "There's no risk of incontinence today, unlike last night in gator country."

"Well," she said, "there is that."

Outside the main entrance of the Strathmore Hotel was a manmade pond about half the size Amos at the waterfowl sanctuary had recommended for swans. There was a fountain in the middle with a statue of a half-naked woman carrying a bowl of fruit. Water spewed erratically from a big cluster of grapes.

As I climbed out of the passenger seat, a beautiful mute swan floated around the pedestal at the statue's bare feet. I jogged over with Keats and Percy. The swan came toward me at about the same speed and its wings snapped up like a fan. It stopped a few yards from the shore, hissing. Behind the big white bird swam six small fluffy grey ones. The so-called ugly ducklings were adorable.

"Oh, my goodness," Jilly said, joining me. "Cygnets!" She scanned the pond. "Where's the other one? I thought you said they mated for life."

"They do." Keats gave me a look with his eerie blue eye and mumbled something I'd already guessed. "I suspect her mate is in the pond at the Briars. This is probably Hera, wife of Zeus, and six little gods in the making."

"He left his family?" she said, as Janelle and Bridie lined up beside her.

"Probably not by choice," I said. "I got a better look at his wings last night and one appears to be clipped. So he didn't fly into the Briars and he most certainly didn't walk that far."

"Let's see what we can find out," Janelle said, turning. "I'll have a chat with the manager."

We followed her up the wide sandstone stairs. She flicked back her curls and straightened her shoulders as we walked inside. I didn't need to see her wide smile to know it was there because the man behind the front desk nearly melted. It was a hot day, but not as hot as Janelle, apparently.

"Why, hello there," she said. "I used to be you." She must have glanced at his name tag because she added, "Jeremy."

"Pardon me?" he asked.

"I worked behind this desk once upon a time. After a stint at the courtyard bar." She gestured to the rest of us. "I wanted my grandmother and friends to see the place I spent so many happy days. It looks nearly the same."

"Welcome back," he said. "There have been some

improvements in the past couple of years. I'm due for a break if you'd like me to show you around."

"How lovely," she said. "We'll wait for you outside."

A few minutes later, Jeremy came down the stairs two at a time to join us. "You can see the first change from here," he said. "Our swan pond is a popular attraction. Maybe too popular since the babies arrived. People are always feeding them and children climb right into the water. We've already lost two chicks, I'm afraid."

"There's no protective fencing," I said, watching cars stream into the lot. It was probably the lunch rush. There wouldn't have been many decent restaurants out here. "A predator could nab the cygnets easily enough."

He glanced at Janelle, dejected. "You know management would never hear of fencing out front. It's not the image they want to project. Even though we lost our male not long back."

"Did he fly off?" Janelle asked. "Abandon his family?"

Jeremy shook his head. "His wings were clipped. He either left on foot or was taken."

"Who would steal a swan?" she asked.

"A prank, most likely." He scuffed the gravel path with a black loafer that was quickly covered in gray dust. "Our clientele hasn't changed. Corporate groups who enjoy the open bar. Mostly men. The night manager has quite a time of it."

"So you figure someone lifted the swan and took it home with them?" she asked.

"Maybe. And obviously he couldn't fly back."

"Did you report it?" I asked. "The police might know where the swan ended up."

Again he shook his head. "Management wanted to let

the matter go. We don't like to attract negative attention here. It could put off guests."

Anger percolated in my gut but I pressed my lips together. Their indifference could work in our favor. This pond wasn't big enough for a family and Zeus wouldn't be safe if we returned him anyway. At the same time, uniting them at the Briars pond was out of the question, where the alligators would make short work of the fluffy little ones. We'd need to stage a rescue and deliver them to the waterfowl sanctuary.

Jilly stepped forward. "This is—"

"Fascinating," I interrupted. "Thank you for sharing, Jeremy. I hope the swans find their way back together someday. It's a tragic love story."

"Tragic," Janelle repeated. "Ivy, why don't you get some shots of the sweet babies while Gran and I take the grand tour?"

"Sounds good," I said, kneeling beside the pond as they went back up the gravel path.

Jilly rested her hand on my shoulder. "When is this rescue going to happen?"

"Tonight, hopefully. Before another cygnet is lost. The only question is *how*. In moments like this, I sure miss Cori and the Mafia."

"Me too," she said. "But I'm not too fussed about getting my feet wet in a pond like this."

"We'll need to extract Zeus too," I said.

"I'll drive getaway," she said. "Send your new best friend Janelle in with the gators."

I laughed. "Not a chance. You're my tried and true wingwoman, so you don't get off that easily. I'll call Amos and figure something out."

Hera circled and the gray fluffballs hopped onto her

back, one after the other. Some of them disappeared into white feathers.

"I'm sorry about what happened, Hera," I told the swan. "If you don't mind my calling you that. I've been keeping an eye on your mate, and I promise to bring all of you together again. Somewhere nice and safe to raise a family."

The swan faced me dead on and it seemed like her beady eyes drilled into my soul.

"Yes, she's good for it," Jilly told the bird. "Ivy keeps her word, no matter how dirty the going gets."

I got to my feet and we walked back to Janelle's old beater. "This is dirty all right. And I'm going to get to the bottom of the swamp of deceit very soon. I'm circling the drain right now."

"You know that means dying, right?" Jilly said. "Could you pick a different metaphor?"

I opened the door for her with a flourish. "We're all dying, my friend. But hopefully we'll age gracefully in a revitalized Clover Grove."

"With plenty of stories to tell our children and grand-children. We'll be remembered as leaders in the culture revival movement."

"Boring," I said. "I'd rather be remembered as a vigilante farmer."

"Suit yourself, cowboy," she said, giving me a high five.

CHAPTER TWENTY-THREE

After we got back to the Briars, Jilly asked us to visit the rec center for a walk-through of the evening's black tie social event. I didn't want to think about parties and dancing. My focus was on rescuing the swans and solving the murders, in that order. The responsibility was starting to feel oppressive. I knew Jilly felt the same way. Whereas I preferred to isolate myself with Keats and Percy to allow mental space for things to come together, Jilly surrounded herself with people and worked off her stress with entertaining. I supported her but wished it didn't mean dressing up and swanning around in heels tonight. Heels a size too large by the looks of things, since I hadn't come equipped for black tie. Jilly knew that, so she asked Janelle to lend me something to wear. It was their first friendly exchange, so I didn't put up a fuss. I'd take the clothes Janelle offered and help stitch their relationship back together. Besides, the only other option was to borrow a peasant dress and hippy sandals from Bridie.

As we left the rec center, Keats snapped into a point. Special Constable Doug was heaving things into the bed of a red pickup truck. There was a heavy plastic bag, a large fishing net, a long-handled tool I didn't recognize, and some burlap sacks. After closing the tailgate, he got into the truck and drove off in the direction of the pond. An urgent whine told us to follow.

"We'll never catch him," Jilly said. "If he's planning to capture the swan, he could be done by the time we get there."

"But we can't let him snag Zeus in a net like that," I said. "He might break a wing or worse. We need to stop him."

"I've got an idea," Bridie said, beckoning. In the small executive parking lot beside the rec center sat Vaughan's golf cart—the one with the gold falcon on the side. "I'm sure he leaves the key in the ignition."

"We can't just drive away in that," Jilly said. "That falcon is a complete giveaway."

"I know the back routes," Bridie said. "I learned early to have a way out of any situation."

"Gran, I like the way you think," Janelle said. "I'll drive."

"Let Ivy drive," Jilly said. "She's used to bumpy rides."

"You think I'm not?" Janelle said. "One good thing about working every single job at a resort is that I can handle any vehicle, including a backhoe."

"Drive," I said. "That leaves me free to watch what Doug is doing."

Bridie took the passenger seat and Jilly and I got into the back with Percy in Jilly's arms and Keats between my knees. We set off down a lane, trundled through three unfenced backyards, and then into a grove of trees.

"He's souped this thing up," Janelle said, slowing to

cross a small creek before gunning it up a hill. "I've never stolen a nicer golf cart."

"There have been others?" Bridie asked, from the front passenger seat.

Janelle tossed her a smile. "Only a few, Gran. Like you say, it's good to have a way out of any situation."

"Pay attention," Jilly said. "That last bump almost threw Percy out."

She had the cat locked in a viselike grip, but that left her without a free hand to brace herself. Meanwhile, Keats whined for a better position to see.

"Time to slow down," I said, as the golf cart crested a small hill. "This is the perfect lookout."

There were several gentle crests in the compound, and this one was well-placed. We could view the pond easily, and yet there was sufficient cover from scrub bush. Doug would only notice us if we made a wrong move and attracted his attention.

Down below, he stood on the dock with the boats and adjusted the brim of his red baseball cap. The swan was out in the center of the pond and made no move to approach. Doug opened a loaf of bread and started hurling big chunks of it into the water.

"You don't feed bread to a swan," Jilly whispered. "It's not good for them at all."

"I hope Zeus knows that," I said. "Because a net isn't good for him, either."

The swan coasted backward with barely a ripple. Doug threw another couple of chunks harder and then gave up. He walked back to the truck and I held my breath as he dropped the tailgate.

Janelle turned to look at me. "What are we going to do if he snags the bird?"

I didn't have an answer for that yet. In a crisis, I tended to rely on instinct. Luckily I didn't need to tap into it now, because Doug grabbed the plastic bag rather than the net. Heaving it over his shoulder, he returned to the dock. Then he took a long look around, as if to make sure he wasn't being watched. We all ducked in the golf cart without anyone saying a word. Even Percy stuck his head under Jilly's arm.

Satisfied, he knelt on one knee, slashed the sack, and poured at least 30 pounds of a granular substance into the pond. Janelle filmed it on her phone.

"Is he trying to poison the swan?" Jilly whispered.

"Probably," I said. "Easier than catching it and risking the wing-beating he deserves."

"If he stole the swan from the hotel, wouldn't he be treating it like a treasure?" Bridie asked.

"Plans change," Jilly said. "Maybe he started out thinking a swan was good for the Briars and things went south. So now he's trying to reverse course."

"Either way, we can't let that happen," I said. "If he's poisoned the pond, it'll take time to disperse through the system. We'll have Zeus out of there before it harms him."

Doug threw the empty bag in the truck, closed the tailgate and got back in the pickup.

"The black tie event is the perfect cover for the rescue," Janelle said. "What now?"

"Proof," I said. "We need to follow Doug and get that bag."

"Easy peasy," Janelle said, reversing the golf cart. "At his next stop, Jilly and I will distract him while you take a look. Gran will stand guard."

Jilly didn't argue about taking direction from her cousin. When the chips were down, she always did the best thing to help the cause. Deploying their considerable family charms in service of the operation made good sense.

The only problem was that Doug didn't go back to the security station as we expected. Instead, he paused for a moment to open the gates remotely and then sailed through.

The doors quickly closed in our faces.

"Reverse and turn right, Janelle," Bridie said. "And be quick about it. There's a breach Doug doesn't know about yet. As soon as he closes one, somebody opens another. Usually Vaughan, who likes to tootle over to Clarington to blow some coin at the casino. It's only fitting we give his golf cart a taste of freedom."

"Shouldn't we take the truck?" I asked. "We'll never catch Doug in a golf cart on the highway."

"Watch me," Janelle said. "I know this turf like the back of my hand from working at the Strathmore. We always found secret spots to blow off steam. I bet I can cut Doug off if we have to and then we'll play it by ear."

Turned out there was no need for highway heroics. Doug only drove about a mile before turning left and heading down a gravel road. Janelle hung well back, as if tailing someone was second nature. She pressed her stiletto down every time he rounded a curve, and lifted it on the straightaways when he might see us.

After a very bumpy mile, during which no one uttered a peep of protest, Doug turned left again. Janelle slowed to a crawl and said, "This is Muldoon's Marina, which isn't much of a marina. The locals come down here to hunt for snakes."

"Hunt for snakes?" Jilly's voice was hoarse.

"Burmese pythons, mostly," Janelle said. "An invasive

species that's multiplying like crazy because they have no natural predators."

"I heard about this," I said. "People tired of them as pets and released them, never realizing they'd decimate the ecosystem."

"Right, so now the government pays a nice bounty for every snake caught," Janelle said. "A big one can bring in four grand or more, and they use the skins for shoes and bags."

"That's disgusting," Jilly said, shuddering as Keats did near water. "Did you try it?"

"Snake hunting? Yep, I'll try anything once. For a skilled hunter, it's easy money."

"I can think of easier money," Jilly said. "Way easier."

"Options are fewer around here," she said. "But there's a good reason it pays well. After the eighteen-foot pregnant mama, I decided not to bother developing my skills."

"Oh. My. Gosh," Jilly said. "If we see one of those, I'll do worse than wet myself."

"Me too," I said. "Janelle, do you think that's what Doug's doing down here?"

"He had the right tools, but there's only one way to find out." She pulled the golf cart into the trees and pointed to a trail that led into the brush.

"Are you really going to bushwhack in heels?" Jilly asked. "Are you nuts?"

"I wish we did have something to whack bushes," Janelle said. "But yeah, I'm nuts enough to do what it takes to get a job done, regardless of attire." She grinned over her shoulder. "Luckily I know a way around the sinkhole. People have dropped in and never returned."

"That's an urban myth," Bridie said.

"We lost a waiter that way," Janelle said. "Guy deserved the deep sleep."

I figured she was joking—trying to get Jilly's goat the best way she knew how—but I winced anyway. If there was a sinkhole around, usually I was the one to find it.

Keats must have come to the same conclusion because he moved out in front of Janelle and started leading the way. Very soon the ground underfoot became spongy, and he took us on a different path.

"Are there snakes here, too?" Jilly asked.

"Sure," Janelle said. "Looking to make some extra coin?"

"We shouldn't be traipsing around here without an anti-venom kit."

"Pythons aren't poisonous. They squeeze their prey till—"

"A paramedic then," Jilly interrupted, picking up Percy.

"At least a rifle," Bridie added. "I'm sure that's what Edna would recommend in her survival course."

"Probably," I said. "But we'd end up shooting each other and we need all hands."

"I'm a good shot," Janelle said, which didn't surprise me.

"Me too," said Bridie, which did.

"Time to expand our skills, Jilly," I said. "In the meantime, Keats has us covered. He's wise to snakes and has saved me from a couple of nasties back home."

He confirmed that with a mumble but it didn't ease Jilly's nerves much. "This is like the set from a horror movie. Cue the zombies."

I moved her up ahead of me, behind Bridie. "Zombies always go for the straggler," I said. "Let them take me first."

"Don't even joke," Jilly said. "Monsters come for you far too often."

"We're here," Janelle said, as Keats circled back to bring us all together. He'd found a little hill where the soil was firm and the view of the water nearly unobstructed.

The water itself was very much obstructed with vegetation. It was clearly part of the swampland Amos had told me about—miles and miles of bog. I wish he'd thought to mention the snakes.

"How do boats get through all that?" I asked. "It's so shallow and marshy."

Janelle stood on tiptoe and pointed. "You're about to see."

A boat was pulling away from a dock, and the only person on board wore a red baseball cap. The craft moved easily and quickly along the surface and appeared to be powered by a large propeller.

"Ah, yes," Bridie said. "I forgot the Briars had an airboat. Doug takes his cronies out for a spin sometimes. That thing ate a huge chunk out of our operating budget and Vaughan approved it. Now I realize it was so that Doug could supplement his income with snake bounties as well as bribes."

"What do we do now?" Jilly asked. "Wait here to see what he brings back?" She slapped at mosquitos. "And risk getting eaten alive or sinking to oblivion?"

"Of course not," Janelle said. "We go after him."

"After him?" Jilly's voice became a squeak and Janelle didn't bother hiding her grin. "How exactly?"

"Never mind, Jilly," I said. "We're not following. It's too risky."

As someone who took pride in trying new things, it pained me to say no. But the landscape here was particularly treacherous and it didn't make sense to put everyone in peril, especially Bridie and the pets. The fact that Keats showed no sign that pursuing was relevant to our investigation backed my decision.

"Not that risky," Janelle said. "I'd really love to know what Doug is doing out there."

"I barely know how to pilot a rowboat, let alone an airboat," I said.

"But I do," Janelle said. "One of my first jobs was in a marina. I even know how to jimmy one if they're all locked. Airboats are a blast."

I managed to squelch my inner daredevil—something Janelle and I clearly had in common. "Let's check out Doug's truck and then take it from there."

Relief came off Jilly, Bridie and Keats in waves. Janelle could lift an airboat and go on a joyride another day if she wanted. If I completed my mission, I might even go with her.

Keats led us along twisty paths and down to the small gravel parking area beside the pier. Doug's truck was the only vehicle there and Bridie stood watch as the rest of us circled it. Finally I hoisted myself up to peer into the bed. As expected, the net, sacks and tools were gone. Only two things remained: the empty plastic bag... and a rifle. Perhaps it was the same one he'd aimed at Zeus a few days ago, or maybe it was a spare. I assumed he'd want one along for the ride in the Briars' airboat.

Grabbing the plastic bag, I hopped back down and everyone crowded around to take a closer look.

"Not poison," I said, reading the print on the back. "On the contrary, it's a product for rejuvenating so-called tired ponds. For producing a healthy biome."

"Maybe Doug is working for the swan, rather than against him," Jilly said.

I took photos of the bag and then put it back where I found it. "I wouldn't be so sure about that. My guess is he's hoping to revitalize it to make residents happy, rather than birds and fish."

"You can question him tonight at the formal," Jilly said, tugging on my sleeve to make sure I wouldn't succumb to Janelle's boating proposal.

"Sounds good," I said. "As long as I don't need to tango with him."

"I'll volunteer, if it comes to that," Janelle said.

"Let me guess," Jilly called over her shoulder as we walked back to the golf cart. "You were a dance instructor at some resort."

"Bingo, Jilly," she said, smoothing her dress, which was still white and bright after our jaunt. Her pedicure would need attention, however. "I ran many a bingo night, too."

"You've got useful skills," Jilly admitted. "So maybe you could dust some of them off to help Ivy tonight when my hands are full."

Janelle's face lit up. "Absolutely."

Bridie smiled, too. We all knew that surrendering my care to Janelle meant that Jilly's grudge against her cousin was easing.

"I appreciate that," I said. "Because Amos said he'd be out of town for at least a few hours on another tricky rescue."

"I'll be there for the actual rescue," Jilly said. "Gran can take charge of the dance at that point."

"Got it," Bridie said. "Although I'd rather be bird-napping. Vaughan tends to get handsy with an open bar."

The rest of us laughed. For Bridie, the prospect of

snakes and an airboat chase had been less daunting than dancing with handsy Vaughan. She might very well make a good apocalyptic soldier.

On the way back, Keats lifted his muzzle to the dank breeze and looked happier than I'd seen him in days. When the breach in the security fence spit us back into the Briars' compound, however, his ruff rose and a low growl vibrated in his chest.

"What's wrong?" Jilly asked, as we left the golf cart where we'd found it.

Once the two of us fell back, I whispered, "There's a threat here, and it's obviously not from Doug, because he's off bagging snakes."

The dog's eerie blue eye confirmed my suspicion. There were bigger challenges ahead than a handsy dancer.

CHAPTER TWENTY-FOUR

When the party was in full swing, I volunteered to circulate with cocktails and canapés as a means to search for Doug without being conspicuous. It was a bold move, because I wasn't known for my grace even while wearing shoes my own size. Jilly had only brought one pair of dress heels, but Janelle's trunk was full of shoeboxes. She set me up in a blue dress that fit perfectly and a pair of navy sandals that did not.

"I'm going down under a tray of rum punch," I told Keats, as he took on the job of herding me through the crowd. Many a guest turned quickly at the light graze of teeth but he was gone before they pinpointed the cause. More than one pair of support hose ended the night in tears.

Janelle met me beside the dance floor with a tray of drinks expertly balanced over her head. That allowed her to slink through bodies, wheelchairs and walkers despite wearing far higher heels.

"Nothing?" she asked, spinning when someone got a little frisky behind her. "Uh-uh, Harold. If this tray comes down too fast, there will be a sudden vacancy at the Briars."

He laughed sheepishly and wheeled off. I admired the way she defused situations without raising feathers. If Harold's hand had landed on *my* thigh like that, it would leave with fang marks from my canine chaperone.

"I was sure we'd get our chance tonight," I said. "Felt it in my bones. Keats did, too. Look at him. His ruff is on the high setting."

"I love the way you two communicate," she said. "If I had a stable life, I'd get myself a dog like Keats."

He glanced up at her and his ears came forward. Smiling at him, she lowered the tray smoothly. She must have pipes as good as mine to carry it like that.

"There's no other dog like Keats," I said. "But the perfect dog for you is right around the corner if you open your heart. What's your dream breed?"

"Belgian shepherd," she said, without missing a beat. "That's what I see in my dreams. Her name is Lilith."

"That would suit you well," I said. "You need protection crisscrossing the country like you do."

"Exactly. And what you said about pet-friendly hotels makes sense. I'm going to look into it."

"Why not slow your roll, Janelle? Set down some roots? I've never been happier since moving to the farm and developing a community."

She gave a quick shake of her curls. "I don't have a big family like yours."

"My community starts outside my family. My friends today were strangers this time last year. And it all started with rescuing Keats. You'd be surprised what doors a dog can open."

"I'll take that under advisement," she said. "I'd like to

be closer to Gran but no matter how underqualified I am the jobs around here are worse. I'm burned out on resort work and the only step left is management."

"You'd make a good manager if that's what you wanted," I said.

"You've seen my rebellious side. I've worked hard to tame it, but there are reasons I kept moving on."

"What would you like to do, if you could do anything?" I asked.

"Run my own business. Help people, somehow." She stared around the room. "I know what it's like to feel lonely and hopeless. So trapped in the past that escape seems impossible. But I'm too old to go back to school."

"It's never too late for a big change," I said.

"Spoken like an HR rep." She softened her delivery with a blazing smile. "I dropped out of freshman year and began my storied career. And do I have stories."

"You'll have another before the night's through," I said. "If only we could find... Casey! We were just looking for you."

"Business or pleasure?" he asked. "Because if someone's looking for a dance partner, there's room on my card."

"We're actually—" I didn't get to finish my sentence before he took the tray of drinks from Janelle's hands and shoved it into my free one.

"We won't be long," Janelle said, spinning off in his arms. She hadn't exaggerated earlier. Her moves under the rented mirror ball were pro level and Casey did well, too. Seeing them twirl reminded me of a time in Clover Grove, when the town—and my mother—fell under a dance instructor's spell.

Shaking my head, I said to Keats, "You know you're hard up when you're nostalgic over an old murder case, buddy. Feels like we're no closer to solving this one and I'm missing home and Kellan like you wouldn't believe."

He was extra gentle as he herded me to a table where I managed to set the two trays down without mishap. My phone was stuck in my bra because the dress had no pockets, so I turned my back to pull it out and texted the team to converge in the parking lot.

Jilly reached me first with Bridie, and Janelle ran up behind them. She moved like a classy spy in a James Bond movie.

"No luck with Doug?" Jilly asked.

Before I could answer, Janelle spoke up. "Casey said he sent him on an errand. Maybe he'll be here dancing when we're done. I made Casey promise to take all the single ladies for a spin and promised him the last dance." She sighed. "The ratio of women to men is heartbreaking."

I had my doubts anyone would still be dancing when we got back. Rescues rarely went as planned but maybe this time would be different.

Jilly gave her grandmother explicit instructions about how to keep the party running well in our absence. Then the two of us got into the truck with Keats and Percy, and followed Janelle's old beater to the gate. Now that we knew Doug was missing in action, it removed one big obstacle. Janelle simply popped out, used the key she had pilfered from Casey's pocket during a dynamic twirl on the dance floor, and entered the security booth. A moment later, the doors opened and we rolled right on through.

"Jilly, I hate to say it, but—"

"Janelle's good," she said. "A great asset to the team."

"Yeah. I'm sorry. If you tell me she's rotten to the core, I'll buy it, because I trust your judgment. But I really want to believe she's changed from the person you knew."

Jilly was silent for nearly a mile before saying, "She may have changed and I hope she has, but it can't undo what happened."

"Everyone does stupid things when they're teens. Except me, I guess. If I'd done more stupid things then maybe I wouldn't be doing them now. I'd have gained more wisdom."

She looked at me and smiled, but it didn't reach her eyes.

"I don't want to tell you what happened, Ivy," she said. "Because if Janelle *has* changed, she deserves a second chance without anyone else knowing the details. I'll only say that she's the reason Gran is stuck in here, likely for the rest of her days."

"Seriously? How can that be?"

"In high school, Janelle fell in with a bad crowd and didn't have the moves or the judgment she has now. One thing led to another and she ended up on the wrong side of the most powerful family in lower hill country. Gran refused to let Janelle take the fall and threw herself in the line of fire. It was probably meant to be a silly stunt, but you see the fallout. Gran's been a bird in a cage for fifteen years. Safe, but not really living."

"Oh Jilly, that's awful. Bridie made that sacrifice so that Janelle could have a good life."

Jilly nodded. "And what's she done with that gift?"

"This isn't the life Janelle wants, either. The fact she's stayed close to Bridie shows how much she cares. Just an hour ago she told me she'd like a fresh start helping people. Maybe seeing you has expanded her horizons."

"I'm trying to keep an open mind but it's harder with Gran stuck in here."

"Can't we do something?" I asked. "To break Bridie out of here?"

"Gran isn't safe while anyone in that family is around to hold a grudge. And that's probably the rest of her life."

I squeezed the steering wheel. "Where are your mothers in all this? Seems like they had a major role to play."

"They started it with their feuding and that's why I could do without seeing either one again."

"I understand the sentiment, as you know well. But my family has changed and yours might, too."

"That was different," she said. "Calvin isn't so bad. He meant well."

"Maybe I'd say the same about your mom if I met her. Besides, we all think our families are different but we're probably more or less the same."

She stared at the dark road ahead. Janelle had left us behind miles back. "I guess that's what scares me about the future."

I waited for her to continue and then jumped to my own conclusions. "About Asher, you mean?"

"About having a family. Wouldn't I become as dysfunctional as my mother and my aunt? What if I wrecked my kids, like they did? It wouldn't be fair to them or to Asher."

Ah. Finally we got to the heart of the problem. Reaching over, I patted her hand. "Jilly, I've known you a long time. We've been through a lot so I know exactly who you are. Smart. Kind. Trustworthy. Steadfast. You turned out that way by choice, so I have no doubt at all that you'd make an awesome wife and mom."

Keats turned from the road to offer his mumbled endorsement.

"Thank you," she said. "That means a lot, both of you."

"I only see one potential problem," I said, grinning. "What if a python came after your baby? Could you handle it?"

"That's what husbands are for," she said. "Snakes and snails and puppy dog tails…"

One dog's tail was telling us an important tale right now. Keats was staring through the seats at the road behind us while his tail bristled.

Glancing into the rearview mirror, I sighed. "We're being followed, Jilly."

"Not again!" She peered over her shoulder at the glow of headlights.

I confirmed it by speeding up and slowing down to judge the other driver's actions. Meanwhile, Keats stayed on yellow alert, ears forward and ruff up. That hadn't changed much all evening. Things were definitely heating up. I could feel it, too.

"I'm going to pull off at the next side road and see what happens," I said. "Can you text Janelle and let her know we'll be late?"

I slowed to be sure we didn't hit the ditch on the turn. The goal was to catch a glimpse of the vehicle as it passed and then find a new route to the hotel.

"What if they trap us on the side road?" Jilly asked, after messaging her cousin.

"Evasive maneuvers," I said. "I've been practicing with Edna. If a zombie's heading my way I want the skills to go over, under or around."

"I wish I could laugh but my heart's clogging my throat," Jilly said.

"It's all good," I said. "But hold on tight. You too, Keats."

I took the next exit abruptly and without signaling.

Before the tail passed, I turned out our lights and stopped. A few seconds later, the vehicle went by at a crawl. There was enough light to see it was a red pickup truck.

"Doug!" My voice overlapped with Jilly's and Keats confirmed it with a mumble.

"What do we do now?" she asked.

"Find another route to the Strathmore," I said.

With Janelle's help, we navigated the side roads fairly well and she was waiting in the hotel parking lot when we arrived. Doug hadn't made it, but he'd likely turn up soon.

"Maybe he's guessed our plan and wants to catch us in the act," I said.

"I say we go ahead," Janelle said. "We may not get another chance."

"Agreed," I said. "You on board, Jilly?"

She looked to Keats for advice. While the dog was still on alert, his ears were up and forward. He was good to go. "Okay," she said. "Let's do this."

Janelle didn't waste another second. She was our decoy and well suited for it. Off she went around the side of the turreted building to the rear patio. She'd called ahead to offer to show the bartender—and the guests—her signature flaming tropical cocktail that packed quite a punch. If we needed more time, she'd be kicking off a dance contest.

We'd planned to change clothes in the truck but with the threat of Doug's arrival, decided not to waste a second. I gathered the gear we needed, while Keats and Percy went to round up the swan.

Kicking off our heels, we pulled on men's rubber boots. Jilly tied her full skirt into a knot. I bid the dress I'd borrowed a fond farewell as I waded into the pond. It would be the first casualty of the rescue and hopefully the only one.

Hera circled the fountain warily with wings raised like a warrior. The fluffy cygnets plopped off her back with small splashes.

I spoke gently to the mother swan and explained our plan, and that she had to go first. I expected one heck of a fight, but she practically swam into my outstretched arms. That said, once I had her secure in my embrace, she turned to watch her babies uttering low, hoarse cries. The little ones didn't understand their orders and scattered, leaving Jilly to chase them down.

"This is going to take all night," she said, plodding after them. They moved like pinballs, colliding and parting and colliding again, cheeping the whole time in distress.

Keats circled on the far side, pushing them in her direction with his energy. Finally, she nabbed one and splashed over to the empty ferret cage I'd left beside the pond. Bridie didn't know Arnie was loose in the house, but I was confident Keats could round him up later.

As Jilly bent to grab another bird, Keats stopped and turned. The unease he had shown all night ramped up to red alert mode. Doug must be coming.

"Jilly, we may need to abort," I said. "Keats is sounding the alarm and we can't leave any babies here without their mother. Maybe it's better to fight this battle another day."

"No," she said, cupping cygnet number two and rushing to the cage. "I'm getting the hang of this now. Five minutes oughta do it."

Keats was far enough away that I couldn't hear the rumble in his chest, though I felt it in my heart. This threat was real and it was bigger than Special Constable Doug Farrows.

"We don't have five minutes," I said. "I see headlights

through the trees now. Someone is coming up the lane and it isn't a pickup truck."

A sleek black sedan slid sinuously into the hotel parking lot. It looked like a government issue security vehicle. The kind a bomb couldn't explode.

"What the heck?" My eyes flicked from the car to Keats, who was now on his belly in the grass. "We've got trouble."

Jilly stopped with a third baby bird in her hands. "Yeah. We sure do."

"Is it the kind of trouble that's keeping Bridie in hiding?"

"I—I think it might be."

"Well, they're parked between us and my truck, so I guess we're going to have a wee chat." I looked over at her and tried to smile. "Bet you wish you didn't have your skirt in a knot."

"And bird poop on my fingers," she said. "On the bright side, someone might want to shake hands before offing us."

"They won't off us. It's Bridie they're after, right?"

"Or possibly Janelle. Either way, they'll keep us around until they get what they want. I'll do my best to help you stay out of it, Ivy. And I'm sorry in advance for what you might see here."

"No apology required. I'm super curious." I adjusted my grip on the swan. "I do worry about the birds though."

Jilly straightened her shoulders and continued to the ferret cage with her catch. "Let's just pretend they're not there and continue till we can't," she said. "They're probably considering the optics of snatching us in front of so many hotel windows."

"Should we call Janelle? Will it help or hinder?"

"Hinder. They know she's here because of her car. But

it's better to let them think she'll come out with weapons drawn instead of dancing the Macarena."

"All right, then. Let's keep pretending that chasing waterfowl in black tie finery is completely normal."

"It is normal... for us," she said, creeping up on the next cygnet.

"I'm impressed with your grace under pressure, Jilly. It's like you haven't a care in the world."

"Whereas I'm wondering if life as we know it is over. If I've brought danger not only to Gran, but the farm. Ah! Gotcha." She delivered another cygnet to the cage. "Now I realize it was silly to think they wouldn't show up eventually. After fifteen years, I got complacent."

Keats started crawling toward the car on his belly and I called, "Don't buddy. This is beyond what the three of us can handle."

He looked back at me, and I could swear his blue eye emitted a light I'd never seen before. His mumble was terse, as if telling me not to count him out.

The black car's high beams came on, blinding me and making Jilly mutter words that rarely dropped from her lips. The last of the cygnets fled.

There was the click of a car door opening and a new kind of dread filled my chest. I'd faced murderers but they were regular humans gone over the edge. This was different. Organized crime, I gathered. Organized sociopaths. There was no bargaining with people like that. All I could do was hold my ground. Hold my dog in place. Pin the cat on the hood of the truck, where he'd retreated to watch. And hug the swan a little closer without crushing her. I could feel her heart racing, or perhaps it was my own. Just when I thought she'd break free, she looped her long neck right around mine. It may have looked like a noose to others but it was surprisingly comforting.

She trusted me to know what to do when I had no idea. I had to figure out how to get us all out unscathed, including my friend who was now running full tilt after the last cygnets. She feinted left and then right, coming up empty. Panic was getting to her.

"Jilly, stop," I called. "They're coming."

"They've been coming half my life," she panted. "I'm not going down without the birds."

My legs started to wobble and I worried they'd collapse outright, leaving me to greet our opponents on my butt in the water. At least there were no alligators in this manmade pond.

Buzzing started in my head. That often preceded a faint but I forced myself to breathe. If I passed out I was no help to anyone. My vision swirled and then cleared. Another set of headlights came into the parking lot. A pickup truck. Had Doug come to join the pool party?

Between my momentary dizziness and the black car's high beams I couldn't make anything out. But I heard doors open and boots hit the gravel. Two people came running toward the pond.

"Ivy Rose Galloway, get out of the water with that bird," someone yelled. "You're a sitting duck, dagnabit."

And with that, I did sit down.

CHAPTER TWENTY-FIVE

E dna Evans bent over and hauled me to my feet. "I didn't mean literally. What kind of soldier sits down on the job?"

"The kind who wants to live to fight another day," I said, trying to get my legs to cooperate. "Help Jilly, please. The people in the black car are after her and her family. It's like a crime syndicate. A powerful one. Possibly even magical."

"Your brother's got her covered," she said, getting behind me and literally hoisting me to my feet. "Ivy, you sound addled. Are you stoned?"

"Stoned! Of course, I'm not stoned. Do you think I'd get stoned before rescuing animals? Or ever?"

Her chuckle was as reassuring to me as my umbrage probably was to her. "The sedan left lickety-split. It's a shame I never got a chance to try my new weapons."

"Asher let you store weapons in the truck?"

"What that boy doesn't know won't hurt him. I told him I packed a complete set of antique china for Bridie and that killed any desire to peek inside the storage box." She perp-walked me out of the pond and then eased me down in the grass.

"Watch the swan," I said.

"As if I could miss it," she said.

"We need to put it in the dog crate Keats doesn't know I have."

He circled Edna, tail low and swishing, almost abasing himself. "What's wrong with him?" she asked. "Is he stoned, too?"

"Just relieved," I said. "We're both grateful. And surprised."

"Surprised Asher and I made it through a long drive without killing each other? You should be. It's not for lack of desire, I assure you. He refused to surrender the wheel under order of Chief Hottie McSnobalot, but when Kellan learned you'd taken Jilly into python country, Asher got antsy. I convinced him that I was better rested for the last leg of the journey, and of course my boot is a whole lot heavier than his. Without that, we wouldn't have made it in time to scare off these so-called crime lords. I don't know where your swans would be without me."

Turning, she shone a powerful flashlight into the pond. Asher was running through the water wearing his Clover Grove police uniform with both arms outstretched. "I'll get 'em, Jilly," he called. "Don't worry."

"I know you will," she said. "Thank you."

Edna shook her head. "He drove day and night for this big moment, only to look like a uniformed zombie. I don't like his chances with Jillian."

I laughed, careful not to jar the mother swan, who was still looped like a living noose around my neck. Our difficulties weren't over, but I could share a light moment with my apocalyptic solider friend. "Asher's chances are good, Edna," I said. "Very good. Don't you dissuade him."

"I want the best for Jillian and you know it. If he lands the birds and wins her heart, I'll dance at their wedding."

Asher gently captured the last cygnets in his big hands and delivered them to the ferret cage. Only then did he turn and sweep Jilly into his arms. She clung to him, rubber boots dangling, and after a dramatic swing that sent one boot flying into the water, he carried her to shore. Tears filled my eyes and I reached carefully around the swan to brush them away.

"Buff your dancing boots, Edna," I said. "I'm picturing a fall wedding in the orchard."

"Will you be wearing your swan cape for the occasion?" she asked. "Because I'll bring my rabbits out of mothballs."

"*My* neck ornament is very much alive, thank you very much. She's going to spend the rest of her days in a lovely waterfowl sanctuary. Now we have to go back to the Briars and collect her spouse. I hope he's as cooperative as she was, but I have my doubts. He's on edge due to recent events."

Edna flicked her light toward the hotel and pinned Janelle in her beam. She was dancing and spinning all the way down the path. When she caught sight of us, however, she stopped and called, "What did I miss?"

"Your calling as a reality show star?" Edna suggested.

"A scary moment," Jilly added, from Asher's arms. "While you were doing the Macarena, the black car came."

Not *a* black car. *The* black car. Janelle's hands dropped to her sides and the wind went out of her sails. "The limbo, actually," she said. "It takes so much focus. That's how I missed your call."

"I didn't call," Jilly said. "It seemed better that way."

Janelle came the rest of the way. "You should have. It's me they wanted."

"It's all good," I said. "The cavalry arrived in time."

She crunched quickly along the path and when her heels hit the pavement, she started clicking toward her old beater. "Change of plans, folks. I need to get back to watch over Gran right now. Doug's on the prowl. There's no one at security and a breach in the fence." Pausing with the door open, she added, "I look forward to chatting later. I assume you're Asher and Edna."

"My reputation precedes me," Edna said, grinning.

"The fatigues were a giveaway." Janelle grinned back before sliding into the car. "My gran is all atwitter about meeting you. You're a celebrity."

Before Edna could answer, the old hatchback roared out of the parking lot.

"Let's hurry," I said, as Edna helped me to my feet. "Jilly, I'm surrendering Hera and the cygnets to you. I'll go collect her mate."

"We've got it," Asher said, still holding Jilly's hand as she stumped toward me with one bare foot.

"Edna, would you mind going with them?" I asked.

"You need me," she said.

"I do, so please get to the Briars as soon as you can. But I can't risk anything going wrong on the way to the sanctuary. Keats will help me with Zeus."

Asher shook his head. "I promised the chief I wouldn't leave you alone for one second."

"I'll call him and chat all the way back, brother. I'm confident Keats and I can handle this alone."

The dog muttered a cheeky "so there," which made Asher laugh. "You're mouthing off to an officer of the law, dog."

"You have no jurisdiction here," Edna said. "I'll carry your gun for you."

"You're wrong, Miss Evans," he said. "The two chiefs had a chat."

"Too many chiefs never helped anything," Edna said, leading the way to his truck. "I'll drive and you can hold the cygnets while Jilly wears the swan noose."

Hera went meekly into Jilly's arms, looping around my friend's neck as she had mine. The dog crate wasn't necessary after all.

In moments, they were on their way. After changing into my work boots, I followed and made good on my promise to call Kellan. He listened without interruption, and because I knew that cost him something, I hurried through it without color commentary.

"Do you know anything about these black sedan people?" I asked at the end. "Jilly seemed terrified. Even Janelle was upset, and she rushed back to guard Bridie."

"Nothing," he said, "and I've done plenty of digging into Wyldwood Springs and beyond. However, they do have a stack of cold cases ten times taller than mine. That's not a town I'd ever want to take on. Their chief sounded, well... overwhelmed would be a good word."

"They need a chief like you," I said. "Especially with a little help from Keats and me." Before he could answer, I added, "Not that I've had much luck with the recent murders at the Briars."

"I looked into the people you mentioned," he said. "There are plenty of bad debts. Vaughan Mills, for starters. Looks like he left Chicago in a hurry. Alba Fletcher disappeared from custody in suspicious circumstances after defrauding her employer. And Elsie Cornwall seems to be in some trouble right now."

"Elsie? Really? She's so sweet."

"Maybe, but her husband isn't. According to a source in Cincinnati, Carlisle got their son to borrow on the equity of the family home and he's about to lose it. That will leave Elsie's grandchildren out in the cold. On top of that, Carlisle bilked a couple of women out of money."

"Maybe Lottie found out about that," I said. "And Elsie did more than steal her crystal ball."

"Crystal ball?" he said. "Wait, don't even tell me. Just come home before you get any deeper in this. Some of the Briars residents deserve to be even more detained than they are."

"But what about Bridie? You found nothing on her? Or Janelle?"

"Nothing yet, but Gillock is turning every stone, I promise. He's diligent and persistent, I'll give him that."

"Okay. You've given me a lot to think about."

"I only gave you one thing to think about, and that's packing your things. I sent Asher to collect you. Edna insisted on coming—partly to escape your unruly llamas. From what I hear, they've been giving her a run for her money."

Lottie's crystal ball may have dished out some truth there. "So, who's my acting farm manager?"

"Cori and Gertie are both on site. Your ark is afloat, although I understand there's a ruckus with the mini horse."

"Clippers? Is he okay?"

"Yeah, as far as I can tell. Cori is talking about an enrichment program. He's under-challenged and I guess the goat castle doesn't work for little horses with big ambitions."

I laughed. Just hearing his voice across the miles

soothed me. Keats hadn't let down his guard, however. His paws were on the dashboard, trying to lash the truck on to our destination.

"So, when can you leave?" Kellan asked.

"After the swans are safely reunited and Jilly is confident Bridie is safe."

"It sounds like she doesn't believe Bridie will ever be safe."

"True. Maybe she'll want to stay down here for a while."

"Asher won't be too happy about that," Kellan said.

"No, he won't." I couldn't help grinning. "Their reunion was like a scene from a rom-com. I expect you'll lose one of your best officers for a time if she stays."

"I'm fine with that if it brings you home. It's a fair trade: an officer for a lady."

I laughed. "I hate to leave a case unresolved, but after dealing with the swan, I'll give it serious consideration."

"Clippers needs you," he said, slyly. "Doesn't that hold more weight than my request?"

"Cori and I can talk about that on the phone." I pondered for a second. "Honestly, I sense the issue here may be bigger than I can handle. If I truly can't help, I'll come home."

"Sounds good," he said. "I'll make a reasonable woman out of you yet."

"Reasonable? That's a big ask, Chief."

"It's a reasonable ask when you're planning a future together. Your issues are my issues."

"You want issues? I can't wait to consult you on the intricacies of farm management."

He groaned. "We'll need a triage system. I prefer to be consulted on any and all criminal activities."

"Fair enough. I'm just about to turn into the Briars, so how about I touch base later, after catching the swan?"

"Ivy, it's dark. You can't tackle that at night when there's wildlife waiting to tackle you. I read about those pythons. There are tens of thousands of them, some big enough to swallow a deer whole. The state holds tournaments for snake hunters."

"That's another reason to get Zeus out of there. Swans don't have many predators, but a big snake sounds like one of them." I glanced over at Keats. "It's now or never, Kellan. I feel it and Keats feels it, too. Don't you, buddy?"

The dog looked away from the highway and delivered a concise yip of confirmation.

"No time for idle chitchat," Kellan said.

"Dog on a mission."

I pulled up to the security doors, hoping Doug had come back from *his* mission in time to let me in. "I'll call you when I'm done, no matter how late."

"Please do. I'll stay at work till I know the whole pack of you are safe and sound."

After one last promise, I hung up and texted Janelle. She was at the party supervising Bridie, and keeping both Doug and Casey busy dancing with the many available ladies.

Instead of getting her to send Doug down, I decided it was better to keep him there. After parking outside, I grabbed what I needed from the truck and followed the dog and cat through the breach in the fence.

Keats mumbled a question and I pondered for a second before saying, "Good idea, buddy. It's worth doing, even if it delays for half an hour."

I stashed my equipment in some bushes and walked up

to the recreation center. Then I circled around it to the property manager's office.

Keats searched for a key, nose down, moving so fast he was a blur in the low light. I was starting to think it would be a bust when Percy meowed from the window ledge. He stretched as far as he could toward the top of the doorframe. Standing on tiptoe, I felt along the ledge and found it.

"Good job, Percy. If I had to clamber through a window it would zap what's left of my energy before I even get to Zeus."

Inside, I kept the lights out and went straight to the desktop computer. Casey didn't seem like the kind of guy to keep paper files.

Unfortunately, he *was* the kind of guy to protect his computer with a password. Maybe that's because Vaughan and Doug were in and out of here, too. Casey probably didn't trust them either.

Was Casey also the kind of guy to be obvious about his password? I'd only have three tries before the system locked me out.

The image of the vanity license plate on his BMW convertible came to mind straight away: HotProperty. I plugged in the letters and got an error message.

"Oh come on," I said. "That's gotta be it. He's so proud of that car."

I added the numeral 1 and got another error message.

I only had one more guess and I tried it: BriarsHotProperty. Crossing my fingers, I hit enter.

"And... we're in," I said. "I am a rock star, boys. So... where do we go first?"

My plan had been to check on Doug Farrows' personnel record.

"I'll check out Larry's record, too," I said. "He left with

an injury right after Lottie was found. Doesn't that strike you as a strange coincidence?"

Keats agreed that it did.

"I should have dropped by to question him earlier," I said. "How about we try him tomorrow?"

The next mumble told me to focus on the task at hand.

"Right," I said. "You know what, though? There's a spreadsheet open in a tab. Let's just take a quick— Oh, wow! It's a record of who's late on their fees. There are lots of people on the naughty list."

It looked like fully a quarter of the residents were in arrears, some by as much as a year. Elsie and Carlisle had joined their ranks two months ago. Had the stress driven her over the edge, I wondered? Something had brought her to tears in Clarington the other day.

Lottie would likely have known about Elsie and Carlisle and some of the others. That might have driven Elsie to eliminate the risk of exposure and shame. But Alice Cheevers? I couldn't see the link. Her name was in good standing in the spreadsheet.

Keats mumbled a suggestion to keep going. He wasn't feeling it yet, and I wasn't either.

"Moving on to Doug. Let's start with email and see if they had any back and forth about the pond. I bet there's something that— Whoa! I did not expect that either. Doug's copied on an order with a pest control company for something called Rotenone. Let's take a look at the browser history."

Keats mumbled a little louder. I was definitely on to something.

"It's a product for eliminating 'problem goldfish,'" I said. "Apparently they're invasive like pythons and will take over the pond and drive out everything else. So now we know what happened to the fish everyone loved. I guess Doug's trying to revive the pond after the slaughter."

I searched a little more. "Wait a second... what's this? And this? There were invitations from developers for offsite meetings. Did Vaughan plan to..." My words trailed off and I stared into space, putting the pieces together. Then I gasped and said, "We gotta run, buddy."

He mumbled that he'd been telling me just that for several minutes. Now it was urgent.

"Gotcha. Just let me send some screen captures to the two chiefs."

It took a couple of tries because my fingers trembled. Now I knew exactly what had happened to the pond... and why. There wasn't a second to lose in getting the next troublesome pest out of there.

A growl deep in my dog's throat startled me to my feet, and I sent the chair rolling back with a clatter. I hadn't noticed that the door was ajar. Someone was eavesdropping and had probably heard enough of my observations to make my life—and potential death—very difficult.

The door opened the rest of the way and a shadowy form filled the space. I could see well enough with the light from the computer.

"Hey there," I said. "Just chatting to my dog about Zeus."

"The gods won't help you now, Ivy. Not Zeus. Not Apollo. Or whatever the rest are called."

It was Casey Cox. Property manager and murderer of goldfish and old ladies.

"How about Venus?" I said. "Because I'm an agent of love bringing two swans together again." I stayed where I was, glad to have the desk between us. On the other hand, there was no way out from here. Stepping back, I sat down hard in the chair and then slid it forward while hitting record on my phone. "The whole family, actually."

"I don't care about the swan," Casey said. "Never planned to keep him long. I just wanted to scare people, but it backfired, like every other plan. People got attached, just like they did with the goldfish. They're just pests, like rats, you know."

"The goldfish, maybe. That's not their rightful home. But the swan is indigenous to the area."

"Whatever. I just wanted the board to vote for closing the pond. I'd put it forward twice and they said no. You can't do a thing around here without bribing people. And what Vaughan wanted for filling the pond was outrageous."

"He's got debts to pay," I said. "Ford, too. And Rollie. And even the Cornwalls."

"Exactly. They're all in hock up to the eyeballs and I'm the one trying to run the place with no funds. My dad wouldn't let me kick them out on the streets where they belong."

"So you wanted to fill the pond and build more housing," I said. "Hence the meetings you booked with developers."

"It was my only way out of this bind and Vaughan wouldn't even grant me that. He said people need water to make captivity bearable." He gave a dismissive grunt. "Like that's my fault. I offered him a nice fountain."

"I get where you're coming from," I said. "Very reasonable under the circumstances."

"When my dad was in charge, people paid their fees. They think I'm a soft touch." Casey rubbed his forehead. "I didn't want him to find out I was running the place into the ground before he died. But then Lottie came poking around. Found her in here one day and later my dad's old ledger disappeared. Unlike you she failed at hacking."

"Maybe all she wanted to do was write an exposé about the people in arrears," I said.

He shrugged. "I don't know but she didn't get the chance. Couldn't find the ledger at her house, though."

That's because it was in her crawl space, I bet, and in Chief Gillock's hands now.

"I've got an idea," I said. "How about I help you convince Vaughan to approve the development? I'm pretty good at making a business case and not bad with PR."

"It's too late," he said. "No one would move here now. Our reputation is shot. Like the swan will be, soon."

"That's an opportunity missed," I said. "Use reuniting the swan family to generate goodwill. It's the kind of story people get behind, trust me. Let's go and do it together."

"I'm not going near that thing. He's attacked already. Nearly burst my eardrum and cut my head. Won't give him another chance."

"Ah. So it wasn't a hoverboard accident."

He shook his head. "It's been one of those domino situations where things keep going south till it all ends in the crapper. Story of my life."

"This can be salvaged," I said. "It starts with rescuing the swan. I'm not afraid of him."

"You should be. He'll take you and your dog under."

"He won't. You'll see. Let's take the swan to the sanctuary together. You get some photos, everyone's happy. Then we persuade Vaughan to do the right thing and your plan moves forward. I'm seeing a swan fountain in the center of the new complex. Maybe even a casino."

He pondered for a second. "Why didn't I think of a casino? That might motivate him."

"I'm full of good ideas, Casey. How about we start making over the Briars' reputation right now?"

Finally he nodded. "Okay. I'll give you one chance with the swan. Raise a ruckus and you know what happens?"

"You drown me, I guess. Like the others."

Pulling out a gun, he said, "My wrist still hurts, so I'll use this instead. Planned to use it on the swan. Maybe that's still the right choice."

"If he goes missing, people will fret. It's a love-hate thing. They love his beauty, but they're scared of him. Moving him to the waterfowl sanctuary gives you the best of all worlds. You bring the family together, and the community is safe from an angry papa. I've been in a lot of sticky public relations situations and hitting people in the heart with baby animals is the way to glory."

He gestured for me to get up and pass in front of him, which was more difficult than I expected. In all my exploits with dangerous killers, I had somehow evaded having a gun pointed directly at me. Not that negotiating with a madman or woman was ever easy, but a gun certainly amped up the pressure.

As I walked ahead of him down the path I slipped the phone back into my bra before he noticed it. Keats walked calmly by my side, while Percy headed off into the bushes.

"If you pull anything silly, you won't be the one I shoot first," Casey said.

"You leave Bridie alone," I said. "She pays her fees on time."

His laugh was more of a grating squawk. "That old bird is nearly as bad as Lottie. But I won't shoot her first, because it wouldn't matter enough to you. Instead, I'll shoot your dog. Then your cat. And then... you."

Keats moved his ears under my fingertips to offer silent reassurance. "You wouldn't," I said.

"After what I've gone through do you think adding a couple of pets to the list would make a difference?"

What *he'd* gone through. Like he hadn't made choices every step of the way. It annoyed me to no end when people refused to take personal accountability. Every villain played the victim, it seemed.

"Okay, I hear you. Could you at least promise me you'll make it humane?"

"I'm not promising you a thing. Besides, I haven't had much practice, so it'll probably be messy."

"You have my full cooperation," I said. "Though I'd much rather you did your target practice on me."

"I'll take that under advisement. Maybe if you come up with a few more PR tips I'll consider it."

I dug deep and found a light laugh. "That's an interesting bargain. I help you with PR if you agree to shoot me first."

"Life is funny, right? I used to laugh, too, until things started spiraling out of control."

"Money trouble is the worst," I said, as he flicked the gun toward the trail to the pond. "I've been there. Still there, actually, because my inn struggled after a murder on my land. Things have turned around for me lately because of exactly what I just told you. People love animals. You can get great mileage from the swan family. Plus I was thinking you could do more with social media. An insiders' Briars channel, to replace Lottie's outdated newsletter."

"There's no need to add another way for these people to gossip."

"They're going to talk anyway. I assume that's why you

killed Lottie. Because she'd talk about your poisoning the pond."

"Among other things. She knew too much. Asked too many questions about our operating budget as a so-called reporter. Vaughan and Ford Fletcher kept their eyes and mouths shut and took what I offered them to stay quiet. Can't tell you how many holes I dug Vaughan out of, but he's stupid enough to be useful and aside from the pond, he never said no to a bribe."

"What about Doug?" I asked. "Is he part of your plan?"

"Only knows as much as I feed him. Poor guy sees himself as a CIA operative and barely has the smarts to operate a hoverboard. I'm surrounded by idiots."

"That has its advantages, no? Larry seemed brighter."

"Yeah. Too bad for him. His head had a collision with a hoverboard the morning Lottie passed. Can't remember a thing right now."

I took the last turn down to the pond, desperately hoping someone was out for a stroll and knowing it was unlikely with a murderer at large. Percy may have gone for help, but since no one really spoke cat here it didn't bode well.

"Do you mind if I ask what happened with Alice Cheevers? I get that Lottie saw you poisoning the pond but I couldn't figure out what happened to Alice."

"I do mind. You talk too much."

"You're not the first to say so. But I figure you're going to kill me anyway, so why not satisfy my curiosity?"

"I hadn't made my mind up what to do with you, but if that's one of your pro tips, I guess I'd better take it."

"I'm not recommending my own demise, Casey. On the contrary, I think I could be very useful to you. I completely understand why you want to dam the swamp, fill the pond and build more housing. You were just trying to get people to go along with that plan by turning them against the pond."

"Everyone gets hysterical over a trash-eating raccoon. I figured dead fish and a vicious swan would have them suggesting it themselves. Who gets attached to a puddle filled with reptiles?"

"People who don't have much else, I guess. How did Alice make waves?"

He pointed at Zeus, who was floating about 20 yards away. "Stupid woman came down here to keep the swan company while you were sipping fancy drinks yesterday. She found me on the dock with the swan in a net. Squawked louder than the bird, so I fed her to the gators. By that time, the bird had gotten free, and you know what happened next."

"Yeah. I went looking for the swan and found Alice."

He jabbed me in the back with what felt like the muzzle of the gun. "You've been a total pain in the butt since the day you arrived."

I laughed again. "My mom says the same thing."

He gave me a harder shove as I stepped onto the dock, almost sending me into the water. It wasn't as daunting a prospect as usual given that I was still damp from the Strathmore adventure.

"Have you got a bag for the bird?" I asked.

"Burlap sack in the rowboat with his name on it," he said. "A ride fit for a Greek god."

"Perfect," I said. "I want to tie up my dog so he doesn't try to come into the water after me. Please?"

"If that makes you feel better, sure." He spun the gun around his thumb and I wondered for a second if it was even real. "Stay focused and the dog might make it back to the farm. Without you."

"I appreciate that so much," I said, grabbing a rope from the kayak Jilly and I had left on the shore the night before.

"I'm not a bad guy," he said. "Everyone likes me, except my dad. Never good enough for him and it turns out he was right. This place is eating me alive."

I looped the rope around a small tree near the water and tied it to Keats' leash with plenty of slack. I dropped my phone beside him and whispered, "A leash never held you, buddy. Do what you think best."

"Less talk more swim," Casey called.

I came back to the dock. "You can't blame a girl for wanting to say goodbye to her best friend."

"If you don't get in the water, I'll drown Jilly, too. How's that for motivation?"

Keats let out a keening wail and I raised my hand. "Quiet, Keats. Let's get this done." I sat down on the edge of the dock and said, "I hate to wreck a good pair of work boots, but I guess I won't be needing them anymore."

Casey gave me a hard kick between the shoulder blades and Keats howled again as I fell into the water face first. I hit my nose on the bottom but it was so spongy it didn't hurt much.

I swam a few yards under water, wondering if I could make it to the foliage where Casey couldn't easily find me. But then he'd kill Keats, Percy and the swan.

Plus there was the matter of gators and pythons. My chances were better in the open water than the jungle.

Probably.

I stood up, flung my hair back and tried to sneeze silt out of my nose. "Water's nice and warm," I called.

"Grab that bird and bag it," he called back, sending a flashlight beam over the water. "Then we'll take a drive."

My goal was simply to stay alive long enough for Chief Gillock to come out. I had no doubt he would after my emails. Could he make it in time?

I walked. I fell. I walked again. The water got deeper and deeper till swimming was my only choice. I had little hope of grabbing the bird and staying afloat.

Treading water near Zeus, I said, "If you can understand me, I want you to know we saved your mate and your babies. They're heading for a beautiful sanctuary right now. If you come with me, I can get you there, too. At least, I think so. We'll have to take out the guy on the dock somehow first. So if you understand and trust me, please follow me back."

The swan glided a little closer and reached toward me with his long neck. I thought he might hiss in my face, but he just stared at me. I kept treading till he pulled his head back, apparently satisfied.

Turning, I swam till I could stand and then walked the rest of the way.

"Well, I'll be darned," Casey said. "The swan is following you like a dog."

"Get the bag and he'll hop right into it," I said. "He wants to leave."

Casey put the gun in his pocket and knelt beside the boat to grab the burlap sack. I looked for Keats and saw that he'd chewed through the rope and crept closer to the dock. I silently asked him to wait for my signal.

Once Casey had the bag, he set the flashlight on the dock and pulled out the gun again. He let the weapon dangle from his thumb as he opened the sack with both hands.

I gently placed my hands on either side of the bird, under his wings. Lifting him up, I stretched out my arms. Casey had to lean forward with the bag, and I could tell he was flustered at seeing his nemesis up close.

"Wider," I said. "I'm afraid he'll bite as he goes in."

He leaned forward even more, grunting from the effort of maneuvering the sack. I eased back ever so slightly to throw him off balance and glanced at Keats.

The dog took off like a rocket. A fluffy orange missile detonated from the bushes at the same time.

There was a screech as teeth met buttock and claws met scalp.

The gun went flying into the water and Casey's arms pinwheeled. It looked like he was going to find his balance again. Zeus must have thought so too, because he spread his wings, knocked me backward, and then flapped into Casey's face, beating hard. There was more yelling, and Casey tipped over on the other side of the dock with the bird still on top of him, hissing and flapping.

That's when Keats shocked me. Despite Zeus having things under control, he took a flying leap into the water and added his teeth to the fray.

I could hear the sirens now but depending on how quickly the gates opened, there was still time for Casey to do some damage with the hands that had ended two women's lives.

I was completely unarmed, but help had arrived on stealthy heels.

Janelle took in the whole scene at a glance and told me to call off the animals.

"Keats. Zeus. Off!" I said, hoisting myself onto the dock.

Meanwhile, Janelle leaned over and offered her hand to Casey.

"Janelle, no!" I yelled.

Casey's eyes were glassy and confused, but he grabbed that hand like it was his last hope.

There was another scream, louder than all the rest, and he fell backward in the shallow water, motionless.

CHAPTER TWENTY-SIX

Janelle straightened, smoothed her party dress, and said, "Ivy, are you okay?"

"Am I—? What did you do to him, Janelle? Is he dead?"

She shook back her curls. "No, although based on what Chief Gillock said when he called, he deserves it."

"The chief called you?"

"Yeah, he wasn't sure if he'd get here in time and was worried about you and the residents, of course."

"But how did you know to come down here?"

"Percy walked right onto the dance floor. And when I stepped outside with him, I heard Keats howling as if his heart would break."

I stared at Casey, who had floated into shore on his back. Now his head rested on the sand and he was at no immediate risk of drowning.

"Did you shock him?" I asked, remembering the electric charge I felt the moment we shook hands.

"Sounds like *you're* in shock," she said. "Casey just

fainted. Now, come and sit down with the animals. The police are almost here."

I followed her off the dock. "Don't let him drown, Janelle. Even though he killed Lottie and Alice."

"Prison will have to do, I suppose. You just stay focused on getting the swan where he needs to go."

I walked over to the park bench with Percy, Keats and Zeus trailing after me. The dog and the swan shook themselves repeatedly, ridding themselves of water and Casey's contamination.

"You three were heroes. All of you," I told them. "Keats, I couldn't be prouder. I know what it took for you to jump in the water like that."

He offered a long elaborate humblebrag that was well-earned.

"And Zeus, I know how awful all this has been. Helpless to fly and not knowing if you'd ever see your family again. Happily, you will and very soon, too."

Keats jumped onto the bench and then climbed into my lap. Since we were both soaked, I didn't mind at all. Zeus settled into a squat, ready to retreat to the water as the situation required. Percy sauntered back to be closer to Janelle and the action.

When the police thundered in on heavy boots, Janelle stickhandled everything, still looking fabulous. I wondered if one of her many resort jobs had been fixing certain affairs that required delicate handling. Maybe she had a buzzer like a tiny taser to protect her from threats like Casey. It was clear this wasn't her first bad guy rodeo. Whatever she had, I wanted it.

Chief Gillock loped over to me. "You okay? Do you want to use my phone to call Harper?"

"Mine's in the bushes if you don't mind getting it," I

said, pointing.

Janelle raised both hands and there was a phone in each one.

"Never mind," I said. "Janelle's got it covered."

"She's something else, isn't she?" His pale face practically lit up. "Maybe she'll stick around and manage the Briars. There's a vacancy."

"That's a great idea." The first sparks of animation warmed me. "The perfect culmination of all her past work. I'll put it forward to her, Chief."

"You do that. And I'll tell Chief Harper that he's got excellent backup in you."

"And Keats," I said. "Don't forget to mention Keats, Percy and Zeus when you talk to him. A citation would be nice. Something to hang on the wall back home."

He laughed. "Kellan said you were pushy."

"Pushy!"

"And persistent. He meant it as a compliment."

"We'll see about that," I said, as he switched places with Janelle.

"Go back to Gran's and change, Ivy," she said. "You're shivering. Keats is shivering. You both need a hot shower."

Keats gave a full body shudder, proving that his loathing for water hadn't abated. A mumble made it clear he made an exception for homicidal events only.

"I hear you, buddy," I said. "And I promise to try to avoid all swamp monsters in the future."

"Easier to manage back in hill country," Janelle said.

"We've got swamps there, too." Turning to the swan, I added, "That's all I'd have to offer you if I took you home, Zeus. But I wish you could be my wingman in the more literal sense. You've got moves."

"Ivy, go," Janelle said. "I know you don't want to trust

me with the swan but Jilly's only five minutes out and I'll stay right here till I officially surrender custody."

"It's not personal," I said. "I think you're amazing and so does Chief Gillock."

"Well..." She pretended to scuff her stiletto. "He wasn't a tough sell. You were."

I pushed myself to my feet and held onto the back of the bench till my legs firmed up. "I hope you and Jilly will patch things up before we leave. For Bridie's sake, especially. But also, you helped save my life and I'd love to throw open my barn doors to you."

Janelle laughed. "I could teach you and Jilly a thing or two about running an inn, but I've got other plans."

"Running the Briars?" I said. "The chief and I agreed it would be the best thing that ever happened to the place."

She stared over at the police as they took Casey away. He was cuffed and on his feet, but none too steady. "I suppose I could stick around long enough to get things in order. But there's somewhere else I need to be."

"The Strathmore?" I asked.

Standing on tiptoe, she smiled. "I hear Jilly now, calling for Percy."

"We all need some creature comforts tonight," I said. "But after I get showered and changed I'm running Zeus down to the sanctuary."

"I'll drive," she said. "Nothing against your truck but this bird deserves a sweet ride like mine."

I laughed. "Please. Yours is bumpier *and* louder."

"I have an automatic transmission, at least. I noticed those stutters as you drove into the Strathmore parking lot."

I cocked my head. "Do you hear that?"

"What?"

"The sound of barn doors closing. Runaway Inn's honeymoon suite is no longer available to you."

"Honeymoon suite!" She pushed curls off her forehead and looked truly flustered for the first time. "What are you talking about?"

"Something I saw in Lottie's crystal ball," I said.

"You did not."

"You and a man in uniform. Clear as day." I grinned at her. "Jilly could never say no to a wedding at Runaway Farm."

"Don't underestimate my cousin," Janelle said. "And get going before someone gets a shock in the backside."

CHAPTER TWENTY-SEVEN

Jilly and Asher were quite happy to turn around at first light and drive to the waterfowl sanctuary for the big reunion. They'd already gotten Amos out of bed to come down and he stayed there to welcome us.

Bridie and Edna were chatting up a storm as they got into Asher's truck. Edna even insisted that Bridie take the front seat.

"I'll probably get carsick back here from Officer Galloway's driving," Edna said, as she rolled down the window. "You could lose the uniform now, young man. You're officially off duty."

"I feel like wearing it," he said. "Although I did change into my spare. It's pretty hot down here."

"It's not hot, it's humid," Bridie said, and everyone laughed.

It was hot *and* humid, and I'd be glad to get back to the sweet spring breezes of hill country soon. I'd wanted to leave right after the swan reunion but was cautiously optimistic that another day or two without murder hanging over our heads might be enough to heal the family rift.

It seemed promising that Jilly not only chose to ride in Janelle's old beater, but also to take the front seat. I sat in the back with Keats on my lap so the big swan had enough room beside me. He hopped in on his own, and I marveled once again at the trust animals could bestow on humans whose hearts were in the right place. That said, when I tried to pat him, he opened his beak in a menacing hiss. Keats made the wise decision to adjourn to the footwell.

There was silence in the front seat for a few miles, but it felt lighter than usual. Finally, after another hiss from the swan when Keats apparently looked at him the wrong way, or with the wrong eye, Jilly spoke.

"I'm glad you're going to stay here with Gran, Janelle. That's really good of you."

"Just for a bit," Janelle said. "I can't stay forever."

"It would be tough to be the only one under sixty in the compound, other than Doug," I said. "Even with a few hot dates to Clarington with Chief Gillock."

"Chief Gillock?" Jilly said. "What did I miss?"

"Janelle's got her very own Chief Hottie," I said. "He was impressed by how well she handled herself during the, uh..."

"Violent attack by a murderer?" Jilly said. "Well, she has had some experience."

"She has?" I said.

"Not much," Janelle said. "A bit more than Gran thinks and a lot less than Jilly imagines."

"Are you a sleuth, too?" I asked. "Is that something else you have in common?"

"No," they chimed at once.

I stuck my head through the seats and Keats grumbled over being squished. "You do have tons in common. Always did, always will. You're both ready to let bygones be bygones. Am I right, Keats?" His agreement was muffled by the cracked leather of the seat. "Time is running short to talk through it in person."

"My bygones are gone," Janelle said. "Jilly thinks I did something I didn't, that's all. She took the side of the town against me."

"I didn't." Jilly sounded a shrill note. "Your own mother said you did."

"She *hoped* I did," Janelle said. "But I didn't. And I couldn't. Maybe I could now, but not then."

I sat back. "This is all very cryptic. Are you catching any of it, Keats?"

He panted a happy ha-ha-ha. In his opinion, the mediation was going great. I wasn't so sure.

"It's best if you don't hear the details, Ivy," Jilly said. "On that, I'm sure Janelle and I agree."

"Yeah. Sorry, Ivy," Janelle said. "I know it's frustrating."

"Not at all." I rolled down the window a little. The old beater's air conditioning didn't have much life in it. "After what happened at the motel, and the cars tailing us and the creepy black sedan at the Strathmore, I think I know enough, which is basically nothing. I'm just a simple hobby farmer and I'd like to keep it that way."

"Good decision," Janelle said. "You're so lucky to have a calling you love."

"You have a calling," I said. "And it isn't hotel or facilities management. It's matchmaking and mediation. Since you got here you keep trying to set people up."

"Without much success so far," she said. "I'd love to help Videa Dumasse find love, but the pool of decent men is so small. I've been thinking about arranging dance nights with similar gated communities nearby. And once Larry's back, we'll hire more security."

"Hoverboards for all," I said. "I still hope to get a ride on that thing."

"I don't know about mediation," Janelle said. "It would be hard to hang up my shingle given the rift in my own family."

"You don't need a clean record to start over," I said. "Mine isn't and neither is Jilly's. No one's perfect and everyone deserves a fresh start. You can't stay here for the rest of your days." I thought about it for a second and added, "This is where the dog comes in."

"What dog?" Janelle said.

"The right dog. Once you find her everything will all fall into place. I may not have your woo-woo talents, but I know this to be true."

"You have woo-woo talents," Jilly said.

"Not at Janelle's level."

"Too much woo-woo only causes trouble," Janelle said.

"You can say that again," Jilly said. She took a deep breath. "But Ivy is right, Janelle. You are a natural match-maker and mediator. Don't let what happened in our family stop you from using your gift."

Janelle almost veered onto the gravel shoulder and caught the car in time. "Really?"

Another deep breath from Jilly forced the words past her block. "I want to leave the past in the past. Ivy's shown me the wisdom of doing that." Glancing over her shoulder, she added, "You're a role model for handling the manure life drops at our feet."

I laughed. "I am something of an expert in manure. Used well, dung can bring glorious growth."

One more deep breath and Jilly looked at her cousin. "Let's try to be a family again. We can't let decades pass between reunions."

There was wriggling at my feet as Keats tried to wag his tail in a confined space. Zeus stuck his long neck between the seats and swiveled to look at each woman in turn, making them both flinch.

"Reunions will be easier soon," Janelle said. "Because I'm moving home."

"Home!" Jilly blurted the word. "To Wyldwood Springs?"

"Home to the old house. It's time for Mom to let me take up the baton. Diplomacy isn't her strong suit, and I'm hoping I can settle a few things in the community."

Jilly reached across what had been a huge divide and squeezed her cousin's arm. "It would be good to have you so close. Maybe Gran can come back, too. Eventually."

Janelle deflated behind the wheel. "It would take better negotiation skills than mine."

"Give it time," Jilly said. "And be super careful. Will your mom agree?"

"I'm going to suggest she take over managing the Briars. That way we've got things covered at both ends. It won't be easy, but I'm ready to try." Turning under the big wooden duck at the waterfowl refuge, she added, "I've spent ten years training for this. The only thing I need is—"

Keats gave a jubilant bark.

"Exactly, Keats. My dream dog. I'm going to find her on the drive back. I feel it in my bones."

"Don't discount a cat," Jilly said. "There's nothing more comforting than a nice purr."

"Except possibly a handsome cop," I said, watching Asher help Bridie out of the truck with a courtly little bow. He left Edna to descend on her own, likely knowing she'd chew off his arm if he'd tried.

"Sounds like you two have it all laid out for me," Janelle

said, putting the car in park. "I'll do my best to make you proud."

"Make yourself proud," I said, getting out of the car. "And your mystical Belgian shepherd. Although I'd keep an open mind about the breed. Think longer and lower."

Keats gave a sneeze of laughter, so maybe he shared my hunch.

Janelle left me to open the rear passenger door for the swan and I expected to lift him down. Instead, he jumped out and waddled ahead with Keats circling in wide arcs behind him. Eventually Zeus turned and let out a hiss and Keats fell back.

We followed the path past several ponds, each with its pair of resident swans. I was beginning to wonder if we'd missed our turnoff when Zeus started running. His wings spread, with their missing feathers visible like broken teeth in an old comb. They couldn't achieve liftoff, but they did propel him forward to a pond where a lone swan floated. One by one, grey cygnets popped out from under her feathers.

"I hope she takes him back," I said. "Amos told me even a week can turn committed mates into strangers and enemies."

"Not these two," Jilly said. "They're madly in love."

The evidence came as soon as Zeus hit the water. He turned from awkward to graceful in an instant. They circled each other for a moment before practically merging into one being as their necks intertwined. It was one of the most touching, romantic things I had ever seen, and tears rolled down my face.

A loud sniff behind me told me I wasn't the only one crying, and when I finally looked away from the snowy pair and their family, Asher was wiping his eyes on his uniform sleeve.

He glanced at Bridie and after she nodded, dropped suddenly to one knee on the grass at Jilly's feet. Her hands clasped and then covered her mouth. Good thing her green eyes were dancing or we might have been worried about the outcome.

If I knew my brother, he'd probably prepared an elaborate proposal on the drive down. But the ring box he pulled out of his pocket was from Haute Baubles. Bridie had ordered it while we were still in Clarington and had it delivered, just in case.

"Jilly," he said, "I thought long and hard and—"

"Asher?" Edna said. "We talked about this. Brevity is a valuable trait, both in good times and an apocalypse."

"Right. Yes, Miss Evans." He gave his head a shake. "Jilly Blackwood, it would be my honor to serve and protect you for the rest of our days."

"In sickness and in health," Bridie added.

"In barns and bunkers," I said.

"Till death do you part," Edna said.

"With all the magic love can bring," Janelle finished.

Keats threw back his muzzle and offered a jubilant, "Roo-roo-roo."

It was a sound I'd never heard from him before and we all laughed. Then we circled the happy couple.

"Did I miss the answer?" Edna said. "Did she say yes?"

"Yes!" Jilly said, competing with another joyful howl from Keats.

After a few minutes, I left the celebration and walked to the edge of the pond again to watch Zeus and Hera swimming side by side with a trail of babies behind them.

They turned to face me with eyes that were still sharp but warmer than cold beads.

"You're welcome at Runaway Farm when your feathers grow back," I said. "I'm building a pond with plenty of room for a running takeoff."

Keats grumbled a rebuke for ruining a fine moment with talk of bringing more water into our lives.

A few moments later, Asher cleared his throat and I turned. "Congratulations, brother. You've won a great prize."

"It pays to aim high," he said, grinning. "I was never afraid to bat out of my league. Mom probably made a better man out of me than Dad would have if he'd stayed."

The word "dad" didn't nauseate me like it did a month ago. "Calvin isn't so bad," I said. "I understand why you kept in touch with him."

His bright blue eyes dropped to the grass. "I'm sorry about keeping that a secret, especially from you. I couldn't explain why, even to myself. It had something to do with Jilly."

"Jilly? How so?"

"I knew I wanted to spend my life with her since the day we met. That got me thinking about family and roots, and what I wanted for my own children someday. So when Dad came calling, I opened the door too fast without thinking about the rest of you."

"It's okay," I said. "We're all changing, right? Let's just swim with the current and not against it."

The famous Asher Galloway smile competed with the swans for brilliance. "Any chance you'd be my best man?" he said.

"Give that job to Kellan, because I'm casting myself as maid of honor."

"Hopefully everything at the farm will settle down before the wedding," he said. "I couldn't believe someone would try to seize Clippers in broad daylight."

"Seize Clippers? What are you talking about?"

His smiled vanished behind a cloud. "I figured someone told you."

"Thank goodness I can count on you when my deputies keep me in the dark. Tell me now."

"I only know that someone walked off with him and faced the fight of their life from Cori and a pig poker. Edna was beside herself that we'd left already. There was a lot of talk of explosives on the way down that I can't unhear."

Turning, I said, "We've got to get back. I can't believe Kellan didn't tell me."

"He didn't want to distract you at a critical time," Asher said. "Besides, Cori and Gertie are standing watch twenty-four seven. Another day or two won't make a difference there, but it will for Jilly and her family here."

One look at Bridie, Janelle and Jilly walking arm in arm along the path, surrounded by bright sun, blue water and multicolored birds, made me reconsider.

"You're right, brother," I said. "She deserves to savor this moment. I'll stick to hassling everyone online. There's a security feed so I can stand watch, too." I looked down at Keats. "That'll teach us never to leave the farm again."

"There's something else," he said. "Teri Mason called me to say her mom wants to speak to you as soon as you're back. It's urgent."

"Teri's mom? Asher, she's basically been unconscious for years. We've never met."

He squirmed, as if his uniform had gotten itchy. "I know. But that's what Teri said, and it's supposedly, well... life and death."

"Huh. Okay then. It's good to know things won't be boring when we get home."

"There's a wedding to plan, too," he said, smiling again.

"I've got a grand idea for that," I said. "And then you can drive down here for your honeymoon."

"Sounds like I could earn a few extra bucks bounty-hunting pythons," he said. "I can handle snakes."

"Tell that to your beautiful bride," I said.

"Why ruin a great moment?" He tossed me a grin before heading back to Jilly.

I sat down on the grass, even though it was speckled with bird poop, and Keats climbed into my lap. He mumbled as I rubbed his ears. "You're right, buddy. Vacations aren't for sissies. It's time for us to get back to work."

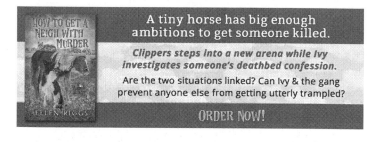

Have you joined Ellen Riggs' author newsletter at **ellenriggs.com/fun**? You'll receive two stories free, including *The Cat and the Riddle*, which is EXCLUSIVE to subscribers. The story takes place after *Swine and Punishment* and sets the stage for a future novel. Don't miss out! Plus, of course you'll see some great photos of my adorable dogs.

Do you want to join Janelle and her grandmother on a magical adventure to find the dog of her dreams? Read on!

Rescuing this sassy dachshund would be a lot easier if he were still alive.

Janelle Brighton is not a witch, although she knows a thing or two about magic. For starters, she can see ghosts, or at least one. She can read minds, at least some. And she can zap people with a little energy burst that scrambles their brains, at least for a while. But she's not very good at any of it. She's either a late bloomer, as her grandmother says, or a dud bud.

That's why it comes as a shock when a jewelry store heist and a murder in Gran's community also reveal a plot against Janelle's life. Someone desperately wants to prevent her from heading back home to Wyldwood Springs to face the ghosts of her past.

Luckily, the ghost of her present—a cocky, chatty dachshund named Mr. Bixby—holds the key to at least one mystery. And if they can rescue each other before the killer rids the world of this slightly underrated non-witch, they may just be a match for magical threats to come.

*Join Janelle Brighton in this **short prequel** that begins* the *Mystic Mutts Mysteries* series, *a paranormal cozy mystery featuring a saucy dachshund, several ghosts and murders to solve*

I Want You to Haunt Me is available now!

Runaway Farm & Inn Recipes

Jilly's Spring Fever Asparagus Gruyere Tart

- 1 lb thin asparagus, trimmed
- 1 pkg all-butter puff pastry, thawed
- 2 tbsp Dijon mustard
- 1½ cup shredded Gruyere cheese
- ½ tsp cracked pepper
- 1 egg
- 1 tbsp milk

Instructions

- Line 2 baking sheets with parchment paper and set aside.
- Steam asparagus about 3 minutes till tender-crisp. Chill in cold water and pat dry.
- Unroll each pastry sheet onto prepared pan. Spread evenly with mustard, leaving a 1-inch border. Arrange asparagus side by side,

alternating ends, on top of mustard. Sprinkle with cheese and pepper.

- Beat egg with milk in a small bowl, and then brush over pastry border.
- Bake in 450-degree oven for 16 minutes, rotating and switching pans half-way through, till cheese is bubbly and pastry puffed and golden.
- Cut each into six pieces and serve warm or cool, while accepting accolades for a deceptively simple treat.

More Books by Ellen Riggs

Bought-the-Farm Cozy Mystery Series

- *A Dog with Two Tales* (*prequel*)
- *Dogcatcher in the Rye*
- *Dark Side of the Moo*
- *A Streak of Bad Cluck*
- *Till the Cat Lady Sings*
- *Alpaca Lies*
- *Twas the Bite Before Christmas*
- *Swine and Punishment*
- *The Cat and the Riddle* **(Newsletter Exclusive)**
- *Don't Rock the Goat*
- *Swan with the Wind*
- *How to Get a Neigh with Murder*

- *Tweet Revenge*
- *For Love Or Bunny*
- *Bought the Farm Mysteries - Books 1-3*

Mystic Mutt Mysteries

- *I Want You to Haunt Me*
- *You Can't Always Get What You Haunt*
- *Any Way You Haunt It*
- *I Only Haunt to be with You*

Books by Ellen Riggs and Sandy Rideout

Dog Town Series

- *Ready or Not in Dog Town* (The Beginning)
- *Bitter and Sweet in Dog Town* (Labor Day)
- *A Match Made in Dog Town* (Thanksgiving)
- *Lost and Found in Dog Town* (Christmas)
- *Calm and Bright in Dog Town* (Christmas)
- *Tried and True in Dog Town* (New Year's)
- *Yours and Mine in Dog Town* (Valentine's Day)
- *Nine Lives in Dog Town* (Easter)
- *Great and Small in Dog Town* (Memorial Day)
- *Bold and Blue in Dog Town* (Independence Day)
- *Better or Worse in Dog Town* (Labor Day)

Made in the USA
Las Vegas, NV
05 September 2021